THE FIGHTING LITTLES

BOOTH TARKINGTON

THE
FIGHTING
LITTLES

DOUBLEDAY, DORAN AND COMPANY, INC.

GARDEN CITY 1941 NEW YORK

PRINTED AT THE *Country Life Press*, GARDEN CITY, N. Y., U. S. A.

To All the Nieces
Florence, Margaret, Josephine, Patty, Susanah, Mig,
and the Divine Flora
From
A Completely Admiring Uncle

THE FIGHTING LITTLES

I

JUNE MORNING SUNSHINE brightening hotly on the lowered window shades of Mrs. Little's bedroom woke her from a dream that she was still beautiful Wilma Filmer, unmarried and being chased by a Russian choir. For some moments after her waking, which was at first only partial, she remained in fear of the choir; then, becoming slightly more intelligent, comprehended that she was afraid of something else but couldn't remember what it was. She didn't wish to remember, either. Apprehension lay upon her shapelessly; but she preferred not to investigate it and tried to get back to sleep again, no matter came what dreams. Recollections wouldn't let her, began to form themselves, and she was aware that she feared something old and something new. Something that had been happening for a long while frightened her and so did something recent—so recent that it had taken place during the past night. "Oh, my!" she said aloud, remembering everything, and decided not to get up until her husband had gone downtown to business, if he'd let her.

The something old that frightened her—the something that had been happening for a long time—was the change in what she thought of as her husband's disposition. During their engagement and for a long time after they were married nobody could have been more amiably tractable. He sought no pleasure without her, except to attend a Legion meeting now and then, or a banquet of his college fraternity alumni; and, generous, he was delighted when she confessed to him that she'd spent a little more on a dress, a pair of slippers or a hat than she thought she ought. Sturdy and energetic in body and mind, he loved his country, his wife, baseball and pounding hard at his business. They were happy in the six-room house where they lived those first years, half way to downtown in their growing city; it wasn't until after the birth of the baby that he showed a first symptom of what later got to be the matter with him.

"Put her back in the crib instantly!" he said crisply to his wife, one day. "I don't intend to have my child picked up and held in that posture; it's not hygiene."

He'd read all the books, and his wife hadn't read any; books made her sleepy. So she gave way and put the baby back in the crib. Several times Ripley Little was like this; but evoked from the young wife more amusement than alarm. In fact, she was pleased by the scientific raising he insisted upon for their little girl.

Affection made him perhaps an overdutiful father, and he was only a little less so when the second child, a boy, was born three years and a few months later; but in general the young husband's amiability, often fondly indulgent, continued, and so did the cheerfulness of the small household. There couldn't easily have been a jollier family when the children were little. Christmases and birthdays were merry festivals, and in the summertime Ripley Little had a hundred devices for making gay— afternoons at the ball park, picnics in a dozen sylvan spots known to him since boyhood, evening dashes in the car for sundaes downtown at the fashionable confectioner's, spending debauches at Schücke's voluptuous toy store, movies, the circus—there was no end to the surprises he had for the children.

He loved to play with them and their toys, and, when they grew old enough for school, he went over their lessons with them, chucklingly solved their problems in arithmetic, freshened his memory to talk history with them, and obviously asked no better of life than to continue these pleasures. He didn't even play golf, declaring that he had too much fun at home with "the little Little family." In those days he loved to speak of his wife, his children and himself as "the little Little family", and he often repeated wistfully his great wish—that his children would never grow older.

He was a born businessman, and, profoundly inspired by the thought that he worked for his children's future, he strove mightily and successfully, was happy in his daily tasks, prospered rapidly. Goody, the little girl, was six years old and Filmer, the boy, just under three in 1929 when their father bought the fine new house, with the shrubberied big yard for them to play in, far out in a semi-suburban affluent neighborhood. The stock market collapse of that year didn't hurt Ripley Little much—he'd anticipated it—and he stood up to the declines of '31 and

'32 manfully; it wasn't till after the banks had been closed in '33 that his confident cheerfulness was really impaired. His wife, never much aware of economics or of public affairs, perceived that he began to have a habit of looking uneasy and to be sometimes irritable in his speech. He was still jolly with the children but inclined to be stricter with them.

This strictness, or at least the attempt to enforce it, increased. He'd been brought up—or now believed he had—to respect his elders, to cultivate quiet and rather formal manners, to reverence religious observances, to possess a feeling of responsibility and to be generally sensible. As his children grew old enough to be supposed to understand these things, he naturally expected their deportment to show that they did, and, more and more worried about his country and his business, he became more fretful when it didn't.

Especially was he sharp sometimes with his daughter; for the young Goody, resembling her mother, who was still a noticeably pretty woman, seemed to be growing up lightheaded, particularly when she came to be fourteen and fifteen and sixteen. As these ages coincided with unpleasant perturbations brought upon Ripley Little by both private and public affairs, he was the more frequently temperish, while Goody, proportionately high-spirited as she grew prettier and prettier, replied in kind. To Mrs. Little her own position daily seemed to be the unfortunate one of an umpire present upon a field of continuous contest—an umpire often appealed to but without the power to enforce her decisions or, indeed, many opportunities to announce them.

She was a peace-loving woman; but not an able one. She'd never known how to cope with what she called "the servant problem", and her vigorous husband had done most of the housekeeping before Cousin Olita came to live with the family. Cousin Olita, born Filmer (not Little) was peace-loving too; but she had a gift, her only one, for making household service smooth. In her youth Cousin Olita had been thought quite a showpiece in a large curvy way, though nobody young would have believed this of her now, and she was still as pleasant looking as she was overbuxom, frizzly-blonded and good-natured. Flat broke at forty-five, she'd flopped upon the Littles, who kept her because somebody had to; but her sunniness and her talent with servants and for marketing were at least partly worth the added expense. Mrs. Little thought that they all might be having a pretty nice time together—she and Ripley and Goody and young Filmer and Cousin Olita—if her husband could ever just forget the New Deal and stop fighting with Goody, anyhow now and then.

He didn't seem able to do either, though he had a wild week of excitement and triumph in the early summer of 1940 when the Republicans nominated Mr. Wendell L. Willkie for President. Ripley Little went so passionately into the campaign that his troubles with the seventeen-year-old Goody were minor until after the election in November, which prostrated him. Recovering partially, he renewed his struggle to form his daughter upon old precepts and was so vehement in the matter that Mrs. Little feared there'd never be peace in the house again.

She reproached herself for her total failure as a reconciliator. Not perceiving that she was merely a buffer in a war between two generations and two nervous nervous systems, she was sure that there was *some* road to harmony if she could only find it. Advised by a friend, she privately consulted a psychiatrist who, himself confused by her account of her troubles, got her all mixed up and frightened. She began by trying hard to tell him about her husband's peculiar system of profanity, how what he said sounded terribly like swearing yet really wasn't.

The truth of the matter, simpler than she realized, was only that Ripley Little sometimes yielded to the ancient urge of many good men to be profane yet not irreverent and to blaspheme without sin. Archaic forms, such as Od's wounds, Od's fish, 'Sblood, Gadzooks, would have been ridiculous in the modern mouth, and the later Jiminy criminy, Jiminy crickets, Gee, Gosh, Golly, Jeepers creepers, or the New England My Godfrey, My Odfrey, and By Orry, these and their like would have been pale upon the tongue of a man so forcible. Ripley Little's style in all of his acts was the natural, so his style in swearing sprang naturally to his lips, although, as his wife said, it sounded dismayingly like the real thing. Mrs. Little's powers of narration, however, were feeble and she didn't make herself entirely clear.

"You see, he says something like jobjam, for instance," she told the psychiatrist. "Sometimes I think he's saying what it sounds like, or even worse; but I don't think it ever is, really, if you see what I mean. He was brought up religiously and likes to set an example whenever he can. When we were first married I never really did hear him say anything like that—not until these last few years. I'd

think I'd hear him muttering these things to himself, and
then sometimes it would come out right loudly—jobjam
and those other things, you see—especially when he's
talking about our young Goody's friends, or her beginning
lipstick or anything, or wearing shorts, you see. For quite
a while I used to think it was profane; but if I listened
closely, then I didn't think so because I could hear it was
just jobjam or job jam the helm——"

"What?" The doctor leaned forward attentively.
"What did you say?"

"Why, job jam the helm," Mrs. Little replied, reddening. "Sometimes I'd get to thinking he said these things
so much that I ought to speak to him about it and tell him
it was bad for him. You see?"

"Yes, perfectly," the psychiatrist replied. "After you
first thought you heard your husband using these strange
expressions, you thought you heard them oftener. I see.
Now let's get back a little. Perhaps you might find it interesting to give me just a little talk about your childhood,
and we'll see if you can remember if anything ever shocked
and upset you when you were very young."

Bewildered, Mrs. Little tried to comply; then interrupted herself to explain that her husband really did say
"job jam" for worse. It wasn't an illusion of hers, she said
repeatedly, and what she wanted advice about was how to
become the kind of woman that could keep peace in her
family; but the psychiatrist, smiling kindly, kept trying
to lead her back to her memories of her childhood. She
felt that they weren't getting much of anywhere together,
and when she left she was so worried about her own men-

tal condition that she decided not to come again lest she be more so.

Going to lengths, she read several magazine articles on helpful wifely and motherly procedures. She even confusedly plodded through part of a book, *The Family,* and, hearing of an instructive play called *Life with Father* in which a wife and mother got away with a good deal in spite of a dominating husband and father, she went to see it; but she came forth hopeless, knowing herself not up to the lady therein depicted.

In regard to her present family life, Mrs. Little found only one comfort: she gave up the idea that she could ever hope to stand between her husband and their daughter, though she'd always keep trying; but at least she hadn't often to try to stand between Ripley Little and their young son, Filmer. That promising boy had reached the age of fourteen, almost fifteen now, without getting Ripley Little seriously upset more than seven or eight times.

The mother realized that maybe this was because Filmer, in his home life, was carefully secretive about himself—except in perhaps too frequent references to the praise he had from his teachers—but at any rate it was a comfort, for the time being. She knew of course that Filmer's adolescence might break out on him and get him into real trouble with his father, the way Goody's had; but, so far, this wasn't happening, thank heaven, and her husband sometimes even praised Filmer's sensible conduct as a contrast to Goody's irresponsibility. Filmer was growing up to be a good quiet little man, the father had gone so far as to say; Filmer knew how to take care of himself and how to treat older people with consideration; Filmer was too bright to look upon life as uproar and motion merely.

"Uproar!" Mrs. Little thought of the uproar that had roused her in the early dark hours of that morning, and again she gasped "Oh, my!" to her pillow.

The sunshine grew stronger upon her window shades; she heard Cousin Olita tap upon Filmer's door to rouse him for the day; then firm footsteps, a man's, sounded along the corridor, descended the stairway and were heard from the hall below. Straight beneath her, in the dining-room, a moment later, there was a thump as of a chair roughly used. Ripley Little was sitting down to his breakfast.

II

In the butler's pantry Gentry Poindexter, colored, tall, Zulu-ish and all in white, spoke with relish to his wife, the Littles' housemaid. "Boss sutny madded up this day, Almatina. You go' hear him cuss like you ain't never hear him yet."

Almatina, preparing a breakfast tray to be taken upstairs, shook her head. "You the dumb-earedest man I ever listen to, Gentry. How many times do I got to tell you it's like Miss Olita says and Mr. Little's cussin' ain't cussin' at all. It sound like it; but it ain't."

"So?" the colored man said. "You and Miss Olita can tell me it ain't cussin' every day for seven months and Christmas; but if you right, then I ain't got no more ability to listen good than a ant's got money to buy him wrastlin' pants." He giggled whisperingly, placed a silver coffee-pot upon a Sheffield tray and stepped toward the door. "Settin' at table ri' now, holdin' up the newspaper 'tween him and Miss Olita so he ain't got to look at her. Ain't makin' a sound; but he go' be buzz-boomin' soon!

Somebody go' start him; but it ain't go' be me. Ain't go' be Gentry tell him whut happen las' night. No, ma'am!"

Thereupon Gentry Poindexter opened the pantry door with his knee, passed into the dining-room and refilled the coffee-cup at the elbow of the stocky-bodied, middle-aged man who sat at the head of the mahogany Georgian table and irascibly stared at a morning newspaper. Cousin Olita bore him company, so to speak; but hushedly. She looked up from her place half way down the table, and spoke in a low voice.

"You might just leave the coffee-pot, Gentry. Mr. Little may like——"

"What?" Little looked over the top of his paper challengingly. "What may I like?"

"Nothing," Cousin Olita said hurriedly. "I only told Gentry to leave the coffee-pot because you may like——"

"Like?" Ripley Little said again. "I'd like to know what's left for me to like. I'm jammed if I see what's left for anybody to like when every time a man looks at a newspaper for nine years he either sees where Hitler's done something worse than he did yesterday or else reads something that means he'll have to hire three lawyers to tell him how to write down everything he does in what little business he's got left with what little money he's got left in a way that won't get him into the penitentiary." He thrust the paper from him. "It seems slightly peculiar to me that you claim to have slept through all the rumpus in this house after midnight last night. I find that hard to credit, Olita, hard to credit." He looked sternly at the colored man. "Gentry, that noise certainly penetrated to your quarters. What was it?"

A film of blankness overspread Gentry Poindexter's face; his eyes became opaque and his whole person expressed nonreceptivity. "Me," he said, "I ain't turn off layin' on my face from ten las' night to six o'clock after daylight."

"What? You mean to tell me you slept through all *that?*"

"When I sleep," Gentry said, "I sleep. No, suh. Whutever 'twas, Gentry ain't hear it."

Little frowned at him. "You didn't hear the siren?"

"Hear whut, Mr. Little?"

"I'm asking you. You didn't hear a police car sirening all over this neighborhood last night?"

"Police? I got nothin' to do with them people."

"It sounded all the way from down the street, getting louder and louder," Ripley Little said. "It didn't stop its noise until it got in front of this house; and right after that a car turned into our driveway and job jam if it didn't sound to me mighty like as if it was the car that had been doing the sirening! Then somebody drove a herd of cattle into the house, turned the phonograph on, and the cows tried to dance. You heard nothing?"

"I ain't hear no cow dance, no, suh, Mr. Little. All night long I sleepin' sweet on my face and ain't hear——"

He was interrupted by the youth, Filmer, who came into the dining-room at that moment and took his place at the table. "Then you must 'a' been dead, not asleep," Filmer said. "I never heard such a disgraceful noise in this house in all my whole days. Bring me my cereal, Gentry."

"Oh, then somebody *did* hear something, after all!" Ripley Little looked upon his son with a frowning slight approval, as Gentry departed. "I'm glad to be corroborated. Gentry and your Cousin Olita talk as if I'm suffering from auditory delusions, Filmer. They'd both take their oath that the neighborhood and this house were so peaceful throughout the night that they slept like lambs and heard no disturbance whatever. Can you tell me what caused it?"

"Easy," Filmer replied. "I could win quiz contests all day on questions like that. It was Goody and Ham Ellers —I know I heard *his* voice—and the rest of her screwy crowd. I didn't wake up till they were dancing right under my room; but they were creating such an outrage I wondered, Father, you didn't go down and stop 'em."

"So did I!" his father said testily. "So do I now! A thousand times I wonder why I permit this family to be subjected to such outbreaks in the dead of the night." He looked crossly at Gentry Poindexter, who was placing Filmer's cereal upon the table. "You can get ready to drive me downtown, Gentry."

"Downtown?" Gentry asked in a surprised voice. "Downtown, Mr. Little?"

Little, rising from his chair, stared at him. "What's the matter with you? Where else do I go except downtown, at this hour? Isn't it your custom to drive me downtown in my car after breakfast?"

"Yes, suh; but I was jes' thinkin' about that."

"You were? Just thinking about it, were you?"

"Yes, suh; I was thinkin' kind o' like this." The colored man, avoiding his employer's eye, discovered a crumb upon the polished surface of the table, removed it conscientiously with a napkin. "Mr. Little, ain't I always says we intitle to be a three-car family, not one them cheap twos? Look at this fine big house, all that nice grass and flower bushes and them trees we got, nice driveway out to the street. By rights we a three-car family, Mr. Little. We——"

"What's the matter with you?" Little inquired again. "Are you going to bring my car around or aren't you?"

"Yes, suh. I was jes' thinkin'——" Gentry carefully removed another crumb from the table, seeming intent upon this duty. "We pure and honestly need more'n jes' one car, Mr. Little, for me to drive you downtown in and go after you in, and only one other for all the scramblin' round Miz Little and Miss Goody does in it, 'specially Miss Goody. No, suh, yes'd'y noon Miss Goody had to leave that other car in Crappio's garage and it won't be out today; Crappio can't say when. That other car been complainin' since 'way las' winter. Them old models hard to get in good condition once they break down. So we ain't go' be able use that one now, Mr. Little."

"I'm not talking about the other car," Little said. "I'm talking about my own car. Are you trying to tell me you've let it get out of commission? It was absolutely all right when you brought me home in it at five o'clock yesterday afternoon. Have you had it out since?"

"Me? No, no, suh! But yes'd'y evenin' drivin' you home I kind o' notice we ain't rollin' so good. Seem like sump'n fixin' to bust; she ain't say whut. Indurin' the night it look like she done it. Yes, suh, sump'n bust; this morning she won't roll."

"What! Do you mean to tell me that just standing in my garage that car——"

"She won't roll, Mr. Little. She out. Madison Boulevard bus line got nice bus, though; yes, suh. Scuse me, suh."

Gentry, carrying two crumbs in a napkin upon his tray, kneed himself back into the butler's pantry, and Ripley Little, still standing, looked intolerantly at Cousin Olita, whose gaze was upon her coffee-cup. "Olita, do you think you can see to it that Crappio gets a repair man here in time to have my car put in condition to be sent downtown for me at lunchtime?" he asked.

"I—I'll try, Cousin Ripley." Cousin Olita drank from her cup, seeming interested in its upper rim as she did so. "I'll do my best; but you know how repair men always are, Cousin Ripley. Of course the Madison Boulevard bus is very pleasant indeed; I like that bus, myself, Cousin Ripley. One always sees people one knows in the Madison Boulevard busses, really nice people, too; so that a bus ride on a Madison Boulevard bus often means really quite a nice sociable time and——"

"That's why I hate it," Little said as he opened the dining-room door and walked out into the wide front hallway.

Sounds from the other side of the white-paneled front door, thirty feet before him, brought him to a halt; and his forehead immediately became corrugated with displeasing suspicions. Footsteps clumped on the floor of the portico outside that door; young voices were heard confusedly and there was a fumbling at the polished big brass latch. Then the door opened, revealing four interestingly damaged male persons, in age between seventeen and twenty-one. Two of them had their right arms in slings; the third, with the aid of a crutch, humored an injured foot; and the fourth had a bandaged chin. At sight of the master of the house all of them paused; then the one with the bandaged chin advanced a few steps, looking serious.

"Listen, Mr. Little, please," this one said. "Where's Plunks?"

"Listen yourself, but not please," Little returned. "I don't wish to intrude upon your private business or manners, Hamilton Ellers; but don't you usually ring the bell before entering people's houses?"

"We thought you'd be gone, sir," young Mr. Ellers explained unthinkingly.

"Ah! Too bad!" Ripley Little said. "Too bad; but I'm not. What's the matter with all of you? Been in a nightspot riot? Never mind, don't inform me; I'm not interested. It's a bit early to receive callers. Kindly permit me to suggest that you return to your homes—or to your surgeons."

"Well——" Hamilton Ellers, abashed but only slightly so, touched his bandaged chin; then passed his hand over his irregular but not uncomely other features. "Well, sir, we'd really like to see Plunks if——"

"That's not my daughter's name." Little advanced discouragingly. "I don't enjoy hearing it applied to her. I realize that my objection means nothing to you; nevertheless, I still retain title to this property. Kindly retire—or unkindly if you prefer. I'm indifferent which, just so you retire. I bid you good-day—permanently if possible. Do I make my meaning at all clear?"

"Well, sir, if Plunks—I mean Goody——"

"I don't?" Ripley Little continued his advance.

"Ye—es, sir." Hamilton Ellers, at least law-abiding, clumped out to rejoin his friends in the portico, closing the door behind him; and Ripley Little, breathing noisily, passed into the living-room and from a window saw the four moving crippledly toward the front gate and the street. They spoke busily together as they went, but seemed downcast.

" 'Plunks'," Ripley Little said, staring through the glass. "That's nice. 'Plunks'!"

"I don't blame you, Father," his fourteen-year-old son said sympathetically from the open double doorway behind him. "I don't blame you for getting mad and talking to yourself."

"Talking to myself?" Little turned. "I wasn't doing anything of the kind."

"Weren't you, Father?" Filmer said. "Well, anyhow, I think you did the right thing. Goody heard you, too. She was leaning over the banisters and she'd have come down and interfered except I think she thought it'd just make it more embarrassing. She's still up there, listening, and it ought to teach her something useful because she certainly heard——"

"I certainly did!" a sweet voice called vindictively from the stairway, and the prettiest girl for miles around—dark-eyed, brown-haired and stirringly graceful—sped down the steps and came rushing into the room.

III

Her violently yellow, scarlet, green and black modernist pajamas were not unbecoming; but her facial extreme beauty was marred by a swollen underlip and a discoloration under her right eye; two strips of adhesive plaster, moreover, were crossed upon her right cheek. "Did I *hear* it!" she cried. *"Now* I know how you speak to my most intimate friends when I'm not there to protect them! You may be my father; but———"

"That will do! We'll go into this in a moment." Little turned from her to his son. "Filmer, have you finished your breakfast?"

"No, sir. I was just getting into it when I thought I'd better come out in the hall and see what———"

"Very well," Little said. "I don't pretend that I'm not glad to have one intelligent and obedient child left, Filmer; but I think now you'd better go back into the dining-room and close the door and finish your breakfast."

"Yes, sir." Filmer, reluctant but flattered, proved that he was obedient, and, after the dining-room door had been heard to close, Ripley Little addressed his daughter, trying to use a quiet and reasonable voice. She stood before him defiant, breathing fast.

"Now let's have it," he said. "What's the matter with your face?"

"Nothing's the matter with it! Nothing to speak of. I merely——"

"Merely!" her father echoed. "Merely? You call that merely? I'm beginning to have strange ideas. Those gilded hoodlums that just tried to break in here at breakfast-time were practically in ruins, and I'm beginning to believe that a police car actually *did* drive up to our front door last night. I——"

"They're not!" the daughter interrupted hotly. "What right have you to call my most intimate friends hoodlums?"

"They are!" The father's temper, already wrecked within, began to operate his voice. "Bandaged gilded young hoodlums, and I'm not going to have them breaking in here day and night, calling a daughter of mine 'Plunks' and——"

"What's the matter with 'Plunks'?" she asked bitterly. "Is it my fault you named me 'Gudrida'? Mother told me she didn't have a thing to do with it; you were bound to christen me 'Gudrida'. I hate being called 'Goody' or 'Drida' and there aren't any lovelier boys in this whole world than Ham Ellers and Bull Thetford and Ruggo Smart and Hot Toddy. You——"

"Look at your face!" Ripley Little said, all reasonableness gone. "Just look at it, I ask you! How'd you get it?"

"That's exactly what I'm trying to tell you. If you'll ever stop raving long enough to let me——"

"All right. I've stopped. So go ahead. If anybody's doing any raving in this room it certainly isn't I. It's difficult to restrain myself sometimes; but——"

"I thought you said you'd stopped." Then, as her father only looked at her over a heaving chest, Goody spoke as rapidly as she possibly could. "It all amounts to nothing at all except the boys had to come early today on account of having to see me right away about something very important."

" 'Important'? Of all creatures living on this distracted earth the four least likely to have anything important in their heads——"

"Go it!" Goody said. "I thought you claimed you'd stopped and wanted to listen. I'm glad, though, you don't think it's important about your car because——"

"My car!" Little started. *"My* car?"

"You weren't using it, nobody was; the other one was in Crappio's and we didn't have any," Goody explained, with an air of strained patience. It was as if she strove to reach the mind of a backward child. "Mother and Cousin Olita both practically the same as said we could because Ruggo's sister had sneaked his car out on him, poor Ham's got smashed by that truck last week, and Bull and Hot haven't got any. So we definitely didn't have any other way to get to the Rosy Showboat. We——"

"It's coming," her father said. "Now I'm beginning to get it. Rosy Showboat! You *had* to get to the Rosy Showboat. Of course! The whole jobjam world would have been upset and Hitler'd have been sitting right in the

White House if you and Ham Ellers and Bull Thetford and Ruggo Smart and Hot Toddy hadn't got to the Rosy Showboat. So you deliberately took my car—and later there was a police car——"

"Police car? Ridiculous!" Goody interrupted. "It wasn't anything of the kind. I suppose you heard the siren and——"

"Heard it? Who in this whole town didn't hear it? It came screeching up the street and then the phonograph started and a herd of buffaloes——"

"Oh, I knew what a fuss you'd make if it woke you up," Goody said. "What's the use? Entirely on account of your forever going into a frenzy over my staying out a few minutes late, I insisted on coming straight home from the hospital where they took us first, and the boys naturally came with me in the ambulance—an ambulance isn't a police car, is it?—and before we went out to the icebox the nice intern that came along with us may have been a little high and he was the one that turned on the phonograph, and the dancing didn't last over half a minute because I knew if it woke you up you'd be like this in the morning and——"

"Ambulance," Ripley Little said indistinctly. "Hospital first, then ambulance. What happened to your face and my car?"

"That's what the boys wanted to see me about this morning," Goody said. "The man in the other car was definitely beside himself. He claimed he could prove that Ruggo was driving with his head swiveled round to speak to Ham Ellers and Bull and me on the back seat when it happened."

"When what happened?" Little's voice was more indistinct. "When what happened?"

"Why, when the man's car *hit* us," Goody replied, as if to the most foolish of all his questions. "What else *could* I mean? So naturally the boys were anxious to find out the first thing this morning if I'd found out if you had any collision insurance on your car because maybe——"

"Jobjam!" Ripley Little said. "Jam! Jobjam the helm! Jam the——"

"Oh, all right!" Goody seemed at the end of her patience. "All right if you have to take it that way. Why can't you be sensible? We all did everything we possibly could. Even while they were fixing us up at the hospital and we still didn't know whether we were alive or dead, we telephoned Crappio to send the wrecking-crew for your car. I'm sorry if you're inconvenienced, Father; but I think for you to speak to just about my dearest friends in the insulting and outrageous way you used when they came here as they did this morning just to try to be helpful and——"

She would have continued; but her father clapped his hands together, making a sound that assisted his facial expression to stop her. "Compared to what I was seven or eight years ago," he said, "I'm a poor man; but I still command funds enough to hire guards if necessary to prevent any of those four car-smashers from setting foot on my premises again day or night. Out of the whole of this community for your constant associates you select the freshest, uselessest, recklessest——"

"I do not!" Goody protested. "They are not, and anyway they select me. Definitely! They definitely——"

"Will you stop!" Little shouted. "Whenever I attempt to exert the slightest authority you try to 'definitely' me deaf. Definitely, definitely, definitely! I'm so sick of that jobjammed word I——"

"Why all the noise?" his daughter inquired. "I'm simply trying to tell you I'm sorry for what happened to your car and discover if you have any collision insurance; but why try while you're definitely beside yourself? If you have any further reason for detaining me from my breakfast, kindly state it. It's getting cold on a tray upstairs and I'd definitely like to return to it."

"Go up and eat it!" the furious father said. "While you're consuming it, swallow this down, too: not one of those swing-crazed speed vandals ever sets a crippled foot on my property again. Definitely!"

"Indeed?" Goody, who had decisively moved toward the door, swung about haughtily. "What's your objection to them?"

"What's my——"

"Certainly! What's your objection to them?"

"Well, I'm dob dabbed!" Little said. Then, conscious that desperation availed him nothing, he once more tried to be reasonable. Compelling himself, he made his voice appealing, as if from man to man. "See here, Goody, let's just try to look at this thing sensibly. If you've got to go places the whole jab time as it seems we can't stop you from doing, why can't you anyhow pick out somebody more intelligent, or at least safer, to go with? There certainly are *some* young people in this town with anyhow a little common sense and good manners and human caution. Why can't you find at least one young man or boy that has some steadiness and sense and modesty and industry and——"

"Who?" Goody asked, and, stepping toward him, permitted herself to utter a slight peal of jeering laughter. "You have somebody in mind, Father? Whom do you suggest?"

"Why—why, anybody except those," he said. "I wasn't thinking of anyone in particular. I only mean somebody superior to those——"

"Well, mention one," Goody returned. "You say there's such a lot. Can't you mention just one? Who?"

"Why—why——" Little goadedly searched through a limited gallery of ill-remembered young faces and in haste selected one with an earnest expression and spectacles. "Why, young Norman Peel, for instance."

"Norman Peel? Did you say Norman Peel, Father?"

"Certainly I did. Norman Peel. Why not Norman Peel? He's—he's——"

"He's what?" Goody repeated her injurious laughter. "You don't know any more about Norman Peel than a whale does about cats. Are your orders that I'm to be Norman Peel's sole escort from now on?"

"I merely mentioned him," Little responded, struggling with his voice. "I mentioned Norman Peel as merely one example of the better sort of young men of this community."

"You agree with Norman, then," Goody said. "Have you ever seen much of him, Father?"

"I see him from time to time, certainly. He's shown energy enough to go into business and I've heard his employers speak of him as industrious. In a way I've had my eye on him for some time and——"

"Oh, you have your eye on him, have you, Father? As a son-in-law?"

"As a young businessman I'd be glad to see in my own employ," Little said, and, sorely aware that Goody had him far off the subject of her defacements, his injured car and those responsible for both, he added sternly, "As a young man I'd be glad to see in my house because he doesn't come bursting into it held together with splints and calling my bandaged daughter 'Plunks'! As a young man who doesn't send me from my home on foot after maltreating my daughter's face, inflicting losses on insurance companies and——"

"Oh, then, you *have* got the insurance!" Goody cried. "Thank heaven the boys won't feel they have to ask their fathers to——"

"That's all that concerns you, is it?" Little said fiercely. "That's all you——"

"I said I was sorry, didn't I? How many times do I have to——"

"Don't exert yourself; once is enough," Little said. " 'Sorry' pays all the bills, puts my car at the door for me and fixes your face all up again! Young people nowadays burn your house down, then just say 'Sorry!' and——"

"Sorry!" Goody interrupted. "My breakfast's waiting." She returned spiritedly to the doorway, stopped and looked over her shoulder. "What do you know about 'young people nowadays'? How could you know anything about 'em when you're always in such a state? Maybe it isn't tactful to mention it; but in my own quiet circle you're rather well known as the terrible-tempered Mr. Little."

"I?" he cried unwarily. "That's absolute slander. How often does anybody ever hear me speak in anger? Twice a year at the most. I——"

"Twice is right," Goody said. "Six months each time."

Upon that, she took advantage of his inability to respond promptly, and departed; but half way up the stairs she paused to call downward, "Norman Peel? Houp-la!" Then she resumed her swift ascent.

IV

LITTLE, remaining near the open wide doorway of the living-room, heard her light footsteps reach the upper hall; then, as spaces were open and the house was quiet, he unfortunately heard something more—his wife's voice, apprehensively hushed but all too clearly audible.

"Is he gone, Goody?"

He felt justified in taking it upon himself to reply, more than loudly enough, "I am not, thank you!"

"Oh, dear!" Mrs. Little's response was the squeak of a snared bird; for in truth she was trapped by her own indiscretion. Unable to return to her bedroom and retain face, she was irresistibly drawn down the stairway to explain herself if possible. She came into the living-room pulling more closely about her the garment of blue rayon she wore over her night dress; but its effect and hers was that of a helpless fluttering. "I only meant——" she began. "I didn't mean—— I only asked Goody——"

"If I'd gone," her husband said grimly. "So you already knew what happened last night. Did you get up and join the party down here when you heard the dancing?"

"Well, I did get up," Mrs. Little admitted. "I mean, when I heard them all go out and Goody came up to bed, I went in her room and got her to tell me about it. Don't you think we ought to be *so* glad, Ripley, that she wasn't seriously injured—that none of them were? It really was a miracle! Really, Ripley, we seem to be a pretty lucky family. Don't you think we all ought to be——"

"Rejoicing?" he asked. "Me in particular, I suppose you mean? No, I don't. Since you ask me: no, I don't. Especially after the interview I've just had with my daughter, I don't. In regard to that interview and the general state of this world and this country, I don't find myself in a rejoicing condition. Do you?"

"Oh, dear!" Mrs. Little sat down flaccidly.

"Up to the time I passed my fortieth year," her husband said, "I lived a pleasant, quiet life. Up to then I didn't even know I belonged to a 'Class'; I thought I was just a citizen. But somebody that'd read books by somebody that'd read foreign books began calling 'most everybody the 'Great American Middle Class' because there seems to have been something like that in Europe; and then, pretty soon, we all got put into new Classes to fight each other. Goody's in the Youth Class, the Female Youth Class that has to fight the Father Class. Away from home I'm not in the Father Class, I'm in the one that got picked on and exploited from the start by all the other Classes, and had to pay for all of 'em, jobjam 'em! Up to when I passed my fortieth year——"

"Now, Ripley, please!" Mrs. Little tried to interrupt

him. "Don't let's go over all that again and get all worked up and——"

"It used to be a nice world," he said, "up to when I found out I belonged to the Underprivileged Class, the greedy few millions of businessmen that ought to go broke so as to make everything even at zero. Then when we all *are* broke, and the country, too, along comes this nice agreeable gentleman, Hitler, with the dear little Japs to back him up and scare the shirt off of everybody in the world that just wants to be let alone to 'tend to his own business—and that's the very time my own daughter picks to do her jammedest. I tell you from the heart that if it weren't for Filmer's being kind of a comfort to me sometimes, I'd be ready to swear we made the mistake of our lives ever having any children at all. I——"

"Now, Ripley, please don't——"

"Please don't what, Mrs. Little?" Mrs. Little quivered; whenever he called her "Mrs. Little" she knew that things were bad. "Please don't *what?*" he repeated. "Talking to Goody I merely expressed a slight natural human indignation because of the destruction of her face and my car by her disbrained associates and suggested that just possibly a city of this size might afford something superior in the way of companionship; and I was openly jeered at when I mentioned, for instance, young Norman Peel. She——"

"Norman Peel, Ripley?" Mrs. Little said timidly. "I don't really know him at all well, dear; but I—I don't think he's exactly Goody's—Goody's type, is he?"

"Wouldn't that be to his credit?" the embittered father asked, and replied to himself, "If what she's already

picked shows her type, it certainly would. Just compare
Norman Peel with her Ham Ellerses and Hot Toddys
and Bull Thetfords and the rest of 'em, for instance.
There *isn't* any comparison!"

"Isn't there, Ripley?"

"Not a dobdab nickel's worth!" Little's irritation was
increased by what seemed criticism on the part of both
Goody and her mother—criticism of his ability to discern
superior worth. In his argument with Goody he'd mentioned Norman Peel almost at random, not being able at
a moment's notice to think of any finer young man; now
he found himself, he knew not how, in the position of a
champion. Automatically he became crossly enthusiastic
in defending his choice. "Just like you and Goody!" he
said. "I wouldn't put it past you both to be against
Norman Peel because his spectacles kept him out of the
draft. I wouldn't put it past you to be against him because——"

"But I'm not," she protested. "I'm not against——"

"You are," he said. "I can see it. In my opinion, for a
boy only a year out of college, and a beginner, Norman
Peel's just about the brightest young businessman downtown. He was in my office yesterday on an errand; he
was only there for as much as ten or fifteen minutes but I
could tell he knew exactly what he was about. Besides
that, he's got a bright earnest face, he dresses quietly—
none of these big checks, no-necktied, slack-panted,
wrinkle-socked, loud——"

"Ripley, please don't get so excited. I don't doubt Norman Peel's a good young man; but maybe it might have
been a mistake to try to talk him up to Goody just when

The Fighting Littles 31

she felt so hurt about Ham Ellers and the others. She can't help their all being in love with her, you see, and I'm afraid it was a little hard on her to have you——"

"So you're at it, too, are you?" her husband asked.

"At it, Ripley? I—I don't know what you mean. At— at what?"

"Attacking me. It's the last straw." He stamped into the hall, took his hat from a table, put it on slammingly. "Well, dob dab!" he said. "I beg you to excuse me. I'm on my way."

Mrs. Little, slack in her chair, whimpered, "Oh, dear! Oh, dear!" as the front door clashed behind him and simultaneously a door opened in the body of the house. Filmer came from the dining-room, entered the living-room and stood before his mother. His expression was serious and perhaps a shade too self-satisfied.

"So it's the same old story," he said. "The same old story." He liked the phrase and himself for using it; so he tried it again. "Mother, why has it always got to be the same old story?"

"What?" she asked. "What old story?"

"I mean," he explained, "I don't claim Goody's a really smart girl; but I don't see why she can't exercise a little obedience and intelligence in her dealings with Father, the way he says himself I do. A little while ago, in this very room he told me I'm the only one that has any and does, and I've even heard him say so when he didn't know I did. I don't see why this same old story has to always go on the same way practically every day. Father's a perfectly well-meaning man if you know how to handle him. You got to humor him and show you understand him and

got a little sympathy, and he'll be all right. All he asks
from this family is a little——"

"Never mind!" His mother, finding his tone intolerable,
interrupted him. "I'm afraid your father only praised you
because he's upset with Goody about something, Filmer.
I'm afraid you forget there've been certain times in the
past when he didn't find you so intelligent and obedient as
he believes he thinks you are now. Aren't you forget-
ting——"

"Oh, those?" Filmer thus dismissed the times to which
she referred. "They were just ippisodes. Listen, Mother;
what is it he's upset with Goody over? Was it anything
else except the hullabaloo that went on last night? Listen,
Mother, was it——"

"Never mind, please. It's nothing you have anything
to do with. You must realize that in these dreadful days
—just look at the newspapers!—we're all very nervous
and when there's any kind of disturbance at all everybody jumps, especially businessmen, and most of all your
poor father."

"*I* don't, Mother. You say everybody jumps. Look at
me; I'm as calm as——"

"Then try to stay so," Mrs. Little said, "and be very
considerate because it's true everybody's nerves are
jumpy. Mine are, for instance, right now, and if you stop
to talk any longer, Filmer, you'll be late to school."

"Always the same old cry," he said. "Always the same
old cry, 'You'll be late to school.' Whenever anything's
wrong in this family and I so much as dare to ask to use
what little brains I got to help——"

"Your 'little' brains, Filmer?" His mother, in spite of

her depression, was faintly amused. "You mustn't be so mock-modest, Son. I'm sure you don't for a minute forget your splendid school record or overhearing Miss Hoapmiller's telling the Principal you were her brightest pupil."

He was hurt. "Don't I ever get to hear the last o' that? Just because I thought it would please my parents and happened to mention it at home I suppose I got to have it dinned into my ears all the rest o' my whole life every time I ever——"

"Do go, Filmer!" his mother begged. "I'm sure you're late already; do go."

"You seem to forget this is the last day of school," he said. "Vacation commences tomorrow and being late the last day doesn't matter a farthing's whistle. Not a farthing's whis——"

"Do go, Filmer!"

"Oh, certainly," he said. "But remember this: it's the last time. Up to September it's the last time I can't be confided in what's wrong in this family on account of I'll be late to school. After today that excuse won't serve. I'll know all about this business before tomorrow anyway. Good-by, Mother."

He left her coldly, and, when he returned in the middle of the afternoon, having lunched at school, made good his promise to discover the cause of the morning's domestic trouble. A long and probing conversation he had with Gentry Poindexter in the empty garage put him in possession of even more facts than had occurred, and he appeared at the dinner table that evening sympathetically ready to be a partisan of his father. Somewhat dampeningly, however, his sister was not present, and Cousin

Olita, answering a frowning inquiry of his, explained that Goody had gone out to dine and dance.

"Where?" Ripley Little asked, and set down his soup-spoon. "Where?"

"At the Green Valley Country Club," Mrs. Little replied, looking at her plate.

"With that face? At the Green Valley Club with that face?"

"Gentry told me about her face," Filmer said. "I went upstairs to look at it; but she had her door locked so I couldn't, and wouldn't open it when I asked her. Well, I don't know I should have done this exactly, Father; but I went around on the roof of the porch to Goody's window and looked in and she was powdering and lipsticking. She's got a black eye and adhesive plaster, and her under-lip's about the size of a red Easter egg and——"

"Filmer!" Cousin Olita laughed. "What a story! Don't exaggerate so."

"I don't know," Little said. "I don't know that it's much of an exaggeration, unless her lip's gone down remarkably since this morning. To me the unbelievable thing is that she'd be willing to exhibit it and her other mutilations before an assembly of people who——"

"Now, Ripley." Mrs. Little, not looking at him, shook her head slightly. "You really don't understand girls of Goody's generation. They love to look like that nowadays in public."

"Yes," he said, "I forgot that. They do, jobjam 'em!"

Filmer restrained an impulse. It was to explain to his father that defacements and other injuries sometimes added to the distinction of one's appearance, offering the suggestion of accidents the result of dash and daring. Appearing on a crutch at a party for instance, Filmer felt, might even imply that one had been doing something pretty fancy with an airplane; and about the next best thing was the look of having got into trouble at eighty miles an hour in a car. The truth was that as Goody hadn't been actually killed Filmer rather envied her the chance to display her evidences of speed and action. He didn't say so, however, and, after a short study of the expression upon his father's broad face, decided to retain by silence the parental esteem in which he complacently knew himself to be held. Filmer's thought was, "You can't tell what he'll do. Most of the time these old people don't take things the way you'd expect 'em to and it'll·be a lot better for me to not say anything right now but just go on being a comfort to him in his own way whenever he thinks of Goody."

Filmer maintained this policy all evening. Quiet, sympathetic, he sat near his father in the living-room and was careful to keep the radio down to the barest audibility. When he rose to go up to bed he bade his father goodnight in the gentle tones of one who comprehends everything. He had a success.

"Goodnight, my boy," Ripley Little said. "Goodnight, my boy."

V

His FATHER called Filmer "my boy" eight or nine times, and Goody nothing at all, during the next several days. This had happened before; and being the favorite child rapidly became, as usual, almost a commonplace with Filmer. His whole first week of vacation, in fact, was rather a dull one; his mind had found little to dwell upon. Precocious spottily, though sievelike with a thousand minute vacancies, that mind was accustomed to absorb textbook formulae more quickly than could most of its competitors; and in his pardonable statement to his parents he had not exaggerated Miss Hoapmiller's praise of him. Now, with no homework to fill the loose hours, and no daily triumphs over an audience of slower intellects, he almost missed the dear old schoolroom, almost could wish himself there again.

Fragrant mid-June and a torrid pea-green morning found him without engagements, stagnant in idea and almost without impulses. Nevertheless, as his aimless feet bore him out to stand in the portico after breakfast, a change took place; for a ruling element of conduct automatically departed out of him with the very closing of the door behind him. This element might be called the habit of domestic guardedness. Filmer indoors, and open to family observation, was one thing; Filmer at school was another; and Filmer outside of either home or school was yet another.

He yawned without shielding the aperture, stretched his arms, and then, moved by a vague prompting, went out to the shady sidewalk, and strolled southward. Beneath a hot blue sky and a few motionless cotton clouds he sauntered, not thinking formed thoughts, yet as aware of himself as if he had been a celebrated personage observed in every look and action.

Though he was short for his age, sometimes mortifyingly so, his style, he knew, was better than merely good. He was hatless, of course, proving his hair's abhorrence of regimentation. His green jersey was not only wrong side front but wrong side out, too, so that the stitchings of "44" could be seen upon his back. His hot trousers, of a purpled blue, were incomparably baggy and shapeless, and no color at all could be ascribed to his once russet shoes. He walked loungingly, swinging his arms more than appeared needful, and now and then he moved his jaws as if he were chewing, though he wasn't. He thought it looked well to appear to be chewing something and the action reassured him, helped him to make the glance of his eye what he wished it to be—disdainful of all life and property except his own.

Turning eastward at the next corner, he came upon a colleague hung spineless in a gateway, a boy who also

wore, skeletonized, "44" upon his back. Unlacing his
limbs, he joined Filmer in the stroll, and, as greeting,
inquired, "Whaddy know, Fil?"

"Nertsy-nerts," Filmer replied fashionably; then, as
they walked on together, he drew forth a package of
cigarettes, lighted one, and proffered the package. "Got
the nerve to smoke yet, Mister Charlsworth Beck?"

"You know what I'd get," Charlsworth said. "Listen,
I thought your father was going to give you a car on
your twenty-first birthday if you never smoke up to then.
So how———"

"Is him saying so the same as me saying so?" Filmer
asked. "If my family want to think promising me a car
six or seven years from now's the same as me taking the
all-tobacco pledge, why, the way I look at it, Charl, it's
simply let 'em sizzle in their own grease."

"Yes, but look, Fil. Don't you want to get that car
when you're twenty-one years old?"

"Might or might not." Filmer was lofty. "Listen. In
the first place I don't hardly expect to ever live to be
twenty-one years old, and in the second place, look, supposing I *would* live that long, look, is it my business to
go puffing around the family? What they don't know
won't hurt 'em, will it?" Again he was heartless. "Just
let 'em sizzle in their own grease!"

"But listen a minute, Fil; look here a minute. The
reason I don't smoke, myself, it's because my mother
can always tell. The only thing ever fixes my breath exactly right is a raw onion, and most of the time you
simply can't find one, and look, I hate 'em in the first
place. What you do about your breath, Fil?"

Filmer remained superior. "Yes, a good many fellows that smoke away from the family have trouble with their breath. I used to worry some over mine till I worked out just the right substance for it. There's just one substance that really does it. It's Eucalina."

"What?"

"Eucalina." Filmer took from his pocket a small flat blue tin box. Charlsworth looked at the box, saw in white letters the name "Eucalina", had a sketchy view of smaller print, "One every two hours until relieved", and his eye caught the final words, lower down . . . "should be regulated by the advice of a physician." Filmer threw away what was left of his cigarette, opened the tin box, took out a small bluish-white tablet, and placed it in his mouth.

Charlsworth looked at him admiringly. "Say, listen, Fil. Isn't that kind of medicine or something? Isn't it kind of risky maybe?"

"Might be—for some people," Filmer said easily, and restored the box to his pocket. "You got to learn to stand the taste; but I'm used to 'em."

Charlsworth's admiration increased. "Look! I've noticed sometimes you smell like kind of inside a hospital or somewheres. Don't your family ever notice you smell that way, Fil?"

"Yes; but there's medicated soap in the hall lavatory at our house and I just say I been washing in it."

"Yes, but——" Charlsworth struggled interiorly with thoughts. "Well, look, f'r instance, Fil. Your family use that same soap sometimes, themselves, don't they? So look; they know *they* don't smell like you do, themselves, so when they notice you're smelling and you tell 'em it's the soap, and they know it don't make them smell, themselves, but you do, why, listen, don't they think that's kind of funny and ask you why you smell when they don't?"

"No, they don't." Filmer uttered a slight scornful laugh. "When I smell and they don't and I say it's the soap, well, their minds don't go on working. They just think, 'That's kind of funny', and quit and think about something else. It's the way their minds work and it's the way most people's minds work." Then he added, "It's why if you got a few brains you can do just about what you like to in this world."

"Boy! That's telling 'em!" Charlsworth said. His friend had used an expression that pleased him and he now made it his own. "Do your own way and just let the family sizzle in their own grease, huh? 'S the way I do, too, Fil." Then he became inquiring. "Look, Fil. What do you do when they say you simply got to do something you don't want to?"

"Me? I say to myself, 'Use the bean, old kid; use the bean.'"

Charlsworth's lips moved thoughtfully, repeating this prescription, committing it to memory. The two boys, sauntering round the block, had now reached the corner of the shady street upon which Filmer lived, and here Charlsworth began to walk more lingeringly. He came to a stop.

"Look," he said. "You heard Antoinette Fry's going to give a party?"

"Her?" Filmer stopped, too, and in all sincerity was

disgusted. "Listen. That dame could give a million par-
ties; I wouldn't be caught dead at 'em!"

"Why? Are you worse sourer on Antoinette Fry than
you are on all of 'em, Fil?"

"Me? I wouldn't look at Antoinette Fry if she was
in the electric chair and they gave me a ticket! I
wouldn't——"

Charlsworth spoke hushedly in warning. "Listen, Fil;
she might hear you!"

He made a nervous gesture toward the house before
which they'd paused; and Filmer, glancing over the hedge
that bordered the sidewalk, saw a girl sitting upon the
verandah steps, prattling gayly to two boys. She was a
beautiful little creature, animated, fair-haired and dainty.
The blonde hair was waved glossily; her gold-figured blue
blouse and her white linen skirt were new and unspotted.
Her short white socks were inconsistently protected by
small but adult high-heeled toeless blue slippers.

Filmer openly sneered. "Look at Bill and Slops listening to that dame like she was the supreme toots of this
world! Not me! She'll haf to show a few brains before
she ever gets Filmer Little to——"

Charlsworth interrupted timidly. "Look, Fil. Say
listen. Look. Let's just go in and——"

"What?" Filmer, insulted, stared at him. "You want
to go in *there?* You ask *me* to go in there and——"

"But I told you I heard she's going to give a party,
didn't I?" Charlsworth said, in apologetic explanation.
"Come on! We'll just go in and laugh and show sarcasm
at everything they say and——"

"Goo' by, siss!" Filmer turned on his heel and slouched

toward home. "Goo' by, siss-boy! Go on in and watch her wag her old toes and wave her old fingernails she's been sticking in her mother's strawberry jam! Goo' by, siss-boy!"

Charlsworth, depressed, joined the lively group on the verandah; and Filmer, having swaggeringly passed before the two next adjacent houses, paused to enact a fragment of drama for which the inspiration came upon him out of nowhere. Chewing nothing faster, but otherwise cool and deliberate, he elevated his left hand in which he held an invisible baseball. Then, enclosing this intangible with his right hand also, he lifted two fingers as a signal, "wound up", elevated his left foot to the height of his head and pitched a miraculous curve. "Hot zinga*zooey!*" he said, and, squatting upon his haunches, became an imperturbably chewing professional catcher, received the ball in an imaginary glove, said "Smack!" and, immediately an umpire, announced curtly, "Striker out!" This, for nobody's benefit but his own, gave him a little satisfaction. He ate another Eucalina tablet and walked slowly into his own yard.

In one of the striped canvas chairs under a tree at the edge of the greenly simmering lawn, Cousin Olita sat knitting. As she glanced toward Filmer, upon his approach, her nose-glasses twinkled affectionately in a disk of sunshine that came through the foliage above her.

"That's a nice boy," she said, for no reason. "Come sit down in the shade; that's right. You've got that medical smell again, Filmer. Your mother and I were talking about it yesterday—— I mean about your having it from the soap when nobody else does. I told her it must mean something about your constitution. It might be one of these new things people have, and before it goes any deeper I told her she ought to send you to some crack right-up-to-the-minute doctor and he ought to give you a nice thorough examination all over. So often lately I've noticed your smelling like——"

"Is it your business or mine?" Filmer asked sternly. "You 'tend to yourself and I'll 'tend to myself. If any doctor tries to examine me he'll see what he gets, kindly remember when you go around discussing my affairs with my mother, please."

Cousin Olita's mind wandered from the smell. "Your sister's having such a nice morning, Filmer. She's gone out riding."

"Riding!" Filmer exclaimed. "Do you mean to state that after what she did to Father's car she's now permitted to run up bills hiring horses while I'm not granted even the most niggardly allowance but haf to depend on handouts and pittancers——"

"Pittancers, Filmer? Don't you mean pittances?"

"No matter what I mean," he said. "Goody and her gang absolutely destroyed the best car this family's got, the one Father uses for himself. He had to have Crappio sell it for junk, and now, on top of that if he lets her hire horses——"

"No, no!" Cousin Olita laughed. "I never can remember when you ought to say 'riding' and when you ought to say 'driving'. Of course I was too young for the generation that used to talk about going out buggy-riding; but when I lived in Urnabula and one of the young gentlemen would try to steal a march and get me away from the others for the evening he'd usually ask me if I didn't want to go out auto-riding with him. Of course 'auto-riding' is probably looked upon as an out-of-dated way of putting it nowadays; but—— What's the matter, Filmer?"

Her question was evoked by the startled incredulity of his expression. "You say some of 'em tried to steal a march and get you away from——" he began; then stopped, not because of tactfulness or to conceal his total unbelief but because of a thought more urgent. "Listen, Cousin Olita, it doesn't make any difference which you think Goody's doing right now, 'riding' or 'driving'; but what's she doing it in or on?"

"What? You mean what's she out riding in, Filmer?"

"That's what I said, didn't I? In or on what?"

"Why, in the other car, Filmer. It got back from Crappio's this morning just a little while after your father took the bus downtown, so Goody——"

"She did?" Filmer rose from the canvas chair in which he'd been reclining and stood rigid. "She's actually had the front to take that car out?"

"Your mother said she could, Filmer."

"What! My mother let her? She actually let that girl——" Filmer was unable to express his desperation by his voice alone; he threw himself full length upon the grass. "Hasn't anybody in this universe got one particle of common sense left, not one single particle?"

"What's the matter, Filmer?"

He sat up and passionately told Cousin Olita what was the matter; for herein was touched the sorest spot in all his bruised longings. Over and over, with acute feeling, the subject had been debated between himself and all the other members of his family and sometimes Gentry Poindexter, Filmer always holding the affirmative and everybody else the negative.

"If it's come to this," he said, toward the conclusion of his present oration to Cousin Olita. "If it's come to where a girl that thinks the radiator's what runs the engine and has no business on earth to have a driver's license, and utterly ruined my father's own car just a few nights ago—— If it's come to my mother granting permission to that girl to take out the only other car this family's got the very minute it comes from Crappio's where her driving laid it up, while I'm not even allowed to touch a wheel when I'm as good a driver as there is in this city, and my family fall back on the mere driveling legalistic excuse that I haven't got a driver's license because——"

"That isn't the only reason, Filmer," Cousin Olita interrupted, knitting placidly. "Don't you remember that day of the family picnic when your father's car was bran' new and you got in it when nobody was looking and started it going and that cow and——"

"Listen!" Filmer said fiercely. "Did those animals receive one iota of injuries? Did my father haf to pay one iota of damages for that cow or that calf? I ask you to answer me!"

"No, they were only frightened; but you know what the new car looked like after the tree kept you from hitting them, Filmer; and don't you remember how the farmer that owned them——"

"Listen! Everybody's got to have an accident when

he's only a beginner, hasn't he? How old was I when I had that accident? I ask you to answer me. How old was I?"

"Well—let me see. It wasn't so long ago. You were——"

"Not long ago?" Filmer shouted. "I was thirteen years old. Only thirteen. That's how long ago it was!"

"Thirteen," Cousin Olita said reflectively. "Yes, I remember; it was about a year ago."

"What! Listen! Do you ever expect to make a mathematician? Use the bean, can't you? What's thirteen from fifteen? Use the bean! What's thirteen from fifteen?"

"Two," Cousin Olita replied. "But the picnic was on Memorial Day, the thirtieth of May, I remember now; and you won't be fifteen for two or three months yet, Filmer. So it's only a little while since you were thirteen, you see."

"I give up!" Filmer said. "I'm practically fifteen; but thirteen from fifteen don't leave two any more. Two whole years *have* gone by in spite o' that, though—but what's the use! Here we've got a Mayor that won't give you a driver's license on merit and lets a girl that don't know a spark plug from a tail-light have one, and *I'm* supposed to do nothing with my time while she rolls all over the United States with her old Ham Ellers just because he's got wavy hair and such a boyish smile! I heard her say he had to a couple her gal-friends, myself. 'Such a boyish smile'! Wouldn't *that* poison the cats I ask you!"

"But, Filmer, why wouldn't Hamilton Ellers have a nice boyish smile? He's only nineteen, maybe twenty. Besides, what makes you think she's out riding with him?

She isn't. As soon as the car was delivered, she telephoned to somebody she likes better and he got the day off from business right away and was here in a jiffy and they jumped in the car and———"

"Who?" Filmer asked scornfully. "Who got here in a jiffy and what's a jiffy?"

"It's a hurry, Filmer. Norman Peel."

"Norman Peel," Filmer echoed. "Why, she never———"

"Goody likes Norman Peel," Cousin Olita said, smiled fondly, and, with a plump hand, pushed higher the cluster of large blonde curls above her pink forehead. "She never really got to know Norman until that party last Tuesday night, she tells me; but she's been talking about him every minute since. I think it's so nice when young people fall terribly in love."

"You do?" Filmer rose to his feet and indelicately made gagging noises. "You think———"

"It's pretty." Cousin Olita, to Filmer's view, looked idiotic—unmitigatedly so. "I've never known Goody to seem so much like being head over heels in love before. It's sweet."

Cousin Olita and her thoughts of love had become repulsive to Filmer; and, to make clear that they hurt his stomach, he placed both hands over it and went stoopingly into the house.

VI

Entrance through an open French window brought him into the dining-room, and here he remembered something. On the previous evening, while "the family" sat elsewhere, he had retired quietly to the dining-room to read a borrowed well-worn work reputed liable to confiscation and known to him and his male circle as Bokakio. Threatened by interruption, he'd hurriedly thrust the volume into a drawer of the small sideboard; and now, as nobody was near, he decided to retrieve it and do a little more summer reading.

The humidity of the weather made the drawer stick, and, resenting this, he jerked the handle powerfully. The drawer yielded; and so, to an extent, did the whole sideboard. A fine old rose-pink glass compote, a trophy of one of his mother's antiquing excursions, slid picturesquely over a polished mahogany surface and dispersed itself upon the floor. It was accompanied by another antique, a Sheffield teapot, which naturally suffered less and only had its spout bent.

Filmer was annoyed. He was often accompanied by breakage—seldom a week passed without his dismembering some useless, prized old thing—but nobody except himself ever became accustomed to it; and he now realized he'd have to listen to a lot of dismal blah-blah about the compote before the day was over. That wouldn't be all, either: the subject would be brought up time and time again in the future, long after he was thoroughly sick of it.

He replaced the teapot, leaving the bent spout in shadow toward the wall, so that his mother wouldn't notice the difference, probably, until the next time she asked somebody to tea. Then, having used a foot to push the ruins of the compote beneath the sideboard, he brought forth the book, closed the drawer, went out to the garage, sat upon a stool, and. resumed his perusal of Bokakio. As he read, he absently smoked cigarettes, lighting one at the end of another, until finally he was surprised to find the package empty. By that time, however, he heard a musical gong belling indoors, Gentry Poindexter's announcement of lunch.

Filmer placed Bokakio carefully under a large box of junk; and then, fearing that he perhaps reeked of tobacco, he washed his hands and face at a sink in the garage and made use of two Eucalina tablets. Remains of these were still precautionarily in his mouth as he came into the dining-room and sat down beside Cousin Olita, opposite Goody. His father was present. Ripley Little often lunched at home, having resigned from his downtown club in May 1940 when one of the new members asked him if he thought the President could be persuaded to accept a third term.

"That the way to behave?" Ripley Little gave the favorite a surprisingly cold glance. "No greeting? No courtesy? Just clop-clop in and flop down in your chair and begin guzzling? No apologies for what you've done? Nothing?"

Filmer looked hurt. "For what I've done? Father, I haven't been doing anything I know of."

Mrs. Little shook her head sadly. "Filmer, of course you know what you did; you couldn't have forgotten it this soon, and I'm sure he's sorry, Ripley."

"Then why doesn't he say so?" Little asked. "He's a mystery. How does he manage to destroy property by merely walking into a room? It must have been so; time and again he does it. There wasn't anything on the sideboard to interest him. How could——"

"I was outdoors when I heard the crash," Cousin Olita said. "I didn't come in, though, because he doesn't often hurt himself much. Maybe he got dizzy and reached for something to steady himself without looking. It *might* have something to do with that medical smell he often has because just a little while before I'd been asking him if he oughtn't to have the doctor for it. I *do* think he ought to, because I notice it gets stronger and stronger." She glanced about brightly. "Don't you all smell it again right now?"

"Smell it?" Little repeated "Smell it? It gets into the food. As soon as he came into the room I began to taste it and since he's sat down I can't taste anything else." After a busy hot morning downtown, Ripley Little had

come home by hot bus, wilted; he'd bathed and donned
a new "tropic suit" of pale linen. Then, somewhat refreshed, he had been told by Gentry Poindexter of
the loss of the valuable compote. The favored child
was responsible, no question; and the father didn't wish
to be hard on him; but the smell, on top of the destruction,
was trying. "You didn't radiate this odor at breakfast,
Filmer. How do you manage to do it now?"

"I guess," Filmer said apologetically, "I guess I must
of got some of that soap on my hands again from washing."

"Soap?" his father asked. "How do you expect to wash
without getting soap on your *hands?* Do you usually wash
with your elbows?" He stared down the table at his wife.
"Can't that soap be changed? He seems to be allergic to
it and maybe Olita's right; possibly he ought to see a
specialist. A good epidermist might be able to tell us why
the rest of us can use that soap without——"

He was interrupted by a little accident. Filmer, nervous,
had applied too much force to the cutting of a chop upon
his plate. The chop, not tender, slippery with the juices
wherein it lay, leaped from Filmer's plate and came to
rest temporarily upon his father's new linen lap.

Little cried out unhappily, and, making the matter
worse with a napkin soaked in ice water from a goblet,
spoke testily of his son, of the price of clothes, and of the
cost of compotes believed to be of Bristol glass; but he
had to interrupt himself for hygienic reasons. "Stop
that!" he commanded. "Jobjam it, going to eat it after
it's been on the floor?" Again he addressed his wife. "Almost fifteen years old and he'll eat anything—anything!"

Does he care where it's been? He does not! Only the other day I saw him drop an all-day sucker on a dob dab ant-hill and then eat it—or at least he *would* have eaten it, ants and all, if I hadn't taken it away from him."

Abashed, Filmer nevertheless defended himself. "The other day? Why, my goodness, Father! When that happened I wasn't hardly over nine years old. I only——"

" 'Only'!" Little said. "Only ruined my clothes! And then going to eat it right off the floor! Why, when I was your age if my father had to talk to me as I'm compelled to——"

Sunny Cousin Olita spoke to Goody in a caressing voice. "You had a nice morning with your new friend, didn't you, dearie?"

"Just beautiful," Goody said, and, as her face was all right again, looked better than beautiful herself. Color was unusually high in her young cheeks; her voice had something new in it—a hushed and honeyed lingering, a rhapsodied little drawl. "Beautiful," she said dreamily. "He thinks we ought to have a hedge in front of the house instead of the fence, to be like the rest of the neighborhood. He likes to sing duets, Mother; so I've called up Madam Wurtza and arranged to begin vocal lessons, two a week. It's only four dollars a lesson. He said——"

"Who?" Ripley Little stared at his daughter. *"Who* is it that wants me to take down our fence and put up a hedge to get frost-killed and's already costing me eight dollars a week for music lessons? Who is this new——"

"He's a friend of mine," Goody replied, not eating but gazing wistfully at the tablecloth. "He says this city ought to have lots better architecture, Cousin Olita. He says for instance our house shouldn't have that side gable on it, and either the Watsons next door ought to paint their porch white or we ought to change ours to yellow. He's right about that, don't you think, Cousin Olita? He says I ought to send for a Chow from the Archblow Kennels on Long Island."

Ripley Little also had stopped eating, though he grippingly retained his knife in his right hand. "A what from where?" he asked. "Say that again."

"A darling Chow puppy, Father. He said to get you to wire for it and to have your bank wire the Archblow Kennels you're good for it and——"

"I'm not!" her father interrupted. "I'm not good for it. If I ever see a Chow in this house I'll be bad for it. In the meantime I'm asking again: Who is this new family adviser you——"

"It's so strange," Goody said, looking dreamier and dreamier. "I've lived my whole life in the same town with him and thought I knew him, but never really understood a thing about his nature until the other night at a party something urged me to stop dancing and walk about the lawn with him, listening to the music. Then all at once I saw how different he is and's almost the first one I ever talked to that takes the serious view of life, and wanted to tell me about capital and labor and Hitlerism and these old American reactionaries and how few people understand the vast problems our generation's had wished on us. He talked about you, a little, Father. He thinks in your business you're maybe following old-line methods too closely. He thinks most of you businessmen downtown——"

"Who does?" her father asked. "Who thinks I'm following old-line methods and wants to tell everybody downtown how to run their businesses?" Little paused for a reply; but, as Goody only smiled absently, he continued: "Let me get this straight. You met a boy at a party who's got you taking music lessons at four dollars a crack to sing duets with him, and's going to solve vast problems and rip out our fence and the side gable and paint the porch different and have my bank support my credit for the purchase of a Chow pup. I ask you who——" Ripley Little's already incensed breathing unfortunately inhaled from the direction of his son. "Job jam it!" he said muffledly. "Move farther away! Move down towards Cousin Olita, can't you? Let *her* have it a while!" He looked protuberantly at his wife. "I was talking to old Colonel Roland O. Whiting yesterday, the Americanest man I know; he's ninety-eight and a half years old, the last of the Fighting Whitings, all four of 'em Civil War officers and lifelong friends of my great-uncle, Brigadier General Cuneo Ripley Little that I was named for, as none of you ever remembers no matter how often I've told you. He said to me——"

"Who, Father?" Filmer asked, confused though his interest was aroused. "Was it your great-uncle that you're named for, or one of the Fighting Whitings that said this to you? Which did, and what did he——"

"I'm speaking to your mother," Little said. "At least,

I'm trying to. In conversation with me yesterday old Colonel Roland O. Whiting declared solemnly that this whole earth's now become an insane asylum, and is he right! Europe, Asia, Africa, a man's own country, a man's own business, a man's own home life—it's all jazz-banged to flinders. It's complete!"

He spoke with sincere conviction. At the moment almost all of the gentler impulses, including the instinctive fondnesses of fatherhood, were motionless within him. Filmer, as much as Goody, appeared to be an inexplicable creature who contained no trace of his own or any other intelligence. Without the slightest sense of responsibility, Filmer ruined a suit of clothes, the taste of food, a fifty-five-dollar compote and ate off the floor, all within the same hour—and he hadn't much more than started the day, at that! You couldn't even tell if he'd be alive by sunset. As for Goody, instead of trying to do something to make up for the car she'd transmuted to junk, she plainly tended to slide into a state of unpleasing lovesickness brought on, apparently, by the half-witted conversation of an adolescent Youth Movement spouter at a dance. Mrs. Little wasn't doing anything to stop any of this, and Cousin Olita seldom came indoors when it rained unless frightened by thunder. Ripley Little felt lonely, all alone among shapes that looked like thinking beings but weren't.

He applied more ice water to his lap, with poor results, and asked huskily, "Since Goody seems unable to mention the sacred name, will somebody else kindly try to tell me just who is this refashioner of our family's destinies, this Walking Brain?"

"Why, I thought I'd mentioned his name," Goody said. "You're getting an entirely wrong impression; it's somebody you like, Father. The other day when you spoke of him to me I was silly enough never to have appreciated him; but it was only because I didn't really know him then. It's Norman Peel, Father."

"Norm——" Little began, stopped abruptly and stared at her suspiciously. His son, misinterpreting the father's expression, believing it to be one of indignation, thought to regain lost favor.

"Norman Peel!" Filmer said jeeringly. "She's telling you straight. That's the new one, Father; everybody says so. She's gone plumb mush over that spectacled, dish-faced——"

"What!" The dreamy Goody came to life; her eyes flashed. "You dare? You who go around smelling, breaking everything and eating ants! *You!* Why, you aren't worthy even to speak the name of——"

"I am too!" Filmer shouted. "Why, even Norman Peel's own cousins say that guy's the most egotistical guy they ever knew; they say he's practically got meego-mania. They say——"

"Mother!" Goody rose emotionally. "If this is to be permitted at your table I for one decline to sit here and listen to it. For one, I ask to be excused!"

"That's merely sex," Filmer said, addressing his father informatively, as Goody left the room. "She'd finished her lunch anyhow and she's been nothing on earth but pure sex practically as long as I've known her. It's all that's behind this eight-dollars-a-week duet idea; though I don't say it's sex exactly that makes her want to buy a Chow—a Chow or any dog at all might be a good idea—but the rest of it's nothing but. For instance, take all this hooey about changing the fence and painting the porch yellow and cutting out the gable: Doesn't that betray she'd ruin our whole place just to——"

"Have you finished your lunch?" his father asked. "If you have——"

"Oh, all right." Filmer rose, aggrieved. "At least I'm old enough to grasp when my few opinions aren't thought to be desired." He left the table proudly.

Little, preparing to go, himself, glanced frowningly at Cousin Olita and then at his wife. "Well, what is it?" he asked. "Was she putting on an act at me? Was she trying to put something over on me?"

"What like, Ripley?" Mrs. Little said. "I don't see——"

"I mean about Norman Peel." His suspiciousness increased. "Just because I happened to mention Norman Peel the other day as a superior young man and——"

"Oh, no, no!" Cousin Olita and Mrs. Little both spoke together, and then Mrs. Little continued, "It's only too genuine, Ripley! I don't think she's ever been so much this way before."

"No, she really hasn't," Cousin Olita added. "Genuine? I should say so! I flatter myself I know the real thing when I see it, Cousin Ripley. It's lovely to watch when it springs up this way, and I think you did a wise thing when you pushed him at her. I'm sure he's all you told her he was and you can always be glad you had a hand in it."

"It didn't sound like him," Little said. "What she

quoted him as saying didn't seem to me characteristic. When I've seen Norman Peel downtown he's always appeared to be a bright young fellow anxious to get on in business and——"

"But that's different," Mrs. Little explained. "When they're with each other they're often almost the very opposite of what they are with us, Ripley. He's a serious young man; but of course Goody'd make him feel much more at home with her than he would with you, don't you think? No, I'm sure she told us entirely truthfully just what he——"

"Yes, indeed!" Cousin Olita added this confirmation. "Goody admires him too much to change a word she heard fall from his lips."

"All right," Little said. "All right, all right! I suppose nothing whatever's been heard from the unparalleled snail, A. P. Crappio? He hasn't condescended to telephone when he thinks our remaining car will be out of the shop?"

"Yes, he has, though." Cousin Olita, rising to go, was benign. "You'll be glad to hear, Cousin Ripley, Crappio sent it back this morning, and it looks *so* nice."

Gentry Poindexter had come in to clear the table, and Little spoke to him. "Bring it around, Gentry. You can take me downtown in it and finish your dishes after you get back."

The colored man went hastily to the pantry door, bearing a single saltcellar on his tray. "Miss Goody already tooken it, Mr. Little."

"What?"

"Yes, suh; jes' see her rollin' out the driveway from

the window. She already out pleasure-drivin'. Guess still go' be bus for you, Mr. Little, yes, suh."

The pantry door swung quickly, removing Gentry Poindexter from the sight of his employer, who turned to speak to Mrs. Little and Cousin Olita. They, however, were no longer in the room.

VII

Ripley Little went out through what appeared to be a humanly empty house and reached the sidewalk, on his way to the bus, before he remembered what had happened to his trousers and began to talk to himself about them and other matters. He returned, made the necessary exchange in his room, and, when he came downstairs, found his son awaiting him in the hall below.

"Listen, Father," Filmer said, sympathetic earnestly. "Cousin Olita claims why you got to walk in the hot sun to the bus and then crowd in and rattle around all the way downtown instead of in a car you're certainly the owner of, it's because Goody's been so used to using it she didn't think. Cousin Olita claims Goody's excusable on account of being in such a hurry not to miss any of the holiday Norman Peel worked his firm for; but I, for one, don't think that's a fair statement or that Cousin Olita uses her bean in the slightest."

"Well?" Little walked slowly toward the open front door. "What of it?"

"If you'd just listen a minute——" Filmer begged,

and his father indulged him; they paused in the doorway. "I could have saved all this and you'd be in that car now if I'd been really given the chance," Filmer said. "I was going to tell you at lunch about it was back from Crappio's; but nobody gave me much opportunity. What I'd like to ask you to remember is she's out with it again while I'm not permitted even to lay a single finger on a wheel. All those hours while everybody else is doing what they enjoy, what do *I* do? Hunt four-leaf clovers in the grass with Cousin Olita? Is that what I get to do, Father?"

There was a quavering sincerity in the young voice, and it touched the father. "Maybe you'd better go to a movie," Ripley Little said. "Here, my boy." He gave Filmer half a dollar, went out to the sidewalk, and, mopping his forehead and the broad back of his neck, turned toward the distant corner where he'd catch his bus.

Filmer was gratified by the half dollar, though he didn't know whether he'd use part of it on a movie or not. For the present, preferring to entertain himself with a little marksmanship, he went upstairs to his own room and returned with a small implement that he owned. This was a "slingshot" or miniature catapult made of a metal fork, two stout strips of rubber and a bit of leather, and, although Filmer had long passed the age (or thought he had) when such toys meant much in his life, he felt that it might now afford him perhaps a half hour's pleasure. He gathered some pebbles and fragments of crushed stone from the driveway, and walked toward the canvas chairs under the big tree at the side of the lawn, intending to sit and shoot at such robins and sparrows as might come within range; but, perceiving that Cousin Olita was strolling in the same direction, he went round to the back yard.

There for a while he amused himself and a few birds by shooting at them; then, remembering that he'd left Bokakio in the midst of an important passage, he put the slingshot in his hip-pocket, retired into the garage and resumed his reading. Much of it was disappointing; but he persisted, plugging ahead through the interminable verbiage of the classic work and feeling himself only a little rewarded for his efforts. At last he yawned, rose from his stool, returned the book to the floor under the junk box, strolled languidly out to the sidewalk and sauntered northward. As he passed before the third house in that direction, Antoinette Fry ran out to the hedge and called to him.

"Filmer Little! Wait a minute, Filmer. Do me a favor? Please do, Filmer; that's a dearie."

"Listen, dame!" Filmer paused. "Don't call me that. Believe me or not, I'm particular who I let have liberties with me. State your favor, if you got to, and I promise on my sincere oath I won't do it."

"You won't?" Antoinette looked at him pleadingly over the top of the hedge, which was just to her chin. "Please! You're going to Zorky's Rialto Neighborhood Theater, aren't you? Well, I had a date to meet Slops and Charl Beck there for the second afternoon show; but I can't because my mother had to go out and she's expecting a long-distance call from crazy Aunt Hannah whether she's coming tomorrow or not, and I haf to stay home to get the call, no matter how long it takes, so I can't meet 'em and it's awfully late now; the second show's prob'ly started. You'll tell the boys for me, won't you, Filmer? I'll think you're simply precious."

"Listen here," Filmer began. "Look, dame, didn't I just inform you I'm particular who I let——"

"Now, Filmer!" Antoinette's blue eyes, over the hedge, all at once became deeply personal, implied a mystic emotion. Only lately she'd learned how to do this; and almost simultaneously she'd begun the premature pluck-ing of her eyebrows, the use of lipstick, the staining of her nails and the wearing of high-heeled open-toed slip-pers. As the hostile Filmer stared at her, she felt a strong prompting to overcome his indifference; the afternoon had been boring, without any boys at all about her. "I—I know what you think of me, Filmer," she said in the hushed tone she was learning to use at the right times. "Couldn't you stop hating me long enough for me to show you how unjust and everything it is? Filmer, *I* don't care whether you give the other boys my message."

"Phooey!" He laughed harshly. "Look, if you knew my opinions about you, Antoinette Fry, you couldn't stand yourself. You'd let out just one screech and die on the grass."

Antoinette was put upon her mettle. "I—I know, Fil-mer. All my life you've just despised me. It's because you've always thought I didn't appreciate you. It's be-cause you think I'm too dumb to see you're different from any other boy."

"What?" Suddenly and powerfully interested, he nevertheless tried to remain scornful. "Look, gal, what you think you're talking about now?"

"You," Antoinette said, making the pronoun long. "You, Filmer." She looked away from him and pathos came into her muted voice. "You—you feel contempt for me because you think I don't mind how you look down on me, and I expect you're going to scorn the invitation to my party next week, even with a magician that gets out of handcuffs, because I'm repulsive to you for not showing I appreciate you're the one different one."

Filmer got red all over, both inside and outside his clothes. There were doings within his chest; faint explosions seemed to take place in his ears. Something brilliant and strange was happening to and in him, he didn't know what; but the thought of going on to the movies became repellent. "Lis—listen, Antoinette," he said thickly, and, retracing his steps to the gate, entered the yard.

He tried to use his accustomed slouch as he approached her; but his legs felt weightless and his knees unmanageable. He tried to seem to be chewing something; but his jaw was undependable. He tried to put utter contempt into his glance; but his eyelids didn't work correctly— they became independent of him and blinked. Antoinette stood before him meekly; but was not the Antoinette Fry known to him. That old dame, three doors up his street, long believed mere meat for squirrels, a yaller-haired maker of sap-heads into sissies, was now in a trice ethereally transformed—a heavenly shape made of prismatic light.

"Lis—listen, Antoinette," he said again. "What is all this hooey about me being all so different and everything?"

She touched his arm, and sweetened stars seemed to burst softly about him. "Let's sit down on the nice warm grass, Filmer, and I'll tell you." They sat and she began to tell him. "Of course in your eyes, Filmer, I'm just nobody; but, whatever you think, I'm not too dumb to look up to you. Everybody knows you're different. Even Charl Beck this morning said you're the most reckless boy in town and don't care what you do absolutely."

"Well, *that* much is so," Filmer admitted. "I don't care a thing I do."

"Well, that's different, isn't it?" Antoinette said. "I think it's marvelous. Charl said you take some kind of tablets that he saw on the box ought to be regulated by a physician. He says you can eat 'em just the same as if they were candy."

"Oh, you mean good ole Eucalina?" Filmer laughed negligently. "That's nothing." He brought forth the box of Eucalina tablets and let her see the inscription on the lid. "You can have one; but it'd prob'ly make you kind of sick, Antoinette. You haf to get used to 'em; they're pretty strong."

Carelessly he put three tablets in his mouth; but Antoinette protested. "Filmer Little! Why, I bet that's prob'ly dangerous!"

"Might be for some individuals." To dazzle her, he added three more tablets to those he already contained. He'd never before eaten anything like so many at once; but he didn't think they'd hurt him, and even if they did—a little maybe—he didn't believe it would be immediately, so what was the difference?

Antoinette touched his arm again. "Filmer, you don't

care a thing you do! Would you give up taking 'em if I asked you to, Filmer?"

"Well——" He ate another tablet. "Well—I might or I might not."

"Please don't take any more, Filmer. It scares me. Give 'em to me, Filmer, so I'll know you're safe." She put her hand upon the box and tugged at it. Her fingers touched his, so did her shoulder; her face came close to his—he was enveloped in an ineffable odor of violet sachet and she in a powerful one of medicaments. His grasp upon the box became flabby; his whole being was like that, too, and Antoinette captured the Eucalina tablets, or, at least, what remained of them. "There! I'll keep this little box, Filmer. I'll keep it in my bureau drawer."

"What——" he asked, breathless and swallowing feebly. "What—what for, Antoinette?"

"Oh, just because."

"Antoinette, I—I guess I *am* pretty different, kind of. When did you first begin to notice I am?"

"Oh, 'way last year some time, I expect." Antoinette was tired of talking about Filmer; she sat with her hands clasped round her knees, and her eyes were dreamy. "Filmer, do you know what I'd like to be like? You know that song Martin Mack sang in 'Sweets to the Sweeties'? I'd like to be like that." She crooned softly:

"You fulfil all the dreams that I admire,
You're as pure as ice but a ball of fire!"

"I'd like to be like that, too," Filmer said, and, not an hour agone, would have made a primitive attempt to slay anybody who accused him of talking like this. "I guess maybe we both are. Yes, sir; pure as ice but a ball of fire."

"It's my ambition," Antoinette said. "Whenever anybody commences talking about me I wish they'd say, f'r instance, 'Oh, you mean Antoinette Fry? She's pure as ice but a ball of fire.'"

"I will," Filmer promised. "I'll say it whenever I get a chance, because sincerely it's the way you are, Antoinette. Antoinette, last year when you first began to notice I'm—well, you know what you said—was it some time particular, like maybe when I was only just walking past your house, or you saw me doing something or heard me saying something to somebody, or when?"

"Well, one of those times maybe," she answered absently, still thinking of her ambition.

Filmer felt that he'd better not eat any more tablets; but he had a longing to do something magnificent. He desired to be splendid before her, wished to show her that he was intellectual and also to do startling things that would prove he was even more different than she realized.

"Antoinette," he said. "Do you like Rembrandt?"

"Who?"

"Rembrandt. He's good. He's my favorite artist." After that, Filmer pulled the forked sling from his hippocket and looked about him for a missile. "I used to have fun with these things when I was little," he said. "I used to go around plugging cars with acorns or maybe buckshot when they went by. Makes people sore; they look back and yell. If I could find a little rock or——"

"You better not, Filmer. Here; try it with one of these if you want to." Antoinette handed him one of the remaining Eucalina tablets. "That'd be just as much fun and won't hurt anything."

"Righto!" Filmer placed the tablet in the bit of leather; and he and Antoinette stood up, looking over the hedge. Then, drawing back the rubber bands of the sling, he aimed at the driver of a passing delivery truck, which was making the neighborhood noisy by backfiring. The tablet insipidly went far of the mark.

Other noises in addition to the backfiring broke the quiet of the afternoon. In the distance, but coming nearer, a motorcycle made uproar, and two boys, turning the next corner, began a bellowing: "Yay, Antoinette Fry! What's detaining you, Antoinette? How long you expect us to wait? All year?"

"It's Slops and Charl," Antoinette said. "I guess the movie's over. You better not shoot your sling any more, Filmer; there's a motorcycle cop coming down the street."

"What *I* care?"

Filmer, though slightly dizzy, he knew not why, had just seen something that inspired him. A familiar shape, an automobile lately restored to efficiency, was approaching. In the front seat his sister sat looking entrancedly at the spectacled neat youth beside her; after hours of driving, that day, Goody had tired, and now Norman Peel was at the wheel.

"Quick!" Filmer said, as the well-known car came near; and he seized from Antoinette another Eucalina tablet. With means so insignificant he expected small result, yet felt that he was well justified in doing whatever he could to annoy Goody and her new attendant. Something like loyalty sparked within Filmer; it seemed right to try to punish them at least a little for taking that car and making his father go all the way downtown on foot and in a bus on a hot day. "Watch me, Antoinette!"

He drew the bands of rubber to their utmost practical tension and aimed carefully. The car, being upon his side of the street and not far from the curb, offered him a fair mark; neither Goody nor the absorbed Norman Peel saw him. The little missile curved but slightly in the air, sped through the open front window of the sedan and ended its flight stingingly against the side of Norman's nose. The coincidence of a simultaneous backfire from the delivery truck caused to flash through the young man's mind for one startling instant a suspicion that he'd been accidentally shot. Brief as the thought was, it moved him to place a hand to his nose just at a moment when that hand was needed upon the wheel of the car he was supposedly guiding. The sedan swerved toward the opposite curbstone, and, after detaching one of its own mudguards as well as crumpling another belonging to a bright new coupé coming from the opposite direction, stopped surprisedly.

VIII

THE OTHER CAR, unintentionally facing about, also stopped; and its occupants, three robust elderly women, descended vociferating. The policeman on the motor-cycle arrived; the elderly women made a mere confusion of clamors round him; but their gestures plainly appealed for justice. Filmer saw all this in peculiar distortion, as through flawed glass; and, dizzier, he sank down behind the hedge—a movement originating less in conscious discretion than in illness. Antoinette, anxious not to be seen in his company, ran out to join Charl, Slops and other pleased sidewalk spectators.

Filmer thought best to stretch himself flat upon the grass at the foot of the hedge, and at once his sensations were such that he took but an academic interest in everything that was going on outside of him. Vaguely he was aware of high altercations; they seemed remote, as did the sound of Goody's voice rapidly verbose with indignation. People seemed to be squabbling somewhere; but he regarded this with indifference. He was pretty sure that something or other he'd eaten hadn't agreed with him.

At the moment of the accident he'd been dizzily horrified, not by its possible effects upon life, limb and property, but by an intuition that later some busybody'd be almost certain to hold him responsible. Now, lying upon sod that seemed to swing to and fro, he was callous upon the point, didn't care whether he'd have to go to jail or not. From head to foot he consisted of commotions, and, as a needless ambulance summoned by an excited neighbor came sirening up the street, Filmer had the impression that a cat was miaowing inside his head, trying to get out. Time passed, and he felt that he was passing, too. At intervals he said "Uf!" faintly; then at last shoes and the lower parts of trousered legs whirled round his face, and Antoinette's blue slippers appeared, swimming streakily among watery green grass blades close to his eyes. He heard her voice like a thin little fife distantly piping.

"Run! Run for his mother! *Run!*"

More time passed. A dentist seemed to be present, prying among his teeth with horrid metal instruments; then a strangling liquid was poured into his mouth; his middle became an insupportable tumult. Later he felt himself lifted, though he preferred otherwise and tried to cling to the grass.

Thousands of people seemed to be milling about him, bearing him along horizontally in the midst of a loudly talkative procession. He was mistaken about this, of course: the people carrying him were only Gentry Poindexter, old Dr. Fitch, Charlsworth Beck and Slops; and the others, who were doing the rest of the talking, were Cousin Olita, Filmer's mother, Antoinette, Goody, Norman Peel and a slim trail of spectators. A few of these chance onlookers accompanied the cortege through the Littles' gateway and would have continued with it doubtless into the house and all the way up to Filmer's bedroom if Gentry Poindexter hadn't addressed them harshly from the portico.

The telephone, ringing in the rear of the hall, went unanswered; but insisted again and again and again upon being noticed. Finally Gentry, on the way upstairs with fresh towels, called down to Almatina, instructing her to tell it to stop making all that noise. "Been dinglety-dinglin' seem like hour," he added. "Ask it: 'You go' keep on till tomorrow, no matter who sick?' You slap it off the hook, Almatina."

Almatina didn't slap it off the hook. She listened to it inscrutably, murmured noncommittal responses; and then, leaving the connection in force, made her appearance before an animated group in the living-room. Those still doing most of the talking were Goody, Antoinette Fry, Norman Peel and Cousin Olita. Mrs. Little fanned herself noisily with the evening newspaper, and Filmer's friends, Charlsworth Beck and Slops, spoke seriously together.

"It's Mr. Little, ma'am," Almatina said, and easily produced a silence. "He call up say he occupy with a bureau. Say a bureau pokin' in his business—— Yes'm that whut he say. I can't help it, say a bureau—and say go' stay downtown so don't wait dinner for him, he ain't got time to eat. Yes'm, and ask me why when he so

busy he had to ring 'phone bell all this long time. I jus'
reply Gentry jumpin' up and downstairs, couldn't come,
been a little trouble here. He ask me whut. I say rilly
couldn't tell him, jes' everybody runnin' in and out. He
say you please come to 'phone quick, ma'am.''

Goody, tense, turned to Mrs. Little. "It'll be better to
get it over, Mother. Above all, you'll absolutely have to
ask him if he had collision insurance on this car, too,
and——"

"Oh, dear! Oh, my! I couldn't! And think, Goody, I'd
have to tell him about Filmer first. Oh, no, I can't!"

With outstretched hands Goody swung to plead with
Cousin Olita. "Then it has to be you, Cousin Olita. It
wouldn't do at all for Norman to try and you know what'd
happen if *I*——"

"Why, certainly, I will," sunny Cousin Olita said,
nodded her semi-golden curls amiably and like a little
man went to perform the duty assigned her.

"Don't be frightened, Cousin Ripley," she said into
the telephone; and, after being interrupted for some
moments, continued the conversation as well as she could
in spite of other interruptions progressively forceful.
"Everything's really all right, Cousin Ripley, and Dr.
Fitch says he's sure Filmer's going to get well . . . It
seems he swallowed a box of tablets . . . Yes, and there
was an ambulance; but we didn't use it . . . No, no, no, it
wasn't the same one with the intern that came the other
time, Cousin Ripley . . . Yes, Filmer's been quite sick;
but there was a young man, a clerk from Healy's drug
store, happened to be going by and stopped to look on
and he said they'd been selling him these tablets because

they thought they were for the family; but Antoinette and the boys got scared by the way the ipecac Dr. Fitch gave him acted on him and they tell us he took 'em for his breath for smoking . . . Yes, cigarettes, and I guess he's certainly lost that automobile you were going to give him when he's twenty-one; but the clerk and Dr. Fitch say these tablets were entirely harmless—except that smell they gave him he always said was the soap, you remember?—unless he practically took 'em all at once . . . Yes, it seems that's what he did; but nobody knows why . . . No, nobody seems to understand that point yet, and, speaking of the automobile he won't get when he's twenty-one, Cousin Ripley, it seems Filmer shot Norman Peel with his slingshot . . . Yes, he shot him just before he lost consciousness . . . Yes—and oh, Cousin Ripley, Goody wants to know if you've got concussion insurance on that one, too, because . . . Yes, that's what she said. Didn't I say collision insurance? . . . Goody's anxious to know if . . . All right, I'll tell them . . . Just one moment, Cousin Ripley."

Cousin Olita set the instrument down and turned to speak to Mrs. Little and Goody, who had followed her, hoping to listen only. "Most of the time he just keeps saying, 'Jobjam it, what *is* all this? What *is* all this?' He says he's got to keep his head clear on account of the new bureaus that are after him now. He seems to think I'm only getting him confused and he wants to talk to Goody first, right now, and then to you, Cousin Wilma. Goody, I'm afraid you'll have to——"

"I decline." Goody was spirited. "I decline! Why should I when I know beforehand everything he'd say—

and the way he'd say it, too? You know I'm not a quitter, Mother; but Filmer's your son, not mine, and Cousin Olita's done her best. It's up to you to try to make Father understand."

Mrs. Little took the telephone and tried. She told her husband all about it; she told him twice, she told him thrice. In return, he told her that he'd just been spending a full hour trying to make the United States government understand why, among other things, he'd paid twenty-four dollars for some gunnysacking in March, nineteen thirty-five; that he was now awaiting a detachment of state officials, and that they'd be going into the intimate details of his business and personal life until far into the night. He used to believe that his offices were *his* offices, he said, just as he used to think his home was his home; but these former convictions were the dreams of a job-jam dotard, heaven help him! Of course he was glad, he admitted, that Filmer was expected to survive; but this time there wasn't any collision insurance as the policy had run out while the repairs were in progress at Crappio's and hadn't been renewed because nobody expected ever to see the dobdab car back again. The telephone added that with two such children a man could wish the inventor of the gas engine had died before being born; and the instrumental buzzings most painful of all to Mrs. Little's ear were caused by the words, "Good-by, jobjam it! Good-*by!*"

... The representatives of the state commission proved to be less thorough than expected. Ripley Little finished with them—for the time being—by half past nine that evening, and, twenty minutes later, rode into his own driveway in a taxicab. His wife and Cousin Olita, reclining upon long chairs on the lawn, were enjoying the moonlight; but Mrs. Little rose nervously as he approached them. "Dear, I——" She hesitated. "I'm afraid you must be almost exhausted, Ripley. We'll get you something to eat."

"Thank you, I had two sandwiches in my office and they're not digesting. Have the remains of our last car been pushed into the garage, or has Crappio sent a wrecking-crew to remove them?"

"But, Ripley dear, you really ought to eat something. Do let us——"

"Thank you; but I'd like to know——"

"It was only the mudguard," Cousin Olita said. "Hardly anything except the mudguard got much injured, Cousin Ripley. They found it still runs perfectly."

"It?" he asked. "It? What still runs perfectly?"

"Why, the car of course, Cousin Ripley. Those women in the other one made themselves as objectionable as they could—you never heard such a cackling!—but the policeman himself said there wasn't enough damage to send anybody to the Chair about. He told 'em, himself, you were good for their bill. I had such a nice talk with Filmer, Cousin Ripley, after the doctor got the poor child's exertions quieted down better. He said he was sorry of course; but in a way he thought he was really acting quite a good deal on your account, Cousin Ripley, because they hadn't any right to take the car and make you walk in the hot sun to the bus and then——"

"I'd like," Ripley Little interrupted, "I'd like to get

my questions answered: Where is that car and who found that it still runs?"

Cousin Olita told him. Her inflection was one of surprise as if of course he ought to have known. "Why, Goody and Norman Peel, Cousin Ripley."

"What! You mean to sit there and tell me——"

"Now, Ripley dear!" Mrs. Little pleaded anxiously. "Weren't *we* different from *our* fathers and mothers, too? You see, modern young people simply *can't* sit around home and do nothing. They just don't know *how* because this is a different age, you see, and the footboard hanging down a little didn't really interfere with using it. Goody was terribly sorry about it; but this time of course it wasn't her fault at all, and they'd promised to be at the Green Valley Club by nine. Of course, too, being out with someone you approve of, yourself, like Norman Peel, she naturally feels—— Now, Ripley, please don't get excited and——"

"Excited?" Little began. "You stand there and tell me not to get excited when——"

He was interrupted. On the other side of the fence, not far from them, a young girl and four boys came scuffling along the sidewalk, chattering, pushing one another and whooping a little, in the usual manner of their kind returning from evening movies. As they passed before the Littles' lawn they found the moonlight sweet upon them and broke into song. The five voices, all insupportably loud and four of them changing, didn't harmonize very well, didn't even mingle agreeably; and one of them, squawkier than the others, startled Ripley Little. He had a grotesque thought.

"Why—why——" he said. "How queer! If I didn't know that he's in bed—— Why, that worst voice sounds exactly like——"

"Now, Ripley dear, please, dear!" his wife begged him. "Darling, please don't get excited! They simply won't stay in bed nowadays, and, after all, he ate quite a good deal of dinner and he had half a dollar you gave him, yourself. I tried; but you simply can't keep them home at his age, not if they're in the least able to get up. Ripley, please——"

She'd have said more; but the young people sang so loudly that she had to wait for them to pass. Filmer walked close to Antoinette; his strong wobbly young voice, bawling earnestly almost in her ear, came also into the ear of his lamentable father:

> *"You were my tootsytoo as we danced in Peru,*
> *You fulfil all the dreams that I admire,*
> *You're as pure as ice but a ball of fire!"*

Mrs. Little, apprehensively observant of her husband's face under the full moon, put a troubled hand upon his sleeve. "You *must* try not to get high blood pressure, Ripley. I've always been afraid a good deal would happen to worry you when the time came for his adolescence, and I'm *so* afraid he's getting it."

"Yes—it's one of the most wonderful things in this wonderful world of ours," Cousin Olita said fondly; and, after looking at her for a moment, Ripley Little went indoors.

IX

HE TRIED HARD to be reasonable about both of his children—"at least just this once," as his wife too hurriedly put it, in a talk with him the next day.

It was easier to be reasonable about Filmer, even though he had certainly been the cause of the new little accident; Cousin Olita's account of Filmer's explanation of his loyal motive for shooting Norman Peel had undoubtedly somewhat touched the father's heart. It was less easy to be fair to Goody because her manner so jauntily assumed that he had nothing to be fair to her about. Another of his troubles was that his mind had become unsettled in regard to Norman Peel.

"But it was you yourself, Ripley, that picked him out as your favorite," Mrs. Little urged. "I think at first she had something like a prejudice against him; but your suggestion gave her the idea of—of investigating him a little, as it were, and when she found how nice he really is—well, he really does seem to be the one. You surely like a young man to believe in himself, and she tells me it's one of the things that fascinates her about Norman. He's so sure he's going far in the world of business and——"

"All right, all right!" Little said. "A touch of self-confidence is no harm. In fact, it may be praiseworthy. But this talk of changing gables and our fence and——"

Mrs. Little laughed. "Oh, I wouldn't take that seriously. You know how young people chatter together, and isn't it rather a good sign, his mind's being bent on how almost everything could be improved a little, maybe? Goody tells me she's sure now you were right about him, Ripley, and that's nice, too; it'd be too bad if you think you have to admit making such an important mistake. I mean——"

"I haven't said I've got any real prejudice against him, have I?" Little asked testily, and then was meditative. "Well, we'll see. I'd certainly be glad to find one glimmer of hope in contrast to this hullabaloo coterie she's had about her, wouldn't I? I don't want to be hasty; perhaps if we see a little more of him——"

"Yes, that's it," Mrs. Little said cheerfully. "That's just it, Ripley."

Little agreed that seeing more of Norman Peel might be it, and a morning or two later, in the bus—for Crappio was still restoring the detached mudguard—he bent a sidelong observation upon the young man who sat across the aisle from him. The furtive study contained no disapproval. Young Norman Peel, quiet-looking, sober in dress, was diligent even in the bus; for, through his earnest spectacles, he studied figures in a small memorandum book and with a trimly sharpened pencil made thoughtful annotations upon the margins of the pages. For a time he wasn't aware of his neighbor across the aisle; then, glancing up and happening to catch Little's eye, he nodded gravely, and again devoted himself to his figuring.

Goody's father rose and, with a genial air, seated himself beside Norman. "Always work in the bus, do you?" he asked. "That's the way to get ahead, is it?"

Norman smiled and put the memorandum book in his pocket. "No, not always, Mr. Little; only when it seems useful. Our people are rather pushed this week, you know. I understand that Little and McGorney are, too, especially with the increase in your South American trade. I hear your customs agent cleared a heavy shipment for you yesterday; I hope you see your way to a profit on it in spite of taxes, Mr. Little."

Little's largely restored approval increased. "Profit?" he said quizzically. "Well, how would you handle it, yourself, to insure a profit—in spite of taxes?"

Norman looked gratified, and immediately sketched a plan that surprised Little with its insight. They briskly talked business the rest of the way downtown; then they left the bus together and, still talking, walked side by side to the tall building in which Little and McGorney occupied one whole floor and Norman's employers another. In the lobby, before an elevator arrived, Little followed an impulse.

"I like your ideas," he said. "You seem pretty sound. Some time we might take up these South American questions together again. I'd like to hear what you——"

"Any time. Any time." Norman extended his hand, and

Little shook it. "Any time, Mr. Little. Any time you say."

"Very well. I'll let you know, Norman."

Little was brightened. He didn't think of Goody as marriageable precisely; but the prospect of having this serious, more adult young man about the house—at times—instead of the usual rioters, was soothing. "We might look him over a bit together," he suggested to his wife. "You might let Goody know I have no objection if she cares to ask him for dinner some evening. He's apparently the kind of young man I'd be glad to see in this house. I've seldom met anybody of his age with as sound ideas as he seems to have. Of course he's only got a sort of clerkship so far; but I wish that some of the young fellows in my own employ had his business brains. I don't doubt that he knows, himself, he's smart; but I wouldn't mind some of *them* knowing it—if they were. Yes, tell Goody she can ask him any evening she pleases."

Mrs. Little told Goody. The affectionate woman, indeed, was so pleased by her husband's at last finding one friend of Goody's who didn't upset his nervous system that she not only told her daughter all that Little had said of Norman but a bit more. In permitting some slight genial exaggerations to escape her lips, Mrs. Little hoped that she was bringing her husband and her daughter together, especially as Goody listened with an evident thoughtful pleasure; but Filmer did his best, or worst, to spoil this encouraging effect. He walked into his mother's bedroom where the private conversation was taking place, and made a loud complaint.

"Norman Peel! Norman Peel! Norman Peel!" he said. "Trying to do a little rainy-day reading in my own room and I can't hear anything but gibble-gabble this, gibble-gabble that. Norman Peel, Norman Peel, Norman Peel! What new atrocity has Norman Peel done now? What's it all about?"

"Never mind, Filmer." His mother tried to wave him away. "Just run back to your reading and———"

"Me?" he said. "Run? What makes you think it's that gripping? Look, if the guy knows his own interests as well as I do he'll remain far distant out of this residence when Father's around. Do you remember the expression on his face the day he called Norman Peel a Walking Brain? Whoo! I wouldn't like to have him speak of *me* and look like that."

"You wouldn't?" Goody asked quietly, and added, "How singular, because that very expression is usually exactly the one he———"

"It is not! I and Father get along———"

"Yes, just like that." Goody held up two fingers close together. "Just perfect, your mutual relations." She turned to her mother. "Isn't childhood marvelous? It disgraces itself utterly with drug-store smell-pills and slingshots and policemen and's all abased and has to confess and promise never to smoke again, and you'd think it couldn't ever lift its head, and then presto! it hasn't the faintest realization that anything at all has happened to it and comes hopping and grinning, trying to poke its little nose into adult affairs and———"

"You better listen!" Filmer was furious. "What's become of Ham Ellers?"

"What? Why, you little———"

"Children, children," the mother murmured.

"Children Goody if you want to," Filmer cried, "but don't children me! Ham Ellers was anyhow something like a regular guy. So what did he do to get the bird?"

"The bird, Filmer?" Mrs. Little didn't understand.

"The bird, the can, the gate, the brush-off," Filmer explained. "Why, Ham Ellers may be loutish but he's fully nineteen years old and he's had more experience of life than——"

Goody laughed suddenly. "If you expect to stooge up to Father by a smear campaign against Norman—Mister Peel to you, Filmer—you'll be sadly, sadly mistaken. Tell him, Mother."

"Your father thinks very highly of Mr. Peel, Filmer," Mrs. Little said. "He admires his intelligence and business ability and good manners and likes him so much that he wants to know him better and we're asking him for dinner here very soon."

"What? You mean Father consents to——"

"Consents? No, he suggested it," Goody said, and laughed again at Filmer, who found no retort ready to hand. In a confused state of mind he returned to his rainy-day reading—now a borrowed Heptameron, as he'd finished Bokakio.

The invitation that so astonished Goody's brother was delivered by her to Norman Peel vocally. The enthusiastic girl quoted in her sweet and eager voice all that her mother had said Ripley Little had said of Norman; and then, like her mother, she went even a little further. Her account of her father's expressed opinion of Norman strongly affected the young man—in fact, gave him a great liking for Ripley Little; almost all of us are susceptible to praise freely translated from the original words of an admirer. When Norman arrived for dinner on the appointed evening he was just then almost as interested in Ripley Little himself as in Ripley Little's daughter; though to a spectator this would have been hard to understand. Goody really was beautiful, even at eighteen.

That is, she had her looks and something more—an unmistakable air of intelligence and also the proud quick gleam of eye that means a readiness to fight lightheartedly at the drop of a hat. She wasn't hard; she was straight and springy and held her chin up, and yet there were about her gentle hints that she could be the kindest girl in the world if she ever decided so to be. In spite of all this, and the fact that she was at her utmost loveliness in a beige dinner dress, Norman Peel gave her only a hurried nod when he came into the living-room looking even more earnest and responsible than usual. He spoke to her mother and Cousin Olita with polite, brief formality, omitted the dressed-up reticent Filmer, and immediately turned to the host, who stood by the mantelpiece.

"Bradford, Holcomb and Todd," Norman said, "have been appointed sole agents for the Budstill interests, Mr. Little. We got that in our place just before we closed. Little and McGorney will be affected, no doubt, and, as for us, I think——"

Gentry Poindexter appeared in the doorway. "Dinner serve'."

"Well," Norman Peel said, "we can take that up at the table possibly." Mrs. Little, Goody, Cousin Olita and Filmer moved toward the door; the two gentlemen followed, side by side. "The selection of Bradford, Holcomb and Todd," Norman continued, "will naturally affect Little and McGorney more than it does us of the Corcoran setup, Mr. Little. I think I can show you why and I'll be glad to go over the figures with you in some detail; but first I'd like to give you a more comprehensive answer to the question you asked me the other morning in the bus than I was able to do at the moment. I hope it won't bore the ladies too much if——"

"Not at all!" Cousin Olita, over her shoulder, took it upon herself to reassure him. "In these days when everything seems to be about war with all its horrors I think it's *so* nice to hear people talking about almost anything else. You go right ahead, Mr. Peel."

"Well, then," Norman began, "the question was one of possible profits on that South American——"

They reached the table. "Let's sit down," Little said. "Mr. McGorney of my firm has handled that matter pretty satisfactorily and it's already past history so——"

"No doubt, no doubt," Norman interrupted, as he sat. "I think, though, that it could have been just a shade improved, judging by what I've heard. I think you could have cleared just about five point thirty-seven instead of four point ninety-eight, and I'd like to give you my figures while they're in my head. If you don't mind, Mr. Little, I'll begin at the beginning and give you my improved outline." Neglecting his soup and keeping a bright gaze upon his host, Norman gave the outline.

For an outline it was exhaustive, and Norman was so absorbed in it that Gentry Poindexter had to be tactfully patient about changing the plates for the courses of the dinner. Elaborating step after step, the young outliner's face glowed, and, emphasizing his points with an enthusiastic forefinger, he kept his eyes fixed almost entirely upon the head of the house, whom he seemed confident of pleasing. Ripley Little, who'd been all over the South American transaction many times with his partner, made responses that tended to become perfunctory; and if it hadn't been for Cousin Olita's now and then saying, "Of course I don't understand a word; but at your age I think it sounds just wonderful, Mr. Peel!" the dinner-table conversation might have been thought pretty dry.

Goody, obtrusively demure, said almost nothing at all; her mother murmured aside to Filmer now and then, about his eating, which made him look dogged—the only effect—and Norman Peel talked on. When the party rose from the table Cousin Olita and Filmer slipped away to a movie, Cousin Olita's treat or Filmer wouldn't have gone; and the other four returned to the living-room for coffee. Still talking, Norman took a chair close by his host when the tray was brought. Goody maneuvered her mother to the other side of the room, beyond the piano, and left the two gentlemen isolated. Norman talked and talked. He seemed to think he'd been called in for a business conference.

X

Ripley Little had begun to be worse than bored; annoyance, indeed, was stoking something like actual heat in his breast. He was having a new experience, one that some people might have thought flattering; but Ripley Little wasn't feeling flattered: he didn't intend to listen to anybody of Norman's age a whole evening.

True, he'd slightly cultivated the acquaintance; but not at all, as he now (erroneously) believed, on his own account. It was exclusively to do Goody good (he thought) that he'd imported Norman as a sample of something rather better than what she picked up around anywhere and brought into the house. Ripley Little looked heavily at Goody's delightful profile as it came into view when she leaned forward under a lamp where she sat with her mother beyond the piano. Norman Peel must be dobdab peculiar, Little thought, and the whole idea of having him to dinner began to look like a job-jam blunder on somebody's part, maybe his and Mrs. Little's.

"I hope I've covered this point to your satisfaction, Mr. Little," Norman was saying. "I hope it gives you an idea of my grasp of the situation, though I won't pretend that I haven't some reason to believe you'd already formed an estimate of what my grasp—I suppose we might call it that—amounts to. The other day my chief, R.B. himself, mentioned your again inquiring about me, and there've been other—other sources, so I'm not going to be mock-modest enough to affect not to know of the favorable interest you've————"

" 'Interest'?" The interruption came from Goody, whose head was now invisible to the two gentlemen as, leaning back, she allowed the piano to intervene. "You *are* being mock-modest, though, Norman," her sweet voice said chidingly. "You understand perfectly that the word 'interest' doesn't tell the half! When a person knows that some other person's really crazy about him, why, honestly now, *isn't* it mock-modesty to call it nothing but 'interest'? Why, only this morning Mother said Father was talking about you again and told her he thought you————"

"Well—well now————" her father interrupted, and laughed uncomfortably. "We needn't go into all that. Never mind, Goody!"

"No?" The sweet voice seemed to wonder indulgently. "Men are always so funny about admitting it. I mean why on earth should they always be so embarrassed when they take these fancies to each other? Women love to tell each other right out, over and over, so why shouldn't men, when they feel that way? Norman, you wouldn't think you'd ever have to be mock-modest with Father again about yourself if you'd only heard him simply raving to Mother about how you——"

"Never mind!" Little, deeply flushed, again tried to cut her off. He felt that Goody was making him look job jammed silly. "Never mind!"

"Now don't *you* be mock-modest, too, Father," the unseen girl persisted gently. "Norman likes you and he knows perfectly well you've had your eye on him for a good while. Don't you, Norman? Hasn't he told you *why* yet, Norman?"

"Well, not in so many words," Norman admitted, laughed deprecatorily and beamed upon his reddened host. "Of course, Mr. Little, I know you're a man who never does anything without a purpose and——"

"Of course he doesn't," Goody said. "Didn't I tell you that you're the first friend of mine he's ever asked to have asked here? That means a good deal, doesn't it —and you surely know what, don't you, Norman?"

"I might say I suspected it," the young man confessed, smiling; and then, though plainly exhilarated, he faced Goody's father with gravity. "Before we go any further, though, Mr. Little, I conscientiously ought to point out that Corcoran and Company count pretty strongly on my staying with them. A firm doesn't raise anybody three times during a depression unless it wants him." Leaning forward, he spoke with a colleague's engaging frankness, "Mr. Little, you know that and I know that. It's got to be given its proper weight, hasn't it?"

"Weight?" Little set down the remains of an ill-enjoyed cigar. "What weight?"

"Mr. Little, let's come into the open," Norman said. "I'm ready to put all my cards on the table if you are. On the one hand, Corcoran and Company intend to make R.B.'s nephew a member of the firm before they do me; but, on the other hand, I definitely owe it to myself to be sure of a clearly outlined advance if I make a change. That's frank, isn't it? Then let's be just as frank about Little and McGorney. The truth is, Mr. Little, the younger element downtown definitely feels there's some dead wood in your organization."

"Dead wood?" Flushing more deeply, Little stared. "In Little and McGorney? You say the younger element——"

"Well, frankly, yes," Norman said. "Naturally, as your daughter tells me, you wish to remedy that and I've been aware that your interest in bringing me here this evening might lead to some sort of proposition. Well, I've been giving definite thought to the idea; but, Mr. Little, in fairness to both of us, we oughtn't to take any further steps without a basic understanding that I couldn't consider it without first making sure I'd have no dead wood over me. It's pretty clear that what your firm needs, Mr. Little, is young blood—it needs youth because this is Youth's day—but if the dead wood in your organization's to be retained, why, in justice to myself I don't see how I——"

"What?" Little said. He rose. His collar had tightened round his expanded neck and his eyes seemed about to become protuberant. "You're trying to tell me that you——"

"Of *course* he is, Father!" Goody jumped up dramatically. "And don't you see how *right* Norman is, too, Father?"

"Is he? I don't get him. Right about what?"

"Why, about its being Youth's day!" Goody cried. "Of *course* your firm ought to have some of it; but at the same time, as Norman says, if dead wood, maybe more than fifty years old, would be put over him in your setup he doesn't wish to mislead you into thinking he'd care to come in. In other words, Father, if you keep the dead wood you'll have to include Norman out. That's the A B C of it, isn't it, Norman?"

"Well, partly," Norman said. "I wouldn't like to have your father think I don't appreciate his——"

"More mock-modesty!" Goody exclaimed. "You've both got so much of it, you two poor men, that you'll never get this thing straightened out if somebody doesn't help you." She danced round the piano to Norman and affectionately put her arm within his. "Norman, I never was prouder of you! You're even grander in your business life than Father's been telling us. What Norman's been trying to make you understand, Father, it's that because he intuitively knows you're going to keep all that dead wood in your business he'd rather wait for the junior partnership in Corcoran and Company than take anything like that with you right now, in spite of how much you like each other. The simple fact is Norman means he declines. In spite of personal reasons, Norman means he'd rather——"

"Sit down!" her father said. "You sit down!"

"What? Why should I?" she asked. "Father, you're

only telling me to because you can't think of anything else to say."

Mrs. Little, half risen from her chair to look over the top of the piano at her husband, thought Goody was mistaken about his not being able to think of anything else to say, and hastily rose the rest of the way. "Wouldn't you and Norman like to sing something, Goody?" she asked. "I could play that accompaniment I was trying with you yesterday if you think I'd manage it well enough. Ripley, I'm sure you'd love to hear——"

"Excuse me," Ripley Little said. "I'll ask to be excused for the rest of the evening."

He strode across the room, and, having done some noisy sliding upon the polished floor of the hall, ascended the stairway, talking indistinctly to himself.

Mrs. Little remained for a time with the two young people, though they decided not to sing the duet; but her gaze was often worriedly upon the ceiling. More and more it seemed to become evident that her husband had gone upstairs for the purpose of moving heavy furniture. . . . When she finally followed and with timidity entered his room, she easily comprehended the cause of a recent crash: the topmost large drawer of his bureau lay upon the floor, displaying an intricate disorder of laundered garments. He rose from ploughing explorations among them, and his expression alarmed her more than commonly.

"Fire Almatina!" he said. "She hides my nightshirts from me. She hates me because I won't be a fashion plate in pajamas like Gentry, so she hides 'em. She hides 'em in a new place every Thursday. I ask you to fire Almatina tomorrow!"

"Oh, Ripley! Now, Ripley, please."

"Answer me this," he said. "Would anybody but a boor go out to dine among ladies and talk nothing but business, business, business? Don't you suppose that when a man gets home in the evening he'd like to have a little change and forget the office for a few hours? What's worse, I'd like to know *where* he got the impression that he'd been brought here to be offered a position in the firm of Little and McGorney?"

"Well, you know, Ripley dear, you *did* say——"

"Did I say I craved to adopt a jabjammed peacock just out of the egg a man can't speak one kind word to on somebody else's account but he thinks you need his advice about dead wood and want him in your *firm?* —merely as a junior partner, that's all!"

"Now, Ripley, please. It isn't altogether his fault. I'm afraid Goody may have rather put some of it into his head."

"Into his what?"

"But *you* said he has a splendid one, Ripley, and Goody thinks so, too."

"She does not! She's been making a monkey out of both of us."

"No, no, indeed," Mrs. Little said in a hurried, protestive voice, "not out of *him*, Ripley. She's never had anybody before with such an opinion of himself. She knew he liked himself; but she didn't dream how much, and they think being yourself is great nowadays. After you came upstairs she was really charming with him, making him feel that the excited way you left was all right because you were so disappointed about his not ——" Mrs. Little interrupted herself as her husband made an impetuous movement toward the door. "No, you needn't go downstairs again; they've gone off to some kind of party she'd heard about somewhere, Ripley; they always do, you know."

"Listen to me," Ripley Little said. "I thought we were through with those hoodlums of hers; but get 'em back. Get 'em back—even Ham Ellers. Get 'em back tomorrow!"

"Back?" Mrs. Little was surprised. "Well—I don't think they've been away, exactly; but of course she'll love having them at the house again. I—I'm afraid, dear, from now on you'll have to get used to Norman's being here a great deal, too."

" 'Too'?" Little said. His eyes, and, indeed, his whole face, seemed to be enlarging. "Too? *Too?*"

"But, Ripley, we'll *have* to be nice to him, you see, or Goody'll claim you——" Mrs. Little stopped speaking, and, with a plaintive outcry, hurried from the room. Her husband had begun to use expressions she'd never before heard from him in all their life together.

"Dob the dob jam!" he said. "Job dab the bastinadoed soapsuds of the bishops to the dab dobbed jumping Hellespont! Job jab the jam——"

"Is something or other the matter, Father?" Filmer, returned from the movies and on his way to bed, stood genially in the doorway, which his mother, in her haste, hadn't closed. He was disposed to become conversational. "Well, it seems this Norman Peel turns out to be a pretty fine fellow, after all. I could tell from the way he handled himself and paid his attentions to you instead of Goody at dinner——"

The door was closed in Filmer's very face. Ripley Little, on the other side of it, resumed in his own way the struggle to relieve his feelings.

XI

FILMER felt almost hurt. Too often, he thought, when he wished to be man-to-man with his father, the extended hand appeared unwelcome and he wasn't taken into the confidential relations to which a son of his age should be entitled. Wasn't he almost fifteen? Filmer didn't realize that he was living through what in many particulars is the toughest of all the ages.

To the minds of people ten years old the age of almost fifteen, though but remotely discernible on the path of life stretching into dimnesses ahead, promises a kind of splendor. The boy of ten says, "I'll be almost a man by then!" On the other hand, advanced youth, conscious of having been richly perfected, looks back upon this period with a belittling amusement: "I was the fuzziest-headed little fool you ever saw when I was about fifteen!"

Filmer hadn't learned that all ages are but way stations, and he'd expected more from almost fifteen than he thought he received. No longer even partly a child, he believed, he was nevertheless frequently treated entirely as one. He was inappreciative of what he had to balance these setbacks—the early summer with all its ephemerally tender greeneries, amethyst twilights, long and warm, and moonrise zephyrs and impromptu showers to bring freshened smells to a young nose. Yes, Filmer Little had summer and sunshine and life and love. For Filmer was now in love (whenever he happened to think of her) with Antoinette Fry. This condition redoubled itself when he was with her, or remotely saw her, or even when he heard her yelling in the distance. To be of feather weight in feet and head, responsible for virtually nothing, to be carefree in the young summertime, and, unaware that others may receive the same message, to hear sometimes from precociously coral lips the whisper, "Filmer, you're different from anybody," what aging Party Chief, what economic royalist, wouldn't make the trade? —for a specified half hour or so, of course.

Naturally, however, there were moments when not even Benito Mussolini would have exchanged places with Filmer. Quite a series of such moments arrived on the bright unfortunate afternoon of the day following Norman Peel's declination of an unmade offer of business advancement. Ripley Little hadn't come home for lunch, and at half past two he called his wife on the telephone.

"Get this right," he said to her urgently. "Just about the most important meeting of my life's coming off here in my office at three-fifteen. This morning I thought it was going to be cooler and left my blue suit hanging in my clothes closet. It ought to be there now if Almatina hasn't hidden it, and in the inside pocket of the coat there are three folded pages of notes I wrote for my own guidance. I was so nervous this morning when I left the house I forgot to bring 'em and I've just remembered where they are. I have to have 'em. Got that?"

"Yes, Ripley; of course."

"I've got to have those notes with me when I sit down with these men," Little continued. "I've *got* to. Get that, Wilma?"

"Why, certainly, dear."

"All right," he said. "I'd rather you'd bring 'em to me yourself than send Gentry. Crappio promised he'd have the car back by noon today. You get into it and———"

"It didn't come, Ripley. He telephoned it wouldn't be———"

"All right, get a taxi. Go to my clothes closet, look in the pocket of my blue coat———"

"Oh, dear!" Mrs. Little interrupted. "I absolutely can't, honey. I'm just starting to Carrie Lane's and she's already furious because I promised to be there at two to make a fourth at bridge, and Gentry's gone—it's his afternoon out—and Goody isn't home, either, Ripley. Filmer is, though. Wouldn't he do?"

"I suppose so. He can take the bus. Get him off right away, will you?"

"Yes, Ripley."

"Wait a minute," Little said. "See here! I don't want him cloppety-clopping into my offices in dirty shoes and drooping socks and with his hair all frowzled up and wearing spotted purple slacks and that jam jersey inside out and backside front. Make him put on a shirt and a hat and decent clothes. He'll have to hustle some, too. See that he does, will you?"

"Indeed I will, Ripley!" his wife promised, and,

hustling herself, didn't take time to impress strongly upon their son the need for him also to move with rapidity. Filmer could hurry when he received that impulse from himself; but when an altruistic speed was desired of him, repeated exhortations were advisable. Mrs. Little, talking fast, put too much stress on the change of clothes. She gave Filmer fifty cents for his bus fare and general pocket money, handed him the three folded sheets of scribbled office paper, insisted upon being a witness to at least the brushing of his hair, and departed flittingly. Filmer, pulling off the offensive jersey, thus unbrushing his hair, had the impression that his father primarily wanted him to be all dressed up and secondarily expected him at the office before very long with these scratchy-looking papers.

Yawning in prompt boredom, he substituted a "sport shirt" for the jersey, got into semi-pressed white trousers that were but slightly soiled here and there, white shoes not too white, a blue jacket, and, reluctantly —it was dead against his style—set a Sunday straw hat upon his head. Sauntering, he left the house and was half a block on his way to the bus before he remembered he'd left behind him the cause of his excursion. He returned, found the three sheets of paper—one under his bed—put them in his inner breast-pocket, and, still leisurely, again strolled forth upon his errand.

Two birdlike voices called to him as he stepped outside the gate, and at the sound of one of them his breath became fitful, his color high.

"Oh, Filmer! Oh, Filmer Little!"

Antoinette Fry, blonde, high-heeled and lipsticked,

came skipping along the sidewalk toward him, and with her, less graceful but always jovial, was her plump brunette satellite, Ellie Turner. "Why, Filmer Little!" Antoinette cried, as they reached him. "Listen, what are you doing wearing a hat?" Dancing, she put her cranberry-tipped fingers upon his blue sleeve, danced him onward with her and Ellie. "C'm on, Filmer! Ellie and I were just coming for you. Charlsworth Beck and Bill and Slops are over at the Toastie Snackie Inn on Green Street and we're going to eat Double Deckers. C'm on!"

Filmer had a conscience that just discernibly pointed elsewhere; but he compromised with it. "Well—I got something to 'tend to; but I guess I got maybe time enough for a Double Decker," he said, and gave himself up to the joy of the moment.

At the Toastie Snackie Inn, when Antoinette, Filmer and Ellie Turner arrived, Bill, Slops, and Charlsworth Beck were already eating Double Deckers—sandwiches built of toast, sausage, pickles, horseradish, cold asparagus and sardines. Antoinette, Filmer and Ellie Turner ate Double Deckers; then all six ate Snackie Sundaes— ice cream plastered over with sliced banana, crushed peanuts and wet ginger cake. After that they all felt hearty but had little more money, and Antoinette proposed an economical entertainment.

"Let's all go out to that new amusement park, Dilly's New Dreamland," she said. "It's not going to have its Grand Opening till tomorrow night and they're still working on it; but they'll let you walk around everywhere and look at everything, and it's great! We got enough money left for fares out there and back; but it's five blocks to the right bus line, so c'm on!" Again her light touch was upon Filmer's sleeve. "C'm on; let's run, Filmer!"

Qualmishness was present in Filmer: Hadn't his mother murmured something about three-fifteen—or was it three-thirty? On the other hand, old people were always prodding you to get to places long before time. Antoinette's wishes meant much to him, more than anybody else's, in fact; and here she was beautifully wishing him beside her. "Well, I guess I can still just about make it," he said, and ran with her.

In the bus Bill, Slops, and Charlsworth Beck, annoyed by Antoinette's attentions to Filmer, became witty at his expense, somewhat heavy-handedly. They talked about him in their loud, hoarse, breaking voices, telling one another about his poisoning himself with Eucalina tablets and having to be carried home and put to bed. They made him conspicuous, so that all the passengers heard not only about Eucalina but much of his hat, a Snackie Sundae spot on his white-flannel knee, other and older spots, certain inequalities of his features, and, above all, the shape and extent of his ears. Filmer found all this annoying; for he more than ever wished to be dignified, in a romantic way, in Antoinette's presence. This desire enfeebled him and was bad for his powers of repartee. "Look at your own faces, you guys," he retorted monotonously. "Listen, look at your own ears and faces, you guys. Can't you look at your own faces?"

With the party's arrival upon the former pasture land where Dilly's New Dreamland was being completed, Filmer's three jealous friends gave rein to crude and boisterous humors; they swept the straw hat from his head, tried to sail it over structures still being painted, and so got it wetly varicolored. When he objected, they were rowdyish with him, bumped him, pushed him from one to another, and finally, making free with Antoinette, grasped her arms and ran ahead with her.

Antoinette, knowing well what ate them like worms i' the bud, was sweet to them in turn, one after another, and neglected Filmer. Left behind with fat joking little Ellie while the others frolicked forward among bustling workmen, Filmer again felt misgivings. The ride in the bus had been a long one, with many delaying stops; it was but natural to feel some apprehension—not that a possible slight tardiness would really inconvenience anybody. He hoped, though, that his father wouldn't throw one of those strict fits and speak to him mortifyingly before clerks and stenographers.

Fortifying himself to bear this, should it befall him, "It's all for Antoinette's sake," Filmer whispered to himself, as he trudged among debris with the chattering Ellie, and he added, "For *her*—even more than that!" His brainwork here is a little confusing because Antoinette wasn't now either benefiting by him or bothering about him. Probably what he somehow thought he meant was that to oblige her by tagging along he'd subsequently bear with stoicism even a louder fuss than his father might be going to make.

Antoinette and her friends had reached the amusement park at not quite four o'clock. When she decided that more than an hour's smelling of fresh paint might make her head ache they flocked into a bus that carried them toward home. Twenty-five minutes or so later, when the others hopped out, Filmer, beginning to feel serious about his future, remained seated. He descended at the downtown terminus, and, being now penniless, walked seven blocks to the tall building that housed his father's offices. He moved with reluctant speed, both urged and deterred by a discouraging appearance of lateness all about him. His shadow was longer than it should have been, and a great many people seemed to have finished the work of the day.

Confronted at last with a row of half-glass doors labeled "Little and McGorney, Inc.", he thoroughly tried them all, found all locked, and, moved by the instinct of self-preservation, slid the three sheets of note-paper under one of these doors. That is, he'd been told to change his clothes, wear a hat and take certain papers to his father's offices. Well, he'd obeyed. The clothes were changed; the hat, though damaged, was on his head, and the papers now lay in the offices; nobody could say he hadn't brought 'em.

All that remained to do was to walk home, about three miles. The June sunshine began to look autumnal; he might be a little bit late for dinner and incur criticism on that account. Well, let 'em; he couldn't help it. Prescience grew stronger, causing him not to push himself: What's the use of breaking your neck when you're pretty sure the whole family's going to be dissatisfied with you anyway?

Ripley Little, who'd at last gone home after disordering a bridge party and having employees telephone to

the houses of all acquaintances of Filmer, known or suspected to be such, proved upon the lad's arrival to be
more dissatisfied, by far, than had been anticipated. In
the very midst of Filmer's oft-interrupted explanations,
the father, huskily uttering sounds remindful of the Old
Testament, turned back from the dining-room door
toward which his wife was imploring him, rushed upon
the telephone and ordered a taxicab. He talked dis-
jointedly and almost unintelligibly about Filmer until it
arrived; then shot away in it, exhorting the driver.

Cousin Olita explained in kind tones to Filmer. "You
see, dear, I'm afraid you won't be his favorite any more;
but you must try to be glad on Goody's account because
she's your only sister and it'll be nice for her if he's all
upset for a while with somebody else."

"Look," Filmer said. "Look, did *I* know I was supposed to get there in such a hurry? What was I supposed
to tear downtown at a hundred miles an hour *for?* Why
did Father——"

"I'm telling you, dear," Cousin Olita reminded him.
"You see, those notes he'd made were terribly confidential
with just himself, and he's been telling your mother and
me, and even Goody, over and over he might as well
be shot as have anybody else in the whole world get the
slightest peek at 'em. Now that you've left them on the
floor of his offices where some of his people might come
back after dinner to finish up work—or maybe *all* his
clerks and stenographers'd read 'em first thing tomorrow
morning—why, he felt he'd have to go and get 'em himself right away, you see. Dinner's in a bad way already,
of course, because he couldn't quiet himself down enough

to eat before you came; but I suppose it'll be a good deal worse spoiled still by the time he gets back. I'm afraid that'll make it all the more trying for you, Filmer dear."

Cousin Olita spoke wisdom: Filmer never spent a more harassed evening, and became so low in his spirits that he forgot about its being all for Antoinette Fry's sake. The breakfast table brought no let-up and when his father, departing, mentioned to Mrs. Little that he'd be home for lunch, Filmer considered walking to some outlying part of the city to look for any job that would provide him with the barest food and lodging.

Lunch was much as expected, and when it was over he went upstairs to his own room and got out his stamp collection in the subconscious hope that it would prove to him he'd at least done something in this world. It didn't. Older than when he'd made it, he couldn't fail to comprehend that it was one of the poorest messes of stamps ever collected.

He sat by his window, looking into the Watsons' yard next door where a fat Maltese cat near her time watched with only academic interest a distant robin hopping about the lawn. Filmer didn't like this cat; in fact, she was repugnant to him, and a complete dissatisfaction with life came over him. His mother loved him, but didn't count; Goody, sickening about her Norman Peel, was objectionable; Cousin Olita, voluptuously sentimental and far from able-minded, was nothing but a trial; and, as for Mr. Ripley Little of Little and McGorney Inc., look at the unjustness of the way he'd been acting—as if Hitler'd be right in the middle of the United States because three unreadable old sheets of paper didn't get to the office exactly on time—and then because they were left there pretty much exactly according to instructions! Filmer'd have preferred somebody from the Gestapo for a father. Yet this was the family he had to live with; and, for intimate friends, he had Charlsworth Beck, Bill and old Slops—and a fine bunch of cheese that was! Friendship! They acted like it, didn't they? Here he was, just about fifteen years old and he'd gone through all his life without one single real friend!

XII

By NEAT COINCIDENCE, there came within the scope of his vision just such a creature as he'd have wished to call his friend. The wide green front yard next door, into which he looked slantingly down from his window, had never been interesting to Filmer, as the Watsons were elderly, over thirty-five; but there drew up to the curb a closed automobile covered with dust, and, after a colored chauffeur had opened the door, there popped out a bareheaded slim youth in a checkerboard black-and-white jacket, yellowish slacks and black-trimmed white shoes—attire instantly admired by Filmer as ideal for motor touring. A bulbous middle-aged woman of twittery voice and fashionable appearance emerged also; the colored man drew traveling bags from the baggage compartment and followed her and the youth up the flagstone path to old Mr. and Mrs. Watson's front door.

Filmer's eye took wistful note of the boy in the checker-board jacket. There was something careless, knowing, man-of-the-worldish and impertinent about him; he had the air of one who only laughs at consequences and is capable of telling the whole Faculty where to head in. Here, Filmer thought, was somebody who made old Slops, Bill, and Charlsworth Beck look like the fried bums they were. A friend like that would be something in life; friendship could be real with such a one.

Old Mrs. Watson rushed from her house, greeted the visitors effusively and led them within. The chauffeur followed with the bags, came out again and drove the car away. Filmer drooped back into his dismalness and wasn't much cheered by re-reading a treatise on How To Become An Entertaining Conversationalist, which he'd lately received in exchange for a money order of small amount.

"Filmer dear?" Cousin Olita's voice called from downstairs. "Oh, Filmer? If you're up there, do come down, Filmer. I've got something *so* nice to tell you, Filmer!"

Filmer came to the top of the front stairway, looked down upon her gloomily. "Nice? What you mean nice? I know what kind o' nice you usually want to tell me. Got another photograph of little Uncle Edward at Saratoga Springs in eighteen seventy-two you want me to look at? Or do I get to hunt a couple hours for your embroidery needle and maybe you'll give me a handsome card-case from the five-and-ten next Christmas if I find it? Listen, I'm reading, so for Sweet Mike's sake what you hollering about?"

"Mrs. Harpeddle," Cousin Olita replied, beginning to explain. "Mrs. Harpeddle's on a long motor trip; she's had nervous prostration ever since her forty-fourth birthday. Mrs. Harpeddle——"

"Who-peddle?" Filmer interrupted harshly. "Listen, I'm reading, so for Sweet Mike's sake——"

"No, it's her son, Filmer. Mrs. Harpeddle and her young son have just stopped off on their motor trip for a little visit with dear Mr. and Mrs. Watson because they're related to them, and I've been over there to call and said we had a nice young boy here, too, right next door, and Mrs. Harpeddle thought you might make such a good companion for her young son while they're here, Filmer; though I expect he's a little bit older than you are and has *such* a nice face, besides. He's out in their yard now, waiting, Filmer, because I told him I knew you'd love being a younger comrade to him during his visit."

"I would not!" Filmer, though revolted by Cousin Olita's way of putting things, came downstairs briskly enough. "I am *not* a 'nice young boy', thank you, and I have no intentions of going to be anybody's younger comrade. Accept my regrets and please politely sob yourself to sleep!"

He passed by smiling Cousin Olita, went outdoors and beheld, as he expected, the wearer of the glorious jacket waiting upon the lawn next door. Filmer pressed through the line of low shrubberies that separated the two yards and approached the stranger, who addressed him graciously. "Hello, hello, hello! A little bird tells me you must be this Filmer Little the gals all talk about, what? Shake."

Filmer was deferential. "Then I expect you must be this Harpeddle, aren't you?"

"Harpeddle?" The other boy, who was weedily a

head and a half taller than Filmer, looked down upon him smilingly. "Skip it! Richard Pinney Harpeddle, alias Dicksy Boy—Dicksy to you. Dicksy Boy's what they call me back home, and I guess you can find me easy enough if you ever turn up in that burg and ask anybody, 'Look, do you know Dicksy Boy?' They'd tell you. Somewhere near fifteen, aren't you, Filmer?"

"No," Filmer said. "I am, practically. What are you, Dicksy?"

"Well, verging on seventeen."

Filmer was solemn. "Listen. Have you got a driver's license?"

"*Have* I! A driver's license? Don't I look it?"

"Then what you and your mother got a chauffeur for, Dicksy?"

"It's a long story, pardner. What you say we sit down and talk it all over?" Dicksy Boy placed his hand upon the shoulder of the gratified Filmer; they walked to old Mr. and Mrs. Watson's verandah steps, and sat. Formalities were over; they were at the age when intimacy is as instantaneous as between convivial men at a midnight bar. "Listen, Filmo," Dicksy Boy said. "I got my driver's license over two months ago, the very day I was sixteen. I got pinched that same afternoon and the judge took my license away for two years the day after." Filmer's breast filled with an almost suffocating hero worship; he murmured "My gosh!" slowly and whisperingly, and Dicksy, pleased by the tribute, continued, "Listen, you can ask me all about it if you want to; see what I mean? Some people I wouldn't answer; some

I would. Yes, sir, it all happened on account of a dame.
Were you ever engaged, Filmo?"

"Engaged?" Filmer was indeed staggered. "Me? No,
I don't expect I ever will be, hardly."

Dicksy Boy laughed. "Yes, I used to talk like that, too,
when I was your age or maybe a little younger. Listen,
Filmo; I was engaged the first time when I was just
thirteen. Yes, sir, thirteen. That wasn't the girl they got
my license away from me on account of, though. Not
that baby. No, hardly! I've quit writing to this one,
too; but I'll tell you about her, see what I mean?"

He unfolded a narrative of sophisticated love, hard
driving, accidents and court scenes; he repeated elaborate
dialogues in which he had borne the wittier part. "Well,
sum it up; sum it up. What's it all amount to?" he said,
serious in concluding these episodes. "I told 'em they
could go eat rhubarb, and Mabel and her old skinny
mother and father, too; so what? Why, I drive a car
just the same whenever I feel like it and I don't when
I don't. That's the sum and substance." Then he inquired where Filmer had his clothes built, and, when
Filmer had acquired "built", advised him to go to Fas-
sett's in New York.

After that Dicksy Boy went on to speak frankly of
what is sometimes called sex. He thought Bokakio and
the Heptameron crude stuff, and Filmer was surprised
to learn that the name of a celebrated memoirist he'd
heard Slops mention wasn't pronounced Cazzanobbia.
Dicksy then told Filmer all about the inner life of night
spots, where, he said, a girl of true worth might often
be found as well as among people your family know.

Filmer listened more than admiringly; a spell was upon him. Something rare and uplifting seemed to be happening to him. Dicksy Boy Harpeddle, deep in life, well-adventured among glam-gals, practically a young man, was already his friend—a polished dresser and talker outshining dumb old Bill, Slops, and Charlsworth Beck as the day outshines the night. An ambition to appear before Antoinette Fry bringing his friend Dicksy Boy with him grew strong in Filmer. Together he and Dicksy Boy could show Antoinette what oafs she cherished in old Slops, Bill, and Charlsworth Beck. It was about time they learned a little something, and for Antoinette to remember who was different from them and stop treating him the way she did yesterday. Thus, when the afternoon shadow of the Watsons' house had extended itself eastward across the grass all the way to the street, and Dicksy Boy asked fastidiously what was the hottest night spot in town, Filmer, rising to go, spoke with a slight embarrassment.

"Well—well, I tell you what, Dicksy Boy, old kid, I'd like to attend a night spot myself; but—but I been having a good deal of trouble with the family lately. It's about the worst I ever been in and they got my allowance cut off—for the time being. I tell you what let's do, instead. There's a—there's a girl lives just up the street here that's got a bunch of heels always hanging around; but, herself, she's—she's the goods-plus. After dinner let's go over there and——"

"I see!" Dicksy Boy laughed. "Want me to look her over for you, what-oh?"

"Well—not exactly. I mean these lugs ought to be

showed where to head in. We could kind of slap down the ears of those individuals and rib 'em and everything, kind of, and——"

"Right *ho!*" Dicksy Boy comprehended with pleasure. "Got you, Filmo; we'll smear the mugs. You come over here for me soon as you've stoked the puss. Right after dinner; see what I mean?"

"Right *ho*, Dicksy Boy!" Filmer said. "I'll be over for you soon's I get through dinner; see what I mean?"

. . . He was a little delayed for the appointment. A thunder shower interfered; it began by seeming to explode just over the house during dinner and it became so outrageous as almost to gain Ripley Little's full attention. (He still couldn't even accidentally glance at his son without stopping eating, or anything else, to meditate obviously upon Filmer.) The elementary uproar continued after the meal, then dwindled; Filmer went forth, and Mr. and Mrs. Little sat by the front windows of the living-room and looked out into a cleaned twilight that felt treacherous.

"Hot and muggy as ever," Little said. "Going to get plenty more of it before the evening's over." His gaze, roving complainingly, rested upon two hatless figures passing along the sidewalk, and its discontent increased. "*Now* where's he going? Where's he going *now?* Over to that lipsticked little Fry girl's again, I suppose."

He referred to Filmer, who, with his new friend, was indeed going whither his father supposed. Filmer, chewing nothing knowingly, swinging his arms and slouching in his best style, felt dramatic. He was about to show

Antoinette and Bill, Slops and old Charlsworth Beck the kind of guy he could go with when he really cared to. Limber, lanky, careless and debonair, Dicksy Boy smoked a cigarette in a pasteboard holder and spoke of a waitress he knew who was a widow. To Filmer there seemed a dark grandeur about him.

Middle age is colder. "Who's *that* he's got with him?" Little asked. "Who's that insect with the cigarette in its silly face?"

. . . At Antoinette's the grass was wet, and scattering drops still fell under the trees; but sounds of youth and attempted music came from within the house. Filmer and Dicksy Boy found Antoinette, Bill, Charlsworth Beck and Slops noisily gathered about a piano upon which Ellie Turner was trying hard to play "Squirt Your Hose On Carrie What's She Care" with both hands. Filmer made the presentation of Dicksy Boy to Antoinette and Ellie formal, and to Bill, Slops and· Charlsworth as scornfully negligent as he could. Slops, Bill and Charlesworth, in the presence of Dicksy Boy's jacket, were quieted down immediately. Antoinette fluttered her eyelashes consciously, and fat little Ellie looked eager.

"Heard all about you," Dicksy Boy said jauntily to Antoinette. "Every single thing, where you buy platinum tonic for your hair, and all. Just look at that hair. Boy! Been motoring in seventeen states and every place I went they all said, 'Listen, Dicksy Boy, wait till you meet Antoinette Fry; just wait till you two get together!' Pepper!"

Antoinette pretended to slap him. "I bet you're a great big liar!"

Filmer was delighted. Dicksy Boy had begun mag-
nificently, a credit to his proprietor. "I'll tell you how
it was, Antoinette; see what I mean?" Filmer said. "This
afternoon I and Dicksy Boy got to talking about going
to a night spot or somewheres tonight; but I told him,
'Let's not. Listen, Dicksy Boy,' I told him. 'Instead of a
night spot, see what I mean, let's us go——"

"Pepper!" Dicksy Boy cried, neither he nor Antoinette
seeming interested in Filmer's account of things. *"Pepper!"*

Dicksy Boy put both hands upon the fat back of the
pleased Ellie, pushed her from the piano bench, gave her
a jolly spank, kicked the bench away, and, playing jig-
gishly upon the keys, used his limber legs and large feet
in a semi-stationary dance of clattering agility. Antoinette
and Ellie screamed in rapture; Dicksy Boy increased his
activity, shouting, "Pepper, more pepper! *Hot* Dicksy
Boy! Peppah, more peppah!" Then, playing with his
right hand and still dancing, he used his left arm to
clutch Antoinette to his side. "Dance, gal, dance! Peppah,
gal, peppah! Pepper in the feet, gal. Peppah!"

Filmer drew a breath of apprehension, feared that
Antoinette might deem Dicksy Boy offensive and that she
might therefore think coldly of his sponsor. Antoinette,
on the contrary, immediately entered into the spirit of
Dicksy Boy's fun. "Peppah!" she cried. "More peppah!"
and, unresentful of Dicksy Boy's arm, did her best to
imitate his drumming feet.

"Peppah! More peppah!" shouted fat little Ellie
Turner, and did likewise.

Dicksy Boy abandoned the piano, threw his other arm

about Ellie, and, bellowing "Squirt Your Hose On Carrie What's She Care", danced both girls with him round and round the room. Frequently they interrupted their so-called singing to shout "Pepper!" or "Peppah!" or "More peppah!" or *"Hot* Dicksy Boy!" and whenever this happened all three were ecstasied with a humor inexplicable to the four spectators.

Standing aside, Filmer tried to laugh as heartily, tried to prove himself with them in spirit; but things didn't seem to be turning out as he had thought they would. He was beginning an experience that uncounted suitors of all ages have undergone since the beginnings of human life and will probably undergo to the end of it. When did anybody ever do himself a good turn by bringing a showy friend to dazzle an impressionable or coquettish loved one? Ay, and what's the discretion of a lover who displays to her a dashing stranger all temptingly aglitter with newness?

Filmer's laughter—the kind that claims, *"I'm* in on this, too"—was feebler every time he felt called upon to produce it.

XIII

Antoinette, flushed and bright-eyed, piercingly sang "Squirt Your Hose On Carrie What's She Care"; so did Dicksy Boy and fat squealy Ellie Turner. Whirling, the three interlocked dancers regardlessly slammed into Filmer, knocked him four feet backward, into the piano. "Peppah! More peppah!" they cried, and Filmer, swallowing, felt that he really hadn't known Dicksy Boy through and through until this evening. You never do know a man until you see him among women; and if Filmer had thought Dicksy Boy was going to be so unbelievably fresh with Antoinette and raise all this hullabaloo in Mr. and Mrs. Fry's house as soon as he got into it he almost wouldn't have brought him along at all.

"Hot Dicksy Boy!" the dancers cried, and dropped sittingly, side by side, upon a sofa, screaming with self-applausive laughter.

Dicksy Boy, between the two girls, spread his legs, squirmed one foot behind the feet of Antoinette and the other behind the feet of Ellie, leaned backward, lifting high all six feet; then, throwing his body forward, brought himself, Antoinette and Ellie, in the one sweeping and humorous movement, upright upon the floor. "*Hot* Dicksy Boy! What do we do next?" he said.

"*I* know! *I* know!" Antoinette danced up and down, pounded Dicksy Boy's shoulder. "Tonight's the Grand Opening of Dilly's New Dreamland. We'll all go out there on the bus. We'll——"

"Bus? Listen, woman!" Dicksy Boy said. "What's the use me having a car that'll do a hundred flat if you ask her? I gave the chauffeur a night off; but he drove her round the alley and put her in old Cousin Rupie Watson's garage and I can get her out okey-dokey. Hot Dicksy Boy! C'm on with me, Antoinette. It's dark now and I'm afraid to go up alleys alone in the black black night! We'll be back for you others in two shakes. C'm on, Antoinette. Peppah, gal!"

"*Peppah!*" Antoinette cried. Dicksy Boy seized her hand and they ran out of the house.

Ellie Turner skipped to the piano and hammered the keys, shouting; then turned, enraptured, to Filmer. "Isn't he the wunnerflest cutie-coot? My, is he a hot boy! How long's he going to stay?" She included Bill, Slops and Charlsworth. "Don't you s'pose if we *all* got together and said he just simply *had* to, we could persuade him to keep on visiting that nice Mr. and Mrs. Watson maybe a month or even all summer?"

In response Filmer was almost as lackadaisical as were Bill, Slops and Charlsworth. They didn't wish to appear jealous or anything, but couldn't brighten up

to Ellie's idea, and she turned to hammer the piano again
—did so until an automobile horn insistently disturbed
the darkened quiet of the neighborhood. A phrase already odious to Charlsworth, Bill, Slops and even Filmer
was heard repeatedly from the street. *"More* peppah!"
echoed fat old Ellie Turner, and ran bouncingly forth.

Filmer, Bill, Slops and Charlsworth followed her so-
berly and by the time they reached the curb she was
already on the front seat of the car, jumping up and
down beside Antoinette and Dicksy Boy. The four others,
girlless—for even Ellie would have been a little something—were forced to pile up behind, churlish with one
another about making room.

"I'm crazy about this burg. I'm going to stay here
forever!" Dicksy Boy announced. "Yes, sir," Dicksy Boy
said. "My mother'll do anything I tell her and we'll
keep on visiting here 'way into September."

"Grand! Grand! Grand!" Antoinette exclaimed, and
Ellie Turner whooped like a simple idiot.

"Now, babies, I'll show you some driving!" Dicksy
Boy said, and within three blocks proved himself every
bit as bad as his word. Filmer, Slops, Bill, and Charlsworth Beck flopped about on one another, had pains
physical, emotional and mental.

"My gosh, Bill," Charlsworth begged, "lean your back
off my face! Anyways I'd like to see it coming when
I get killed. Can't you sit all over somebody else a while?"
Bill obliged by sitting thumpily upon Filmer, who was
now positive that Cousin Olita's loopy neighborly politeness had worked him into one of the biggest mistakes
he'd ever made.

Dicksy Boy, having reached a main-traveled thorough-fare, ran through a red light and began to do some spectacular out-and-in snaking among other cars. Every time he attempted one of these fancy feats, Antoinette and Ellie squealed hysterically; then servilely echoed the hero's abominable cry, "More peppah!" It was enough to sicken anybody of condiments for life.

The spontaneous warm friendships of youth, like those between adults at the midnight bar, can be chilled abruptly. "I'll tell you something you won't like," the rocking Filmer said, muffled by a shoulder blade of Bill's. "The dern doggone fool hasn't even got a license. The judge took it away from him."

"My gosh!" Bill, Slops and Charlsworth said, virtually in concert and not with admiration.

Because of a series of coincidences none of which could happen again in a thousand years, the car reached a twenty-five-cent parking lot opposite Dilly's New Dream-land's whitely illuminated main entrance without causing a death, and drove in. The occupants jumped out; Dicksy Boy took Antoinette and Ellie each by an arm and ran ahead with them. Filmer, Bill, Slops and Charlsworth ran, too, for they had a reason; and they were all suggestively at Dicksy Boy's elbow when he paid seventy-five cents, plus tax, for three admission tickets.

"I'll treat the women," he said, laughing. "Hot Dicksy Boy!" Antoinette and Ellie skipped through the turn-stile, and, with Dicksy Boy, were immediately lost to sight.

Bill, Slops and Charlsworth Beck naturally had less than twenty cents between them, after yesterday's orgy at the Toastie Snackie Inn and the bus rides; and as for Filmer, he'd been a bit lofty with the facts when he told Dicksy Boy that his allowance was cut off "for the time being"—Ripley Little didn't believe in allowances, and the past twenty-four hours hadn't encouraged Filmer to apply. Fair-sized drops of rain plopped hintingly upon the four boys as they stood looking at the turnstile and at the long extent of white board fence seven feet high.

"Listen," Slops said determinedly. "I don't stand for this treatment; not for a minute! We got to crash the gate. We got to back in."

"Back in?" Filmer repeated. "What you mean, back in?"

"Certainly, back in," Slops said. "I don't stand for this treatment."

Opportunity was already awaiting him. Upon the falling of raindrops many of the more thoughtful people within the glowing enclosure of the fence decided simultaneously to go home, and, to relieve pressure, a wide double gateway not far from the main entrance was thrown open. "Me first," Slops said, and, as if casually, he approached the outcoming throngs. When he reached them, however, he turned about, so that he faced in the same direction that they did; and then, swinging his arms and leaning forward as if, like them, he engaged earnestly in the process of hurrying away, he brilliantly walked backward. Filmer, at first incredulous but gradually enlightened, saw Slops thus successfully enter the exit gate of Dilly's New Dreamland by the simple means of backing in.

"Now me!" Bill said, and in every detail imitated the performance of Slops.

Charlsworth Beck, to whom this technique was as new as it was to Filmer, nevertheless backed in neatly; then Filmer tried. Being the last, he feared observation and guiltily walked forward as well as backward, losing so much time thereby that when he reached the gateway the departing crowd was sparse and his backing and filling became conspicuous. Large hands grasped his shoulders from behind, a hard knee was applied to him coarsely and he moved only forward, this time with speed. Reproached in ugliest terms by a hoarse and whiskied voice, he heard the gates slammed shut but didn't turn to see who closed them. Instead, gulping, he went to the parking lot across the road, where Dicksy Boy had left the car. Here a man soured by old suspicions loudly refused to admit any person whomsoever without a card proving ownership of one of the vehicles within; and shelter had to be sought elsewhere. For Filmer there was none, and the rain now came down as if the lakes of heaven had capsized.

Filmer stood in it for an everlasting hour, leaning against the tall fence near the wetly packed main entrance. The boards at his back seemed to flow; the ground became an ooze of mud about his once whitish shoes, and finally he said aloud, "Listen! Look *here!*" in the tone of one who remonstrates against exorbitance. At once, as if these words had influence among the rolling and stormy heights, the downpour slackened to a drizzle.

Again the gateway through which his three companions had backed was thrown open. Once more, crowds came hurrying forth, and at the tail of the scrambling proces-

sion walked three figures not of adult size, dripping
moodily. Filmer sloshed forward to them.

"Listen!" Charlesworth Beck addressed him complainingly. "What you been doing all this time here? Look,
have they come out yet?"

Filmer spoke with feeling. "Listen, you been in there
where they *were,* weren't you? *I* wasn't, was I? *You* were,
weren't you? You——"

"We *saw* 'em, didn't we?" Slops retorted. "They went
in a place that says Dancing Twenty-five Cents. We got
on some barrels and looked through a window at 'em
dancing."

"Us, the best friends she's ever had!" Bill said. "Us
out there in all that storm, and we could hear 'em yelling
'Pepper!' so loud the whole crowd in there stopped to
watch 'em, and if you want my opinion it's somebody
ought to tell her father and mother she ought to be protected from going with a great big sap that'll get her
talked about from everybody looking at her he's got her
so reckless!"

"Go ahead," the heartsick Filmer begged. "What happened next?"

"A great big punk in a rubber coat came along and
chased us off the barrels," Slops informed him bitterly.
"Kept following us and shooing us with a club. Dilly's
New Dreamland management better look out or they
won't get much patronage if *that's* the treatment they
expect to hand their public!"

The weather, in slowing down to a drizzle, had only
been fooling blackheartedly. Flash and bang-whack came
together, down swished water; and again Filmer, Bill,

Slops and Charlsworth were bathed with their clothes on. "Listen," Bill said. "Look, let's all go and take turns sitting in his car on the driver's seat, dripping on it and——"

"We can't." Filmer described the suspicious man in charge of the parking lot. "And would that guy even tell you if the car's still there? All he'll say is, 'Show me my numbered check or go on away from here!' He's a nice guy, that guy is!"

"I don't stand for one minute more of this treatment," Slops said. "I don't know how many miles it is home; but I'm going. Fat chance to thumb a ride, us this wet; but I'm going."

Charlsworth Beck and Bill were of like mind; and so was Filmer, fully. The four boys began to trudge morosely down the long and splashing road toward home. "What you want to keep talking about it for?" Bill asked spitefully. "If you expect they're still in Dilly's Dreamland whyn't you go back and wait for 'em, Filmer? He's *your* friend, isn't he? It was *you* brought him over to her house, wasn't it? *You're* the one that——"

"Did *I* know how he was going to turn out? *Did* I?" Filmer defended himself hotly. "Look, s'pose I did get him over there, just for my old Cousin Olita's goofy politeness, where am I *now*? Did I *gain* anything by it? Kindly answer me, please. Did *I* gain anything by it? *Did* I?"

Silvered at intervals by oncoming headlights and inconsiderately treated by mud-spurting tires, the four morbid figures plodded soggily on through the watery dark; and their conversation was, more and more pungently,

all of Dicksy Boy. Thus, insensibly, the four drew together in spirit. Times were few when, like M. Dumas'
musketeers, they were all for one and one for all; but
such an hour was with them now. Filmer felt that compared to a pepper-yelling fish-faced slob that couldn't
keep a driver's license, Bill, Slops and Charlsworth were
pretty nice fellows. They all felt that way and were indulgent one with another. When Slops said that what *he*
hated the most—and what her father and mother certainly ought to be told by somebody—was the way that
great big can of garbage was making her conspicuous,
nobody picked on him for his usual weakness in pro-
nunciation.

Antoinette had to be protected from getting talked
about in public places, all agreed, now that this big circus-
dressed foot-pounder was going to stay all summer. If
her parents didn't show sense enough to look after a girl
like that, somebody else would have to get busy. Filmer
made the first suggestion.

"I live right next door to him," he explained. "We
got a bay window that looks down almost in Mr. and
Mrs. Watson's side yard, and my mother's got an old
fountain-pen filler with a rubber bulb that'll squirt fifteen
or twenty feet. If he ever goes around their house that
side when he's starting to Antoinette's I'll fill that filler
with ink and lean out the window and——"

"Listen," Bill said. "Look. At Behring's grocery there's
some cheese left over from Germany that prackly keeps
customers out of the place. The way I look at this whole
business, if we could rub some of it on his clothes——"

"His hair'd be better," Slops interrupted. "It'd be hard to do without his noticing; but it'd be better."

"Then every time all summer he opens his mouth to say anything," Charlsworth said, "we all ought to yell 'Swill! Swill! Swill!' "

"Yes, that'll help," Filmer assented. "Then we ought to——"

They continued to devise measures for Antoinette's protection, and the harder it rained, the more plans they made to save her. They had plenty of time to elaborate details before at last they came sloshing wearily into their own dark and soaking neighborhood.

XIV

At his own driveway gates Filmer left the others and walked toward the house, heavyhearted but thinking what nice fellows Bill and Charlsworth and Slops were, after all. He walked slowly—because what was the use of hurrying when he couldn't get any wetter?—and it was in his mind that he'd find that old fountain-pen filler tonight and charge it with ink so's to be ready for Dicksy Boy the first thing in the morning. "Oh, pardon me, Dicksy Boy," he planned to say, prophetically dramatizing the black squirting. "I didn't notice you were there, because I happened to get so wet last night the water isn't out of my eyes yet. Let's go over to Antoinette's; I got some friends of mine waiting around over there to see you, Hot Dicksy Boy. *They'll* help you clean off all that ink!"

Thus Filmer gave himself a bitter, slight pleasure; but, ascending the portico steps, he had a misgiving about his reception indoors—a prevision not inaccurate he perceived as with squishing shoes he entered the hall. His father and mother came immediately to the living-room doorway, and he didn't like the expression worn by either of them, though his mother's was only lamentant.

"Oh dear me, you're just a living lake, Filmer!" she cried. "Get to bed as quickly as you can. Rub yourself hard, and I'll come up and bring you a hot-water bottle to——"

"Hot-water bottle? I won't! Mother, I absolutely——"

"Filmer, please! It'll keep you from catching cold. Child, child, didn't you know better than to——"

"Know better?" Ripley Little echoed. "Asking *him* if he doesn't know better? Filmer, do you realize what hour of the night it is?"

"Sir?"

"I asked you——" Little began; then changed his theme. "What's the use? He associates himself with a mental defective, a moron who ought to be kept put away, makes a companion of him on a forbidden excursion, and then, for reasons no human being could fathom, deserts the party and chooses to walk home all the way from Dilly's Dreamland in a cloudburst! What's the use?"

"Sir? How'd you know—— I mean what makes you say——"

"Never mind!" His father waved him to the stairway. "Get your clothes off, if you don't want pneumonia. Dry yourself! Dry yourself! Get to bed! Get to bed!"

"Yes, sir."

Filmer ascended to his own room and had almost finished preparing himself for the night when Cousin Olita entered breezily, carrying a filled hot-water bottle.

"Take it away!" Filmer made this a command. "Take it away and don't come and sneak it up against me after you think I've gone to sleep! Take it out, and don't you know better yet than to walk into people's rooms while they're undressing?"

"But you're practically in your nightclothes, now," Cousin Olita said. "Your mother thought maybe *I* could persuade you; so *do* let me just put this——"

"No!" he shouted. "No! Go out and take it out with you. I'd as soon sleep with a boiled lizard. I won't——" Suddenly he moderated his tone. "Wait a minute. Look, Cousin Olita. Listen. Did you hear what Father said to me down in the hall when I came in?"

"Yes, I was sitting in the living-room with them, Filmer. Your mother was trying to reason a little with Cousin Ripley about you and Goody, because of course both of you children——"

"Me?" Filmer said. "I don't see what *I*——"

"Oh, yes." Cousin Olita shook her head. "You see, coming on top of Goody and the Chow——"

"Chow? What Chow?"

"Why, don't you remember?" Cousin Olita asked. "Goody's been days and days talking about the Chow she wanted to get from Long Island, and just before she went out this evening, why, of course she had to tell your father that it's probably come, because she'd been notified by the kennels that it'd been started. Well, it seems it isn't a Chow pup, you see, because she knew beforehand what your father'd say when it made difficulties. So it seems it's already over two years old; but he was just as upset as if it wasn't, and he and Goody had quite a little time over it together, and after she'd gone it turned out that she'd signed your mother up to tell him about the visitor, too, so——"

"Visitor?" Filmer interrupted. "Do you mean the one next door? Dicksy Boy?"

"No, no. That all came later," Cousin Olita informed him. "Your mother had to tell him about Goody's going to have a visitor, a dear sweet young Southern girl that Goody knew when she was away at school. She's a real little beauty with lots of go, it seems, and they simply adored each other and she's coming very soon and it'll be *so* nice; but your father's always had *such* a prejudice against visitors—unless they're relations of the family— so what between hearing about the Chow and Goody's friend both coming, and of course he still feels terribly over the way you didn't get to his office on time with those confidential notes and then afterwards put 'em un- der the door where anybody——"

"So he had to bring *that* up again, did he?" Filmer said. "Still bringing it up, still bringing it up!"

"Yes. So when it all came out about the Harpeddle boy, Filmer, why, of course he——"

"That's what I'm trying to ask you about," Filmer said, "if you'd ever give me a chance. I mean what'd he mean when I came in and he commenced talking about me associating with a mental defective, somebody that was a moron and I went on a forbidden excursion with? Was he hinting——"

"Oh, no, not hinting," Cousin Olita explained. "You

see, all *that* came on top of the worry about the Chow and Goody's visitor. It was already getting late when it came out about the distress you caused poor Mrs. Harpeddle, Filmer."

"Who?"

"Mrs. Harpeddle," Cousin Olita said. "You see, first they sent Mr. Watson over here to ask what any of us knew about it, and then later I went over there to see if I couldn't do something, and found everything in *such* a state! Mr. Watson had gone on from here to the Frys', you see, Filmer——"

"Mr. Watson did? To the Frys'?"

"Yes, and so when he told Mr. and Mrs. Fry about the Harpeddle boy, Filmer, why, Mrs. Fry thought she'd heard from upstairs that some of you were yelling something about going out to this Dilly's New Dreamland, and poor Mr. Fry took umbrellas and raincoats and got in his car and drove all the way out there, and, after splashing all over the place, he found them and brought Antoinette and Ellie Turner home with him."

"He did? You mean he——"

"He certainly did," Cousin Olita said. "I'm afraid it seems I was terribly mistaken in what I told you about that poor Harpeddle boy this afternoon, Filmer."

"You certainly were!" Filmer agreed. "What *is* all this about me causing his mother distress? I certainly wish I had. What——"

"I'm telling you, Filmer. Poor Mr. and Mrs. Watson feel just as terribly about it as anybody. You see, they hadn't seen their cousin, poor Mrs. Harpeddle, for years and years, and then to have all this happen——"

"Have all what happen? My goodness! Have all *what* happen?"

"Why, all this that did happen, Filmer. She says the whole Harpeddle family's had so much trouble with this young son that poor Mrs. Harpeddle was having a nervous breakdown and right in the middle of it they saw the only thing to do was to get him away from home and out of the town where they live, so she started on a long motor trip with him, keeping him always in the back seat with her. When they got here to the Watsons' she thought it was a nice safe place and she could have a few days' peaceful rest—and then to have him slip through the alley into the garage and take the car out when it's so terribly important for him never to touch it and he was absolutely forbidden———"

"He was?" Filmer said. "He is?"

"Oh, absolutely, Filmer! Mrs. Watson says Mrs. Harpeddle says the judge says that if he ever hears of his driving a car in the next two years, if it's only ten feet, he'll send him to the reformatory *absolutely* and———"

"Send him where?" Pleasure lighted Filmer's eye. "Did you say———"

"Oh, my, yes indeed, Filmer! It seems his family have always had the worst kind of trouble with him—couldn't get him past the fifth grade in school—and finally it all came to a climax with this awful trial in the traffic court, and an uncle of his had to use all kinds of political influence, and Mrs. Watson says the only excuse for him is he doesn't seem to have mind enough to be responsible. His poor mother had both Mr. and Mrs. Watson pacing the garage with her, waiting for him, and when they heard the car in the alley they turned the lights off and when he drove in he turned them on—and there they were! He tried to be bold as brass, in spite of everything Mr. Fry'd said to him out at Dilly's Dreamland, because, you see, he isn't really very bright, Filmer, and still thought he could smooth it all over with his mother; but they took him in the house and she worked and worked on him till at last she got him to crying and———"

"Got him to what?" Filmer was excited. "He did? Honestly? He did?"

"Oh, yes indeed he did!" Cousin Olita said. "After his mother'd talked and talked about the judge, she got the Watsons to bring a Bible and took her oath he'd not have another penny out of her for the next six months. She told Mrs. Watson that always does it and said it was the same old story—her son finds wild boys to go with wherever she takes him. She said she thought it would be different here; but no, he always finds them. She said she thought the worst thing in the whole affair was your all playing on his weakness till he sneaked the car out and then your slipping away and leaving him 'way out at that Dreamland place with two strange girls on his hands. Mrs. Watson tried to speak up for you, Filmer, but———"

"*Me?*" Filmer, who had slid into bed, made a movement as if to rise. "Listen, I'm going straight over to Mr. and Mrs. Watson's———"

"Filmer! You can't!"

"All right, then; I'll go over the first thing tomorrow morning and I'll———"

"No, you'll have to bear it, Filmer dear," Cousin Olita said. "They'll be gone before you could get there. His mother said there was always just one thing to do and so she'd get him away as quickly as she can from the companionships he's started to form. She made him pack and they're going to leave by six tomorrow morning. Now won't you let me put the hot-water bottle——"

"I will not! Are you sure——"

"Oh, yes; they'll be gone right after daylight. Good-night, Filmer."

In the dark Filmer lay frowning. Dicksy Boy wasn't going to stay all summer; he wasn't going to stay at all, and what could have been better news?—and yet, and yet Filmer experienced a regret that was partly bafflement. The infamous Emperor Caligula's gayeties were such a curse upon the earth that to all except himself every hour he lived seemed an hour too long; yet, when he was liquidated by a self-appointed committee, a great many other people were disappointed: they were sorry that he hadn't lived anyhow long enough for them to go ahead with what they'd planned to do to him. This was almost precisely Filmer's condition, as he edged toward slumber.

He still felt like that the next morning when he approached Antoinette's at about half past ten o'clock; but in the sunny air there were indications that his associates in the previous night's adventures had turned their thoughts to other matters. From Antoinette's yard there were heard girlish squealings and basso-falsetto uproars in the unreliable voices of young males about to become manlier. When Filmer reached a point where he could look over Antoinette's hedge he saw that Bill and Charlsworth had old Slops down upon the grass nimbly rolling him, and that Antoinette and jolly little Ellie were looking on, pretending to be horrified. Antoinette ran to Filmer as he came through the gateway.

"Filmer darling!" she cried. "Come make Bill and Charl let poor old Slops alone! They're all just acting simply *too* screwbally this morning!"

"Antoinette, listen," Filmer said. "Listen, Antoinette. Antoinette, look. Did you hear about this Mrs. Harpeddle that's his mother and Mr. and Mrs. Watson catching him last night when he had the front to think that even after your father went out there and got you he could still sneak his mother's car back into——"

"Yes, we know all about it, Filmer. Mrs. Watson was over to see my mother this morning and——"

"Look, Antoinette," Filmer interrupted. "Antoinette, listen. Then you know—you know he's gone, don't you?"

"Yes, wasn't he horrid?" Antoinette said carelessly. She tucked her arm within Filmer's and drew him forward. "Please, Filmer! Do please come make those two awful boys let poor Slops alone."

Nothing loath, Filmer advanced with Antoinette sweetly urging him. "Listen, you mugs!" he said in a dignified way. "Bill, you and Charlsworth are peculiar individuals; you're acting like great big bums only about eight years old." Bill and Charlsworth had already allowed Slops to rise, and the three stood staring satirically at Filmer, who, on that account, decided to include Slops in his speech of reproof. "Great big bums only about eight years old," he repeated. "Yes, all three of you! I guess, though I might expect to see such conduct in mental detectives and morons and——"

"Oh, you might?" Slops said sneeringly. "Listen a while, will you, Big Boy Little! Look, whose friend was he, anyhow? Who brought him here in the first place? Who came strutting in here to Antoinette's last night all swelled up and sponsoring him and——"

"That's neither here nor there," Filmer, somewhat taken aback, responded; and then, inspired he knew not whence, he asked hotly, "Am I my brother's keeper?" This was so good that it surprised him; he felt certain that it would bear repetition, perhaps frequently. "Am I my brother's keeper?" he said, with even more heat. "Kindly answer me that, will you? Am I my brother's keep——"

"Swill! Swill! Swill!" Charlsworth, Bill and Slops bellowed suddenly.

Filmer strove to be heard. "Answer me, please: Am I my broth——"

"Swill! Swill! Swill! Swill! Swill!"

The treachery of Charlsworth, Slops and Bill went even further. No matter what he tried to say, they interfered in the same manner; and then, when Antoinette, pronouncing them bum ruffians, again took Filmer's arm and would have led him away, they tripped him up and rolled him as old Slops had been rolled. It was a rowdy morning, and, though before it was over Filmer helped Bill and Charlsworth to roll old Slops again, he felt rather disgraced by it. He wanted Antoinette to think him something higher than these clowning nitwits who never gave him a chance to be alone with her to talk about what a person that's different from other people does talk about.

He was troubled, too, because he hadn't yet been able to get her to tell him exactly when she'd first noticed it.

XV

He was back at the Frys' in the afternoon, of course; arriving about three o'clock and, recklessly, again accompanied by a creature he counted upon to add to his own prestige with Antoinette. Goody was unfortunately not at home when her Chow, an adult though runtish specimen, had been delivered. This was at about half past two; and, when Mrs. Little had settled the express company's C.O.D. account, Filmer's plea that the poor undersized animal needed exercise after being in a crate all this time seemed reasonable. He made an amateurish collar and leash out of clothesline, and, for a while, tried to give the Chow a needed loosening-up in large circles about the ample yard and shrubberies. The Chow, kennel-soured and not born too gracious anyhow, didn't like the collar, didn't like the rope and didn't like being bawled at encouragingly while dragged by the neck. He might have learned to be a better dog if he'd had a different experience that first day in his new home.

Antoinette received him with outcries of joy so loud

that Ellie Turner was soon there, and so were Charlsworth Beck and Bill. Charlsworth and Bill were con-
temptuous, supposing this new Chow to be Filmer's, nor
did he undeceive them; but Antoinette and Ellie were enchanted.

"He looks exactly like a darling beautiful little reddish
wolf," Antoinette declared. "Let's get up a photoplay
like Snow White and the Seven Dwarfs. I'll be Little
Red Riding Hood and he'll be the Bad Old Wolf all
dressed up like a grandmother. Yip-p*ee,* Little Red Riding Hood and the Bad Old Wolf!"

"Goofy!" Ellie said. "Aren't you over being seven
years old yet, Antoinette?"

"No, I want to!" Antoinette insisted. "I've got the
dearest little red hood ever was and I want you to see me
in it, and my mother's got a red cape, too. Just think how
he'll look when we get him all dressed up like a grandmother! He'll be darling; anybody can see he's perfectly
photogenic. Bill, you run get Slops to bring his birthday
moving-picture camera right away. He told me yesterday
it was all mended again. Get him! Run! I'll do the rest."

She skipped into the house and was dancing out within
five minutes, wearing the red hood and her mother's scarlet cape; she brought a basket, too, and displayed herself
in charming poses, singing, "Oh, I'm Lit-*tul* Red Riding
Hood!" and shouting, "Look! How do I look now?
How'm I doing when I walk like this?" Meanwhile Bill
returned with Slops and the camera, for which she posed
in exquisite motion; and then, when she tired of prancing,
she took from the basket a few things that her mother
didn't know had been removed from a chest upstairs.

"Take a gander!" Antoinette cried. "Here's the funniest darling old lace cap with lappets my mother's great-grandmother or somebody used to wear and her silk mittens and her cute little old taffeta basque. I've got lots of rubber elastics and the strongest kind of safety-pins, so now we'll dress the Bad Old Wolf up to be the grandmother he ate. Everybody help!"

Everybody helped, which may have been one reason why the Chow acquired the conviction that in his new surroundings he had need to fight for his very life.

At about four o'clock he was more or less in costume and partly upon Antoinette's lap when this delusion evoked from him contortions so agile that he seemed to possess the strength of seven and the speed of seventy. Bitten hands grasped at him too tentatively; he went away, and, but little impeded by what he wore as he made a great leap over the Frys' hedge, was round the nearest corner before anybody could reach the sidewalk to see which way he went.

Filmer, uneasy and under the correct impression that the vanished creature was a thing of some price, had now once more to bear the ingratitude of his friends. While Antoinette brought disinfectants from the house to pour upon their injuries and her own, one and all assured him that he was lucky to be rid of such an animal. The best thing that could happen to Filmer, they said, would be if he never found him, and, as for themselves, did anybody think they were going to wear their feet off hunting for a dog that had bit them all up?

Setting forth to trace the Chow, Filmer went in wrong directions exclusively. Inquiries addressed to pedestrians

and to colored men mowing lawns or clipping shrubberies brought him converse with nobody who'd seen a reddish kind of Chinese-looking dog dressed up like Old
Times. Continuing discouragement, however, didn't make
him give up the search until late; he had a warrantable re-
luctance to return home without any news at all. He was
positive that he'd have a scene with Goody, and there
might be others, tediously, with everybody else; and
when at last he did come sluggishly into his own yard,
toward dinner time, he found that he'd at least been
right about the scene with Goody.

She'd been what she called frenzied for three hours.
She'd reached home at about the time the Chow had left
that neighborhood behind him, and when her mother told
her that Wu Wu—name supplied by Goody, quoting a
letter from the kennels—had arrived but was now out
somewhere with Filmer, for exercise, Goody said even
Cousin Olita'd have known better than to let that boy do
such a thing. She went hurrying forth on foot; for, although Crappio's had at last returned the Littles' sole
remaining car, her father had driven himself downtown
in it, announcing that henceforth it would spend its days
in a parking lot near his place of business, except at night
when it would be locked in the home garage. Passing the
house of the Frys', Goody saw friends of Filmer's there,
busy before a small camera; she applied to them and was
told that they all thought Wu Wu was Filmer's property;
they wouldn't have dreamed of getting Wu Wu so excited
otherwise. They had an impression that Filmer'd gone to
look for Wu Wu somewhere.

Goody made a running tour of several blocks without

discovering any trace of either Filmer or Wu Wu; then she ran home and made use of the telephone, calling active friends of hers to go forth upon the search. One of these, of faithful heart, had been successful. Young Hamilton Ellers mounted a fast bicycle, and, after covering much territory, he'd come upon Wu Wu eating something bad in the lot behind the Glue Works and still wearing some of Antoinette's ancestress's taffeta basque safety-pinned about his middle. Having delivered the animal to its pleasingly grateful owner, Hamilton Ellers had laughed off her suggestion of the Pasteur treatment but had gone as quickly as possible to a drug store. Thus, when the foot-dragging Filmer entered the Littles' driveway gates, Wu Wu was already within the house; and Goody, who'd been looking from a window, hurried outdoors to meet her brother. She created the scene with him as spiritedly as if Wu Wu were still a wanderer.

Informed by Cousin Olita, from a distance, that dinner was getting pretty spoiled, both entered the front door almost shouting; but the hall already contained more noise than they were making. Ripley Little had just tripped over Wu Wu, and Wu Wu had bitten Ripley Little on the shoe. Subsequently, at the table, Ripley Little praised Filmer for trying to lose Wu Wu.

This seems to have been the beginning of the feud between Wu Wu and Ripley Little. Wu Wu, uprooted from everything previously familiar to him, distracted by thunderous hours of railway travel in vibrant dark enclosure, then dragged by the neck to be manhandled and suffocated in repellent fabrics, had made for himself a little interval of liberty, only to be captured and borne through the air to a place where great weights smelling of repulsive leather polish were applied to his ribs; and this last was, to Wu Wu's mind, the climax. The great weights and the leather polish he correctly attributed to Ripley Little, and thenceforth connected all the worst that had happened to him with this person. Ripley Little thought Wu Wu a dangerous dog, and Wu Wu thought Ripley Little a dangerous man.

During the day after that of Wu Wu's arrival, the small Chow consented to be somewhat tolerant of almost everybody in the household; he found himself to be really congenial with Gentry Poindexter, and didn't wholly object to Mrs. Little or to Cousin Olita or to Almatina. He felt an instant affection for the cook, reticently accepted overtures even from Filmer, and, coaxed, coddled and fed by Goody, properly adopted her, found her his light of the world. As the head of the house didn't return until evening, Wu Wu decided that this place might be all right after all and began to look upon it as his own property. He was asleep in a relaxed attitude on the floor of the dark upper hallway when his dreams were shattered by that same dangerous intruder who smelt of leather polish.

The former encounter was repeated. Little, upstairs to refresh his appearance before dinner, stepped on Wu Wu, and Wu Wu, though no fool, was certain that the foot on his face hadn't come there accidentally. This time he bit Ripley Little just above the ankle, then sped down the stairs screeching for Goody's help and consolation.

Goody, rushing from the living-room below, knelt, took Wu Wu in her arms and shouted upward a number of descriptions of people who aren't even sorry when they've kicked a helpless little dog. Her father, at the top of the stairs, denounced Chows and used gestures that caused Wu Wu to bark up at him passionately from Goody's arms. Goody repeated herself, added criticism of people who won't let their own families use a car or buy a new one for them; and Little tried his best to be heard over both Goody and Wu Wu. His short-necked and somewhat strangulated voice was at a disadvantage; nevertheless, it was easily in the money.

Mrs. Little came fluttering from her room imperfectly clad; she got her husband into his bathroom, applied lotions to his injury and promised him that he wouldn't have hydrophobia. "Nearly broke my jam neck over him," Little said. "Then he attacked me again, and now, the way she puts it, why, he had a right to because I kicked him! Didn't I tell you last night I *knew* he was going to bite me again? He'll bite anybody that comes near him. I knew it the minute I laid eyes on him. Dog? Not a drop of dog in him; not a drop! He's half red-widow spider and half oriental panda; yet she'll swear it was my fault till the jobjam cows come home!"

"Now, Ripley, please!" Mrs. Little begged. "Goody only heard Wu Wu yelping and she naturally thought—I mean she doesn't mean——"

"She means I ought to *like* to get my foot bit off by something named Wu Wu. Why, job jam it, if it was really a dog would its name be Wu Wu?"

"Now, Ripley, please!"

"Talks about a new car," he complained. "What for? So she could let Wu Wu drive it? I've been thinking for a while we were maybe getting a little peace in this house because it's been seeming not wholly given over to being a swing asylum for her percussion instrument maniac boy-friends that try to shake ceilings down and pound the last few entrails out of poor old half-murdered pianos. Why, jam my——"

"Now, Ripley, please don't start yourself up again. You're not really hurt and Goody knows it or she'd be sorry."

"She knows it, does she? How, Mrs. Little, if you please? How?"

"Why, by the way you were bell—— I mean, by the way you sounded. Now, Ripley, you mustn't get yourself started up again just when there's such a nice thing going to happen for all of us."

" 'Nice thing going to happen'?" Little permitted his trouser-leg to resume its place over his injured ankle and looked at her suspiciously. " 'For all of us'?" he said. "You're sure that includes me?"

"Why, of course, darling."

"When's it going to happen?"

"Tomorrow, Ripley. You know that."

"I do not. What is it?"

"Why, it's Henrietta Pellar."

"What's Henriettapellar? Another Chow?"

"Ripley! I *told* you she's coming."

"Oh, yes," Little said gloomily. "I remember—the 'dear lovely young thing from just over the Mason and Dixon line' that was in Goody's class at school. No, you didn't tell me she's going to get here as soon as tomorrow. Do you think it's too late for us to wire her parents to keep her home where she belongs?"

"Ripley, I *know* you'll be as nice to her as you can, dear, on Goody's account and—and that after this, too, you'll be careful about stepping on Wu Wu again and——"

"On Goody's account?" Little asked. "You mean I oughtn't to step on him on Goody's account? What about *mine?* Doesn't Father ever get to have any feelings, not even when he's bit? If I'm nice and cooing to her visitor and stop getting macerated by Wu Wu on Goody's account, do you suppose maybe she'll let up on me day and night about buying a new car to be turned into a hospital-feeder?"

"But, Ripley, at her age——"

"I've got an age, too, haven't I?" he urged. "I've got *some* age, haven't I—or isn't Father allowed any such perquisite? No, I guess not, and I'll bet my dobdab head that from now on if I ever start to sit in one of my own chairs to read a newspaper I won't get three-quarters of the way down without having to leap like a gymnast because her jobjam Wu Wu's already there and snarling he'll tear out my pancreas if I sit on him! Already I can't walk through my own upstairs hall without her claiming he's got a right to bite my jobjam feet off. On top of a Chow, you inform me my house is now to be filled with a frizzle-headed jitter-squawker that'll bring all the rhumba-thumping, boops-a-daisy ice-box raiders in town to——"

"No, no, no!" Mrs. Little laughed. "Henrietta isn't frizzle-headed at all. She's the darlingest little brunette, sweet as kittens, and you'll just love her!"

"Kittens? And I'll just love her?" Ripley Little looked piercingly at his wife. "I know exactly what you mean; I'd rather be dead than try to live in the same house with one of those."

"Now, Ripley! Do get ready for dinner, dear. It's waiting and——"

"Look at you," he said. "Not going to put on even a jobjam petticoat?"

"Oh!" she exclaimed, and ran to her own room.

XVI

Driving home at five in the afternoon, Little's mind was less upon the traffic than upon the beautiful girl he expected to meet when he reached his house. By this time, he supposed, the place would probably be all choked up with boys and noise and Wu Wu and Southern accent and whatever'd happened to Filmer that day and all the rest of it. Thus he was surprised to find a quiet house awaiting him, Filmer placid, no other young people within sight or sound and Wu Wu not actively demonstrative. As Little came into the living-room the Chow merely gave him a single glance of dislike and retired upstairs to Goody's sheltering bedchamber. Mrs. Little, looking up from her Bundles for Britain knitting, explained the peacefulness.

"We're all in love with her and so'll you be, Ripley. Oh, yes, you will; you'll see! Even Filmer couldn't resist her; could you, Filmer?"

"He doesn't think it's manly to admit it," Cousin Olita said, as Filmer only grunted; "but of course he couldn't.

It was so lovely to see all the gay young things together, Cousin Ripley, like a bouquet of flowers—like rosebuds dancing in the sun and——"

"They don't," Filmer told her gruffly. "Rosebuds don't dance. And do you call Bull Thetford and Ham Ellers and Ruggo Smart and Hot Toddy and Norman Peel rosebuds, kindly answer?"

"So?" Little said. "Then they've all been here, have they?"

"Oh, yes indeed!" his wife answered. "Goody had them all flocking in—oh, yes, certainly, Norman Peel too, dear—just after Ham and she brought her from the station. Then there were Ruggo Smart's twin sisters, besides—Eunice and Patricia——"

"Cousin Wilma means the ones they call Cuckoo and Screwball," Cousin Olita explained in the manner of a translator. "Eunice and Patricia Smart are such charmingly pretty twins—so strapping big and sweet and full of animal spirits!—I shouldn't think they'd like being called Cuckoo and Screwball."

"You shouldn't?" Ripley Little asked. "What good would it do 'em if they didn't—in that outfit?"

"I believe they do, though, Cousin Ripley," Cousin Olita said. "Goody says they'd feel the rest didn't like 'em if they stopped calling 'em Cuckoo and Screwball. I remember a girl in my set we called Old Snoot but not to her face. That seems to be the difference."

"Patricia and Eunice were just as delighted with darling little Henrietta as anybody," Mrs. Little continued. "As Cousin Olita says, it was really fun to watch them start frolicking right away." She laughed. "They never do stay put nowadays. Just before you came, Ripley, they all trooped out and nobody knows when we'll see our two back again. They were going to eat at the Hi Toots hamburger stand and the Doughnut Dunker just off the park, and then movies and goodness knows what seemed to be in prospect. I think you don't need to worry about having a quiet evening, dear."

Little said that was a blessing, and the evening was indeed as eventless as his wife had promised. At ten he went upstairs through a silence broken only by his own muttered responses and a low growling evoked from Goody's bedroom by the sound of his footsteps.

... At twelve he woke with a first impression that he'd fallen asleep under a chute at the stockyards; but he realized that in such places the tramplings of the herds are not accompanied by jitter-music, and besides, the disturbance that wobbled the house was going on not above but below him, in the living-room and hall downstairs. The poor old piano was at work and the boys had brought their percussion instruments. Something believed to be dancing was taking place, accomplished by syncopated floor-thumpings; and there were sounds that he recognized as being within modern youth's definition of the word "singing". A fresh young female voice, unfamiliar to him, yelled excruciatingly:

"Ib dib! Abba ubba ducka! Fisha eata pie!
Swish me! Kish me! Roll me in your arms!
Hippa! Dippa! Beat them fire alarms!
Ock! Bock! Oradoodle! Utch! Bluck! *Yip! Hi-yi!*

As the voice wasn't Goody's nor either of the terrible voices of the twins, Screwball and Cuckoo, too well known to him, Ripley Little rightly identified his midnight serenader as the guest in his house, Miss Henrietta Pellar. Cheers and floor-thumpings followed her effort. Long and hysterical were the bawlings and squealings of "Ya-a-ay, Henrietter!"

More dancing ensued, seemingly by two-ton centipedes; the floor of Little's bedroom vibrated, and finally, when he'd just about decided to go downstairs in his good old-fashioned nightshirt, roaring, there was a lull. It followed jocosely animal-like howls and a clumping toward the rear of the house: the icebox raid was on, and for the next hour or so Ripley Little had fitful snatches of sleep. From one of these, at about three, he was thoroughly roused by the sound of a large drum and a pair of cymbals rolling down the front steps; then there was quiet, though a half-whisper half-coo, passing his door, said audibly, "Honey, I do hope those cute boys' noise didn't get your poor old dadda waked up squawling mad, the way you say he does."

Goody's voice, responding, was less restrained; she didn't seem to care. "It's all right. He never minds anything so long as Norman Peel is there. Don't you love Norman, too, Henrietta?"

Ripley Little conquered his impulse to call through the door. He had things in mind to say; but it seemed wiser to go on bearing them, instead.

. . . He didn't meet the visitor at breakfast—the girls were resting, Mrs. Little said, so to be fresh for a party that evening at Screwball's and Cuckoo's—and it was not until after his return home in the late afternoon that he had his first experience of Henrietta. A moment earlier a prediction of his came perfectly true: with a newspaper in his hand, he almost sat down upon Wu Wu in the large living-room chair Wu Wu joined him in favoring. Wu Wu snarled a last-instant warning; and Little, after convulsively recovering his balance, called Wu Wu a jab jammed bastinadoed son of a bullfinch.

In the hall a heaven-thrilling voice cried, "Oh, oh, *oh!*" and a lovely person walked in. Charmingly smallish, she looked childlike, had the big-dark-eyed warm and trustful gaze of a gentle gazelle; her wavy brown hair showed a fine nimbus of gold in the late sunshine from the western window, and her movements were as lyrically graceful as those of Goody herself. She came unhesitatingly to Ripley Little, looked up archly into his eyes and shook a reproving forefinger close to his face.

"You sinful man!" she said. "I heard you cursing poor little Pussy. Oh, my me!"

"Who?" Little asked. "You heard me cursing who?"

"Yes, suh; cursing poor little Pussy. Dint you know Goody and me gone and changed Wu Wu's name to Pussy? Don't you like Pussy better your ownself, Mr. Little? Pussy a lot cuter name for a Chow, we think. Anyhow, he's Pussy from now on. Ain't you shame cursing a poor little dog with a sweet little name like Pussy?"

"Uh——" Little was confused. In a way Henrietta seemed much more attractive than he'd expected—and then in another way she didn't. That is, intrinsically she seemed attractive; but he didn't like her using so much archness on him. He never liked feeling that he was being blandished. However, he contrived a smile, said he hoped she'd enjoy her visit to his daughter and protested that he hadn't cursed Wu Wu.

"Now, now!" Henrietta shook her delicate forefinger in his face again. "You going to act the big tough-minded man that won't ever change his opinions and bound not to call him Pussy, no matter how many poor sobbing ladies beg you?"

"Well, Pussy, then," Little said, indulging her. "It's a horrible name; but I don't know that it's much worse than Wu Wu. You're mistaken, though, about my——"

"About you swearing so hard?" Henrietta laughed. "Don't you be embarrassed one minute, Mr. Little. We young generation nowadays talk right out our ownselves sometimes, sex and sex alike, oh, my me, yes! What I heard you call Pussy made me feel mighty at-homelike, and if you'll only keep it up I ain't going miss my own loving dadda so much. When he rips loose, Mr. Little, people really hear something—he's got command o' worse than almost anything you gentlemen up North'd be liable to use." She'd been looking Little in the eye all the time; now she confidently took his hand. "I do hope you're going to love your little Henrietta, Mr. Little. She just loves everybody, her ownself."

"Uh—do you?" Henrietta's warm upward gaze, continuing, made Little uncomfortable; he feared she showed a disposition to curl up against him. "That's—uh—nice," he said. He detached his hand from hers, as if absently, and, taking a chair not occupied by Pussy, coughed and shook out his newspaper.

"Henrietta loves everybody in this house," Henrietta said. "Goody and Mrs. Little and Cousin Olita and Pussy and that dear little yodel-voiced Filmer, and she *hopes* there's somebody else, the top of 'em all, that's going to let poor Henrietta love *him*. You think maybe it's going be arranged for, Mr. Little?"

More uncomfortable, "That's—that's very nice," he said. "I'm glad you—uh—find things pleasant here." He coughed again and lifted the newspaper.

Henrietta came and sat on the arm of his chair.

"I do truly love to talk to the older men," she said. "I bet you got no idea how tired a girl gets of all this chipper-chapper she has to do with boys her own age. Besides, you don't know it, Mr. Little; but you and me practically dear old friends already."

"We are?"

"Oh, my me, yes, indeedy! Dint Goody talk to me all through school about her family same's as I did her about mine? Hours and hours I'd tell her about my loving dadda and she'd tell me about hers, and our mothers and all our brothers and sisters and everybody. Why, when I walked in here yesterday it was just like walking in home. Everybody so sweet to me I been feeling ever since I got here I'm just one the family. Don't you *dare* tell Henrietta she and you ain't old friends already, Mr. Little! What you say to that?"

"Well—I——" he began. "Of course I hope in-deed——"

"You better!" She laughed and tapped his shoulder with her small light hand. "You better hope indeed! A little bird kind of whisper in my ear you suppose to be one of the quick-temperedest gentlemen in the whole United States, Mr. Little; all the same I bet you mighty sweet in your heart o' hearts. Yes, suh! In your heart o' hearts I bet you're good as gold if the right person comes along and knows how to go at you. You tell me: Ain't it the trufe?"

It wasn't exactly the truth. Little's middle-aged impulse was to rise and change his chair; Henrietta was making him feel more and more uncomfortable, and he feared that some member of his family might walk in and see him in his present disadvantageous attitude. Even that jobjammed Pussy, who was still in the best chair and watching him with morose red eyes, made him uneasy. There was something galling in Pussy's gaze, something most unfair that seemed to say, "Oh, yes, I'm onto you!" Little realized that it was ridiculous to resent a Chow's opinion; nevertheless he wanted to hit Pussy.

Henrietta prattled on. "I bet spite of all the noise you make you just a sentimental dear old schizoid," she said, and her soft little fingers gave his reddening cheek a feathery pat.

"What?" he asked. "You bet I'm a schiz-what?"

"A schizoid," the laughing Henrietta answered, patted his cheek again and swung her feet childishly. "It's one them funny things Goody and I had in our psychology class. I just know you're a darling precious old schizoid —so really softhearted you think you got to go round barking and gruffing at everybody to keep 'em from finding out what a sweet tender loving little old heart you really got—right in there." She placed a small curled

forefinger on his chest. "Right in *there!* Henrietta knows.
You tell her."

"I'm afraid you're mistaken." Little tried to withdraw
himself into the back of the chair. "I certainly am not a
schiz——"

"Yes, you are! You live in a funny little old dream-
world of your own and——"

"In a what of my own?" Ripley Little was now as
antagonized as he was embarrassed. "I don't do any such
thing. I——"

"Yes, you do! You live in a funny old dream-world of
your own and it——"

"I do? I don't," he said. "You're entirely mistaken; I
never heard worse nonsense, Miss uh—Pellar."

"What you calling me? You going keep on Missmissing
me, honey?"

"No, Henrietta," Little said quickly, for she seemed
to threaten him affectionately; he was afraid she'd kiss
him.

"Yes, you *better* hurry call me right!" Henrietta cried.
"So what'll *I* call *you?* Of course my dadda at home's my
own bes' true-and-loving dadda; but I'm going to call you
my Dadda Little."

"Your—you are?"

"Dadda Little," the fearless Henrietta said, and her
arm slid trustfully from the back of the chair to his shoulder. "My Dadda Little. So look, Dadda Little, now you
got *two* sweet little daughters in your home, me and
Goody. You like it?"

"Uh—oh, yes, of course," he felt he had to reply to

the direct inquiry. "Why, certainly." Well he knew this to be untrue; he didn't like it a jobjam bit and never in his life had he found himself in a falser position.

"Course you do, Dadda Little! There! So now you and me all in cahoots together and going do everything each other wants. For instance, I'm going praise Normie Peel up to Goody every chance I get."

"What? What for?"

Henrietta laughed. "Dadda Little, they *all* know everything's right with you so long as Normie's there. Why, Goody says——"

"It doesn't make any difference what she says, I——"

"Now, now! You want to make *both* your two little daughters happy, don't you? Of course you do! Quit pretending Normie isn't your pick, because you just putting-on; and look how Goody's trying to please you being sweet to him! Aren't you going try to please her and Henrietta in *return*, Dadda Little?"

"I don't think so. In what way?"

Henrietta swung her feet, pressed his shoulder with her arm, placed her loving face almost nose to nose with his. "Dadda Little, aren't you going to buy your sweet Goody that beautiful new green convertible she says she's had the agent bring here four times and you wouldn't even look at it out the window? Aren't you, Dadda Little?"

"I am not!" The words seemed to explode from Little, such was his vehemence. Courtesy to a guest can be overstraining; politeness or no politeness, he rose, dislodging Henrietta, and stood with his back to the wall. "I certainly am job jam not!"

"Yes, you is!" Henrietta reached him in a jump, seized

his left hand, set her cheek against his coat sleeve. "Yes,
you is, you sinful Dadda Little! I'm going be busy every
minute in this sweet home working on you. Right now I
got to go dress for the party; but don't forget!" She ran
to the door, turned there, threw him a kiss. "You and
me in cahoots, Dadda Little!" she cried. "Don't fordet!"
Then she prettily scampered into the hall and up the stairway.

Mrs. Little came in, a few minutes later, and found
her husband trying to read his newspaper, but in a bad
condition. His face was still red; his neck was swelled
and his breathing labored. "See here!" he said. "How
long is she invited for?"

"Now, Ripley, please! I told you she's staying over the
Fourth."

"How *long* over?"

"Now, Ripley——"

"Goody's sicked her on me about that jabjam car,"
Little said. "She's sicked her on me and she tried semi-
infantile persuasions on me that'd make a horse blush.
She says she's going to call me Dadda Little and——"

"Oh, my!" Mrs. Little murmured, and looked frightened. "Oh, my!"

"Listen, Mrs. Little! If she does that before people or
where anybody can hear her——"

"Now, Ripley, please. I'm sure she wouldn't. Oh, my!"

"Listen, Mrs. Little! For the rest of her time here I'm
going downtown to a hotel."

"Please don't talk like that; please don't, Ripley!"

"All right," he said fiercely. "All right! I'll stay. But
if I've got to be subjected to——"

"Oh, indeed you won't, dear," Mrs. Little assured him. "They're dated up for almost every minute she's to be here. Right now, for instance, they're flying off as fast as they can. You won't have to even see her again to-night."

"Maybe I won't," he said. "I'll bet my dab soul I hear her, though!"

XVII

He was not in error. Modern youth, entertaining itself, has become inexhaustibly migratory, pathetically believing that in constant change of background lies the only true happiness; and among the residences this night visited by a party from the party after the party was that of Ripley Little. He woke to screams of "Yip-p*ee*, Henrietter!" There were thumpings, cheers, unbearable whistlings, ecstasied outcries. "Henrietter! Henrietter! Do your stuff, Henrietter!"

The hour could be called advanced, being toward four of the morning, and Little had hoped to feel bright for important business on hand that day; but Henrietta did her stuff. When again—and again and again—he heard "Swish me! Kish me!" the middle-aged man overhead ached to comply with the request for the swishing.

Once he got as far as the side of the bed, sitting upright with his feet on the floor; but he gave up his idea and relapsed, groaning. His experience of Henrietta in the afternoon had made a coward of him. With a fatal

prescience he knew what she'd do. He said to himself
that he didn't care a hot dabbled continental cuss what any
of those screech-and-speed child-maniacs downstairs
thought of him; but he wasn't going to be called Dadda
Little before them in his nightshirt, even if he stopped to
put a bathrobe over it.

. . . Mutual insomnia drew father and son closer when
the morning had come. Filmer's almost losing Wu Wu,
now Pussy, had already helped to restore the lad to his
previous favor, and the complaints of the two that the past
night had been an outrage formed a sort of duet in congenial dissonances. Just before he left, Ripley Little
gave his boy a dollar.

"Get rid of it today or tomorrow, my boy," the father
said. "Don't wait till the day after that, because I don't
want you to spend it on the Fourth of July. I've no doubt
there'll be uproar in this house; but outside of it a man's
got a right to hope the country has sense enough, at least
this year, for a sane Fourth. You can't have a safe *and*
sane Fourth, because there's no such thing as safety left
in the world; but with all the bang-whack-bang smashing
that's going on across the water, and nobody over here
knowing what to do except to make speeches about everybody else's being wrong, it seems about time to leave out
the fireworks. Do what you like with the dollar, Filmer,
except don't spend it on the Fourth."

"No, sir," Filmer promised, and, a few minutes later,
spoke severely to his mother. "Father couldn't be righter,"
he said. "All this rowdyism like last night ought to stop.
It seems pretty peculiar that with Hitler going on and

everything, decent people have got to be kept awake—and then the very ones that do it stick in bed and sleep till noon! Why, you take the way this household acts, let alone all the gibble-gobble he has to bear from Cousin Olita, I wonder Father can go downtown and preside over his business without a doctor. Looking at the way this household behaves——"

"You're a member of it, aren't you, Filmer?" Mrs. Little reminded him. Then she added, "I'm afraid he *will* be getting upset over the Fourth of July, though. For one thing, I hear your friends the Frys intend to give quite a fireworks party. They've never seemed very intelligent, the Frys."

"Listen!" Filmer said. "If you call 'em my friends in one breath and employ the next to go throwing slights on their intellect, is that showing logic? I don't say they're my friends and I don't say they're not; but I do request a little logic in your treatment of them. If you haven't got any, why, just say so and we'll stop referring to it."

"Referring to what, Filmer?" Mrs. Little asked absently; but, without awaiting a reply, sighed and murmured, "Oh, I *do* hope we can get past the Fourth without too much——"

She didn't need to finish the sentence. Her prayer was that her husband's temperament could be soothed and coaxed along through their merry young visitor's stay—kept merely simmering and bubbling under cover, as it were—without openly blowing up. Her hope increased during the next two days, especially as both nights were passed in an unreverberant house, Goody and her circle entertaining Henrietta elsewhere.

Ripley Little caught nothing more than glimpses of the visitor. Indeed, she and Goody, away to dine, to lunch, to dance, to swim in the Country Club pool, or for tennis, returned to the house only for the fastest possible changes of dress or to sleep through the mornings; and on the Fourth, after three hours' slumber, from five to eight, they were off to a breakfast and later a sporting excursion that couldn't possibly end before midnight. Mrs. Little breathed with more assurance; her husband's holiday at home promised to be an unusually serene one. The day passed with fewer popping sounds in the neighborhood than she remembered upon any previous Fourth, and when the Frys' fireworks party began to be heard, at about nine o'clock, the sounds it made were mainly but fizzings. It was almost ten when Gentry Poindexter came plunging into the house, and, shouting, ascended the stairway leapingly.

"We got to get to the roof!" he shouted down to his employer. "Roof, Mr. Little, roof!"

"Is it on fire, Gentry?"

"No, suh. He out on it. I got a clothesline. He might be slippin'!"

Having climbed the two flights and reached the upper night air by way of the manhole on the roof, Little discovered that Gentry Poindexter's pronoun designated Filmer.

At twenty-five or forty, Filmer wouldn't have done what he had done—not unless he had remained almost fifteen when he was twenty-five or forty, as some people do though often only with the assistance of liquor. He'd left the Frys' fireworks party before it was over, and returned home, gone up to the attic, ascended to the roof, and with difficulty had climbed to the top of a chimney, carrying with him four skyrockets purchased with the dollar his father had given him two days earlier.

Dangerously maintaining himself upon the chimney, he'd uttered vainglorious outcries until he had the attention of most of the fireworks party. They could see him, from the third yard up the street, a small figure over and between tree tops, and waving arms against the high night sky. He called loudly: "Look! Look, Bill! Look, Slops! Look, Charl! Look, Ellie! Look, Antoinette! Antoinette, look! *Look,* Antoinette!"

Then, with everybody who saw him shouting remonstrances, and distant red fire illumining him, he attempted to set off the first of his rockets, which he'd placed uncertainly against a projection within the chimney. The rocket fizzed fire, and, seeming to dislike Filmer, turned upon him, burned his left ear severely and dislodged him from the chimney. His fall was not to the ground but to the slanting slate roof of the gable Norman Peel didn't care for; and here Filmer remained, mentally confused and aurally agonized, until hauled up by his noisy father and Gentry Poindexter at the end of a tripled clothesline.

Later, after old Dr. Fitch had gone home, Ripley Little's bedside manner was undesirable, especially when Filmer insisted that he had to get up and go back to the party. The son's theory that his character was perfect and that his reputation for probity couldn't be attacked got nowhere with the father, who became more impatient every time Filmer plaintively repeated, "But I *didn't* buy those skyrockets on the Fourth. I bought 'em the very day you gave me the money, and you only said not to buy 'em on the Fourth of July. You didn't say *'for'*, you said *'on'!*" Moreover, Filmer's explanation that he'd ascended the chimney in order to make his rockets go that much higher didn't clear up his motive to Ripley Little. Yet how simple it was, and how strange it is that often the simplest springs of human conduct appear obscure!

To one person, however, and this one the last to be expected, Filmer's motive was as open as the day. When he came down to breakfast the next morning, his father had gone and the visitor was still abed; but Mrs. Little and Goody and Cousin Olita were at the table.

"Dr. Fitch said he didn't think your ear'd be serious, dear," his mother said, glancing at the large bandage;— "but don't you think it'd be wise for you to stay in bed till we see whether anything's going to develop from it or not?"

Filmer was stern. "I do not. What's more, I had no business to be made to go to bed last night. If Father hadn't been so upset lately over the way respectable individuals can't get to sleep in this house at night——"

Goody looked up, smiling tenderly. "It seemed to be entirely about you that he was so upset this morning, Filmer dear. Is your ear really inside all that wrapping, child?"

"Child?" Filmer said. "Child! Is it my ear or yours? Mine, I beg to believe, isn't it?"

"Yes indeed, child. To tell the truth I've never cared for it at all."

"Children, children!" Mrs. Little said. "Filmer, your poor father simply can't understand——"

"Are you," Filmer asked, "or aren't you supposed to be my mother? Just because my father has to continue raking all this up ad nauseam is it your province to abut him in it?"

"To what?" she said. "Never mind. Your father says your doing such a thing at your age——"

"Listen! Haven't I explained at least three thousand times my age hasn't got a single thing to do with it?"

"Of course it hasn't." Cousin Olita, the one who comprehended, thus came to his aid. "He's perfectly right, Cousin Wilma," she said. "People fall in love at any age. That was why Filmer climbed up on the chimney and set off the rocket to get noticed, you see."

Goody was quick. "To get noticed by whom, Cousin Olita?"

"Now, Goody!" Cousin Olita shook her head amiably. "You ought to sympathize with him."

"Listen!" Filmer spoke uneasily. "What's all this balderdish? I'm tired of all this talk about my ear. How long'd he say I haf to keep this bandage on, Mother?"

"Who was it?" Goody asked. "Who was it he climbed on the chimney to be noticed by?"

"Now, Goody," Cousin Olita said, "you haven't a bit more right to be in love with Norman Peel than Filmer has to be in love with dear little Antoinette Fry."

"What!" Filmer had believed his own condition so private to himself that he was badly staggered. "What—who—who says I am?"

Cousin Olita beamed upon him. "Why, all the other boys are in love with little Antoinette Fry, too, Filmer. Her mother says she's a regular little genius for knowing what it takes, and says it's *so* funny to watch you all half-fighting each other over her! Everybody in the neighborhood thinks you've got it the worst, though, Filmer. That dear little Antoinette Fry——"

"'That dear little Antoinette Fry'!" Filmer interrupted, satirizing hotly. It was horrible to hear slushy-mush old Cousin Olita speaking loosely of Antoinette; and to be taxed with love, to have his most precious inwards profaned, bandied about—he made his voice as abominable as he could. "Dear little Antoinette Fry! Dear little Antoinette Fry! You make me sick and so does she! I HATE dear little Antoinette Fry!"

"No, Filmer dear." Cousin Olita was on her way to the door. "It makes *me* feel a child again to hear you say it, though; it's just the way my two little brothers talked when they were your age. Wait till you're a bit older and bigger; you'll be *proud* to——"

"I will not!" he bawled. "I'm already older and bigger! I'm not going to stand everybody going around gossiping about me, and I——" Then, as Cousin Olita was out of hearing, he turned quaveringly to his mother. "Her mind always did go wandering from pillow to post. Now she hasn't got one iota left."

Goody looked at him waggishly. "Don't you think her trouble is she's love-starved, Filmer?"

"You shut up!" he returned, unpardonably primitive. "Her trouble is she's an old maid, same as you."

Goody shrieked joyously. "An old maid? Cousin Olita? You heard him, Mother?"

"Why, dear me, didn't you know, Filmer?" Mrs. Little

said, and kindly explained. "Cousin Olita's been married three times. She's had three husbands, dear."

"Cousin Olita has?" Filmer asked, surprised, though throughout his life his interest in Cousin Olita had been less than negative. "I never heard her say so," he added. "Did they leave her any money?"

"No, they just left her," Mrs. Little told him absently. "I believe she had some property of her own; but she got engaged again after the last one, and he made a bad investment for her. That was when she came to live with us."

"She did?" Filmer said. "What's her name?"

Goody's mouth opened. "What's her what?"

"Her name, stupid, her name."

Goody made a loud outcry. "Oh, my soul and slippers! It's Filmer, the same as yours, because she always got her maiden name back. Is he honestly my brother, Mother; isn't he adopted? Here he's lived in the same house with Cousin Olita about half his life, and did you hear him? Asking 'What's her name'! I knew there were colossal dumbnesses in this world; but I didn't think I'd ever live to have a brother that——"

"Liss-*sun!*" Filmer shouted, and made the dining-room resound with proclamations of the dumbness of Goody's Norman Peel.

Goody's rejoinders were lively, and Mrs. Little's repetitions of "Children, children!" ineffective. Debate was on: Whether Filmer was any brighter than the average, as he claimed and offered to prove by his school records, or whether Norman Peel was the dumbest person now alive or dead, or whether Norman had the brightest mind on earth and Filmer the dumbest? Argument became so descriptive and biographical that kindly Cousin Olita unfortunately returned to the dining-room as a peace-maker.

"Goody dear," Cousin Olita said. "Suppose Filmer *is* as dumb as you say he is, isn't he still your brother? Filmer dear, stop and think. Suppose Goody said little Antoinette Fry's worse dish-faced than you say Norman Peel is, wouldn't you love little Antoinette Fry all the more and be her stout young champion and——"

Filmer made no effort to contain himself, and, in his pain, found equals for Norman Peel in Cousin Olita's three husbands and her final fiancé. "I bet they were!" he shouted. "I bet ten thousand dollars they were all four of 'em as dumb as Normie Peel himself! I bet that's why you married 'em and where you learned to talk the way you do! I bet ten thousand dollars——"

He was now so outrageous that no one else could be heard at all, and when Gentry came in to arrange a new place at the table, Filmer was alone in the room, but still arguing.

"No use you creating all this wham-bang," Gentry said. "Ladies on they way upstairs; so why waste you vigor hollering 'Li'l Antoinette Fry! Li'l Antoinette Fry! Li'l Antoinette——' "

"You be silent!" The command was haughty. "You've commenced shoving yourself forward as a favorite character around here; but there are subjects I'll see you learn to hold your tongue on!" Then, as Gentry couldn't repress open laughter, Filmer became sterner. "You expect me to submit to my private affairs getting intruded into by every mere splotch of ignorance? You'd better learn to——"

"Who's that, Filmer honey?" the soft voice of Henrietta Pellar inquired, as she came in and took the place Gentry had prepared for her. "Who's a mere splotch of ignorance? You weren't talking about me because I'm such a bad late little sleepyhead, were you? No, I know you got too much chivalry—a young man that'd get his ear all bundled up that way just to please his heart's best darling."

Filmer, who hadn't eaten much so far and wished to eat more, nevertheless rose. "Who's been talking to you?" he asked, placing as much restraint as he could upon himself because she was a guest in the house. "Who's been gibble-gabbling about me and——"

"Why, nobody but just some little bright-eyed hummingbirds, Filmer honey. Just some I met on the stairway as I was coming down. Of course upstairs in my room I *did* hear somebody down here kind of whooping and carrying-on and squealing 'Little Antoinette Fry! Little Antoinette Fry! Little Antoinette Fry!'" Henrietta laughed in the friendliest way. "How little *is* this little Antoinette Fry, Filmer boysy?"

"Listen," Filmer began. "If this crazy gossip's——"

"Now, Filmer honey!" Henrietta's friendly laughter was continued. "Dint I just ask you how little your little Antoinette is? Why don't you take the answer from Orlando in Shakespeare and tell me she's just as high as your heart?"

"I don't care to," Filmer said. "I don't care to take any

answer from any Orlando in Shakespeare, thank you courteously!"

"Filmer boysy?" Henrietta looked up at him, not laughing. "Who been abusing you so hard? You sit right down and finish your breakfast and tell Henrietta. Tell Henrietta."

Filmer gulped and sat. "Well—everybody around here's such a dumbunny——"

"*Course* they are, honey," the goodhearted Henrietta said. "Everybody but just you and me. What business you going to follow when you get out o' college, Filmer? What you most like to be in this world? Tell Henrietta."

Filmer didn't know but told her anyhow; he believed that at last he'd found one grown person who thought he was worth listening to. Some of the things he said came near throwing the intelligent Henrietta into a fit, so she later informed Goody; but she was doing her good deed for the day and gave Filmer a soothing hour.

XVIII

Everybody in the house loved Henrietta, except Ripley Little. It's difficult to love anybody with whom one must be always wary for fear of being entrapped into making a purchase directly against one's better judgment; it's also contrary to nature—nature in a middle-aged man —to experience a warm affection for a person whose presence in a house makes any night's sleep never to be counted upon.

"You swore to me 'over the Fourth'," Little said to his wife. "What's 'over' mean? The Fourth's over, isn't it? It's been over several whole days and nights, at least according to my calendar."

"But, darling," she protested, "of course Goody has to give her a *real* party. That won't be till Thursday and—— Now, wait, Ripley! I know you were rather disturbed last night again; but it wasn't nearly so long as the night before and Goody always tries her best to make them considerate of you and quiet and——"

"Thursday!" he interrupted. "That's to be the 'real

party', is it? Thursday! And now between nights of the Hellespont broke loose and days of not being able to enter my own house except like a sneak thief——"

"What for?" Mrs. Little asked, and, reddening a little, added timidly, "Of course, Ripley, they'd hardly be home at all, and so the boys wouldn't be round much either if—if we only had another car, one that Goody could use——"

"Well, dob dab!" With eyes threatening to become both protuberant and bloodshot, he stared at her. "That's a wife!" he said, and stalked out of the room.

However, he lived through two more days and nights identical with those he'd predicted, though he several times told Mrs. Little he couldn't. During Goody's "real party" he was not present; but he heard the latter end of it when he arrived after the long and annoying poker game he'd joined in town. True, he could congratulate himself upon not having been much exposed to Henrietta, who was too popular to catch him for another tête-à-tête. He had only the briefest of passing glimpses of her until Saturday morning when she and Goody, having early appointments, once more appeared at the breakfast table. Then for the first time she had a chance to call him "Dadda Little" before people. Mrs. Little, Gentry Poindexter, Filmer and even Cousin Olita looked alarmed; and Goody spilled coffee from her cup.

"Why, you precious honey darling Dadda Little!" Henrietta cried; and moved her chair, plate and utensils close to his. "Here you and me living in the same house day and night and hardly seeing the least little thing of each other! I bet you think your poor old Henrietta's mighty neglectful of you. You been grieving, Dadda Little?"

"I——" he said. "I——"

"I bet you have, Dadda Little. So if I keep *on* neglecting you how'm I going coax that beautiful new green convertible out of you for Goody? There's going to be a big change. You and me got to get together, Dadda Little! Don't you believe I'm going to let these chipper-chapper boys take all my time and keep us apart. No, suh, from now on you and me thick as thieves like we started. What you doing?" She fluttered dainty hands in protest, as he rose. "Where you going? Aren't you going finish your breakfast, Dadda Little?"

"I've eaten it," Little replied in a strained voice. "It's too bad; but I've got a great deal of business and——"

"Business, Dadda Little—on *Saturday?* Don't tell me you gentlemen up North——"

"Yes; yes, we do," he said. "We have to. You fixed that for us, down South, last November, and now Hitler's doing the rest. Good-by!"

On Sunday, having slept late into the morning, he breakfasted in bed; then rose, and, looking long in the mirror after he'd shaved, thought he found his face much altered. He dressed and walked heavily into his wife's room.

Yawning frequently, she was seated before her dressing-table, completing a languid arrangement of her hair. "I hope you——" she began; then changed this approach. "I mean you really *must* have got *some* sleep after they left, Ripley dear."

"Take a look at me," he said. "Just take one look if you want to see what young people's happiness can do to a man. Kindly note the black circles under my eyes. See any signs of my cheeks beginning to sag? They're there, all right. Oh, yes—a few, a few! Put all these nights I've been going through on top of all the fighting with you and Goody about buying a jabjam new jobjam automobile——"

"But, Ripley, I've hardly said a word——"

"Oh, no, not a word! Here we're supposed to save gasoline and cut out new cars, for Defense, and yet——"

"But, Ripley, other people are buying 'em and the factories are still——"

"There it is," he said. "You still claim you haven't spoken a word for a new car? You're wearing me down between you, wearing me down. Are you *sure* she's going home tomorrow? Will you take your oath she is?"

"Why, Ripley, of course she is, dear. And you needn't worry about lunch today because they've already gone over to Cuckoo and Scr—I mean Patricia and Eunice's and——" She interrupted herself hurriedly. "Look out! Don't sit on the bed, Ripley! Goody left Pussy with me and he's under there."

"Job jammit," Little said wearily, as he left the room. "Don't you suppose I can hear him?"

. . . It was his habit on Sunday afternoons, when the weather was pleasant, to smoke a cigar after lunch in a bosky nook upon the border of the lawn. Here a clustering of shrubberies sheltered from the observation of neighbors a comfortably cushioned wicker chair under a

striped umbrella. As usual, he went to this chair today, at
about two o'clock; and he smoked half of his cigar before
a deepening drowsiness caused it to fall from his relaxed
fingers to the turf. Much lost slumber made its demands
upon him and for two hours he slept heavily and audibly.
He was still at it when the young people arrived.

They came on foot, chattering but not whooping—two
lovely girls and seven lumbering boys—and they walked
from the driveway gates almost to the house without
waking him. Henrietta Pellar, dancing ahead, twittering
a swing-song, suddenly stood still and held up a finger for
silence.

"Halt, childses!" she said. "Stop and hush. Listen. Oh,
my me, what *is* that funny noise?"

Goody pointed to the shrubberied nook; though from
where they stood nothing could be seen of it except the
bushes. "It's only Father," she said. "He's asleep."

"Goody, I don't believe it!" Henrietta's eyes enlarged
in wonder. "One person alone couldn't; he must have
friends with him." She advanced, tiptoeing, and the others
followed. In a moment she paused, and so did they, for
Ripley Little in his chair was fully disclosed to them, and
the noises he made were disquieting. "Goody, I don't believe poor Dadda Little's just simply asleep," Henrietta
said, after a short reconnaissance. "Why, just *listen!*
Doesn't part of it sound like he's choking and kind of
strangling? Do you think he could be maybe unconscious
and kind of trying to call for somebody to rouse him?
He doesn't *look* right, either; that's no natural slumber.
I declare I think you better get some ammonia, Goody,
or just water if it's quicker, and try if we can't——"

"I wouldn't," one of the boys, a near neighbor, said uneasily. "Honest, I wouldn't. It'll be a lot better if we just let him stay the way he is and go in the house. We better——"

"No indeedy!" the largehearted Henrietta cried. "I just *know* that's no natural sleep." She stepped forward, calling: "Dadda Little! Dadda——"

"Don't!" Goody interrupted her earnestly. "Henrietta, don't! Nobody knows what——"

Henrietta was already beside Little's chair; she put a pretty hand upon his forehead. "Dadda Little, are you sick? Dadda Little!"

Little's mouth closed. He opened it again to say *"Buh!"* then opened his eyes, too. He looked glazedly at the anxious and tender young face close to his, not recognizing it. "Who?" he asked. "Whuh—what——" Comprehension came into his slowly widening gaze; his whole countenance spasmodically reshaped itself, returned to the normal, and he knew Henrietta. "My dob!" he said.

"Goodness, Dadda Little! You frightened me!" Henrietta cried, and, impulsive in her moment of relief, jumped affectionately upon his lap.

"Here!" Little gasped. "Look here!"

Henrietta waved an arch hand at the group of staring, incredulous young people. "Go on away, you all! Dadda Little and me, we going to have a nice talk together. We——"

"Here!" Little said. "Get off! Listen! Get——"

"No, you don't, Dadda Little!" Retaining her seat, though he made efforts to rise, she put her hands upon his shoulders and laughingly pushed him back. "Dadda Little, if I didn't know better I might almost think you been keeping out o' my way on purpose lately. You don't want poor little Henrietta to believe *that*, do you? No, suh; now I got you, we going have a good long chipper-chapper!" Again she waved coquetishly to the others. "Listen, you prying childses, haven't you got any manners? How often I got to tell you go on away?"

Fascinated, they didn't even consider her suggestion. Over her shoulder Little saw seven staring male faces, not one of which he'd ever thought an agreeable sight, even under the best circumstances. Worse, he saw the charming face of his daughter; it was flushed, and his gorge rose with the perception that she was trying not to laugh.

"Here!" he said angrily. "Let me up!"

"Sit still, Dadda Little." Henrietta's voice was the dove's. "You don't want your dear little adopted daughter to travel all the way home tomorrow on the smoky old steam-cars, getting cinders in her poor little eyes, crying all the way—pretty near two hundred miles—do you? Crying what about? *You* know, Dadda Little! Because you dint let poor Henrietta persuade you to buy that whizzy new green convertible for Goody. *Now* aren't you going to promise you'll——"

"No, I jabjam certainly——"

"Yes, you *is*, Dadda Little!" The laughing Henrietta pressed her cheek to his, and for the briefest instant glanced up questioningly from under her soft lashes at the absorbed male watchers. "How'd you like to be Dadda Little?" this glance really asked; but it was only a by-product. "Say yes this minute!" Henrietta cried. "Dadda Little, I swear to my goodness I'm never going stir one inch till you do! If it takes a year and no matter what fuss my parents make about my not coming home, I'm going sit right here till you say yes!" She leaned back, wooing him with the gaze of a young fawn. "You going say yes, Dadda Little?"

"No, I'm not!" he shouted, and desperately took advantage of her relaxed position to struggle to his feet; though he remembered to be at least gentleman enough to save her from falling. "Excuse me, job jammit!" he said, and stalked across the lawn.

His face burned and he realized infuriatedly that the back of his neck, also of fiery aspect, was found interesting by all of the curious young eyes that followed him as he went toward the house. Henrietta, incorrigibly intrepid, was calling to him to *please* come back, Dadda Little; but, making no response except to breathe harder, he entered the front door and stamped up the stairs to his own room. There, alone, he spent the next fifteen or twenty minutes in a preoccupation with self-expressive utterances and gestures.

A lovely young voice calling, "Pussy! Here, Pussy, Pussy!" came to his still scorching ears, and, though revolted, he could not resist his impulse to look out of the window. On the lawn below was Henrietta. Surrounded by doting boys, she had captured Pussy and, seated upon the grass, held him in her arms. "Angel Pussy-wussy!" she said, with her cheek upon his unwilling head. "Don't Pussy love its Auntie Henrietta?" Then from under soft eyelashes there was just a flicker of an upward glance at her audience to see how much they wished that they were Pussy.

Pussy, trying to release himself, was as reluctant to be used in that manner as his predecessor had been. Pussy unaffectedly didn't care to be the object of Henrietta's coquetries. In fact, both Pussy and Mr. Little felt jab jammed embarrassed while receiving them, whether they were employed for the amorous provocation of onlookers or not.

A popular modern interpretation of our behavior is that it's in great part directly contrary to our true natures; thus many might believe that Ripley Little and Pussy, fondly petted by a beautiful young girl, really liked the experience. They did not. Neither had any tortuous self-suppressions, and both were accustomed to expressing their subconsciouses with sincerity; nor did the similarity between them end there—nor did Ripley Little's startled comprehension of it. He perceived that in relation to Henrietta he was in precisely the same class with Pussy. This does not mean that he wished to be more to Henrietta than Pussy was; it means that his temper wasn't improved by being classed with Pussy in his own house. Also, he didn't see how he could be called Dadda Little any more and retain his sanity.

Mrs. Little, occupied with a peaceable book in the living-room below, heard him clumping down the stairs, and, accustomed to footstep-reading, put down the book and murmured, "Oh, my!"

He came in, already talking. "Hot dabble it, Wilma, you took your oath she'd go home tomorrow! You took——"

"Now, Ripley! Please don't let yourself get so ex——"

"Listen, Mrs. Little! She said a while ago she was going to stay right where she was till——"

"Right where she was, Ripley? You mean she meant she'd stay——"

"Right here!" he said furiously. "She means she's going to keep *on* visiting us. She means she'll stay here till I'm worn down and badgered into buying that jam bastinadoed hot dabbled convertible Hanson's been trying to sell me. Get it!"

"What?" Mrs. Little jumped up. "You say——"

"Get it!" Little shouted. "Call up Hanson. It's Sunday; but call him up. Tell him my spirit's broken! Tell him I'm licked! Tell him we'll take it!"

"Why, Ripley!" Mrs. Little's face was suffused with pleasure. "Why, Ripley dear——"

"Get it!" he shouted again, and stamped out and up the stairs, jab-jamming himself every step of the way to his own room.

XIX

THE FLOWERED AND CANDIED departure of dear little
Henrietta Pellar was succeeded by a lull, whole July days
and nights long, a time of peace and politeness in the
Little family. Goody laughed and sang about the house,
even when her father was in it, was considerate of every
lightest wish of his, or at least careful; and, struggling
with himself, he self-protectively repressed many impulses to tell her what he thought about Norman Peel.
She and Mrs. Little were both happy with the new car,
though Mrs. Little seldom had more than a matutinal
use of it, and Filmer, after a few orations upon the public and private injustice exemplified in that girl's practically owning and always driving a machine of which
he should and could be the master, seemed to be trying
to do better generally—at least, so his mother pointed
out to the others.

It wasn't quite true: Filmer wasn't trying to do better
generally; he was only more preoccupied with something
that he had on his mind. For a clear comprehension of

what he had on his mind a slightly elaborated consideration of him at this special period may be helpful.

Being his age, he naturally desired all human society to regard him as indifferent to its opinion of him. His height was five feet and an inch; he weighed a hundred and four pounds; and his face in repose was what is called appealing; but he wished everybody—including strangers who saw him momentarily—to think him the most hard-boiled person alive. Although the jumpiest of girls couldn't have been much more sensitive, this hard-boiled impression was what he dearly, dearly wished to create.

At home his sensitiveness, though often noisy, was less acute than elsewhere; at home, like a bird made secure by its own protective coloration, he often had such callousness to criticism of himself as to be unaware of it. The members of his family were not, so to speak, his Group; to criticism from his Group he was as sensitive as a cat to flung water. For Antoinette Fry and her circle, for their standards of taste, Filmer ordered the conduct of his life, the look and manner of his dress and the operation of his facial expressions.

When his family criticized his Group he was indignant; but when the Voice of his Group (that is to say, Antoinette) criticized his family he felt disgraced. When Antoinette said, "I wonder why your sister wears that goopy blue blouse so much; it looks like the Gay Nineties," Filmer didn't pause to realize that Antoinette wasn't an authority on that period, her mother having been born subsequent to it. No, he hurried home to entreat Mrs. Little to do something about Goody's awful clothes. "Why can't she dress like the right people?" he asked;

and Mrs. Little would have lapsed into a mental prostration if she'd understood that he meant Antoinette Fry.

Filmer's sensitiveness wasn't unique, of course. Mrs. Little was pleased with the new car on Goody's account but also because Mrs. Watson, next door, often saw it waiting in the Littles' driveway; and one reason Ripley Little hadn't wished to buy a new one was that the daughter of T. A. Jafford of the Jafford Trust Company drove a four-year-old Ford.

Mrs. Little, Goody and Filmer would have thought Ripley Little inexplicable if they'd known he cared what any such mummy as Mr. T. A. Jafford would think; and Ripley Little, Goody and Filmer would have believed Mrs. Little touched in the head had they suspected that she gave a thought to Mrs. Watson—and if Mr. and Mrs. Little and Goody had dreamed that Filmer was glad to have a new car in "the family" because of the effect upon little Antoinette Fry and four or five other children, they'd have thought the hoped-for blossoming of his intelligence postponed again, probably permanently. In such matters, Mother Nature may be hinting that nobody's sensitiveness is worth a dime to anybody else, and all of it, therefore, ought to be abandoned; nevertheless Filmer had a right, as it were, to his own, and his was usually harder on him than that of his elders was on them.

Thus, not only his ambition to seem hard-boiled, whether or not he could actually be so, but the specific sensitivity to Group opinion must be well remembered if his mid-July activities—and what was then on his mind —are to be understood. The Annual Welfare Fund

American Costume Fair, a high occasion of the summer, was near; and Filmer's plan for making a public appearance there was what preoccupied him so weightily. These plans were private; he looked upon questions about them as intrusive, though he retained the right to know and criticize those of the ladies of his family, since theirs might be detrimental to him.

"What I'm going as," he said, two days before the Fair, "it's whose business?" He addressed Cousin Olita, who'd brought some sewing to one of the canvas chairs upon the lawn after lunch. Goody reclined gracefully near by, and Filmer sat upon the grass with his back against a tree. "It's whose business?" he repeated. "Mine or this whole gossiping neighborhood? Reply, please."

Cousin Olita, however, had become interested in something else. Upon the shady sidewalk, a neat figure topped with the twin glitters of a pair of spectacles moved distantly into her view but not into that of Filmer; his back was toward these tokens that Norman Peel was approaching. "Filmer," Goody said suddenly, "this morning Cousin Olita gave me that water pistol she bought to scare dogs with when she takes Pussy walking and——"

"She did?" Filmer was roused. "Listen! Cousin Olita, you said if you ever gave that water pistol away I could have it. You promised me——"

"You can," Goody said surprisingly. "You can have it right now, Filmer, if you care to look for it. I left it somewhere—probably in Father's room, I think——"

"Boy!" Filmer hurried indoors, ran upstairs to his father's room, and, after several diligent minutes, found the water pistol upon a closet shelf. "Boy!" Filmer said;

for the water pistol, superficially, looked very like a lethal one and was a necessary part of his planning for the Annual Welfare Fund American Costume Fair. Then he happened to glance out of a window and was astonished to see Goody, accompanied by Norman Peel, gliding out of the driveway in the new car.

"Oh, murder!" Filmer sighed. The car's top was down, and Goody not only wore the blue blouse but turned northward, making it certain that if Antoinette Fry was in her front yard, or at a window, her opinion of Filmer for having a Gay Nineties sister would again be lowered.

He put the pistol in a hip-pocket and returned to the open, gloomy.

Cousin Olita, sewing, laughed. "Thought you'd fall for it," she said.

"Thought I'd fall for what?"

"For the water pistol, Filmer. Goody got me to give it to her this morning and she put it in your father's room where she thought you'd be some little time finding it— because of course she didn't want you upsetting *her* room. Then she told you about it exactly when she'd planned to, just when Norman Peel——"

Filmer didn't understand. "What's all this gibble-gabble?"

"I'm sure it isn't your face, Filmer," Cousin Olita explained in a kindly way. "I think all it is, Norman Peel's very critical, of course—you remember about the gable and changing the fence for a hedge—and probably he's lately just happened to say something to Goody about he wonders why you wear that old jersey inside out so

much with the '44' on the back and these balloony pur-
plish trousers you seem so fond of and——"

"What?" Filmer couldn't believe that she was saying
what she was saying. "Are you trying to——"

"Yes, it'd be more your clothes than anything else, I
think, Filmer. Maybe, too, a little that habit you have of
half shutting your eyes and looking sideways and chewing
whether you've got anything in your mouth or not. You
see, Filmer dear, Goody's *so* sensitive, especially about
any of her family."

"Listen!" Filmer stepped toward her. "Listen!"

"She was *so* pleased," Cousin Olita said, busy with her
sewing. "She was afraid you might be around and she
planned it just right. He didn't see you at all."

"Didn't *see* me?" Filmer's mind wrestled with baffle-
ments; then he laughed jeeringly. "Didn't see me; that's
a good one! Your bean's slipping; she was afraid I'd
maybe say a few things about Ham Ellers just to cheer
'em up. Nurse the bean, Cousin Olita; nurse the bean.
Anyhow, I got the gat."

Cousin Olita, dreamy, changed the subject. "I wonder
if you really understand about the Fair, Filmer—how it's
to help show this is a wonderful country of ours and we're
expected to dress in American history costumes and be
American types and keep on acting that way, too, in
character, after we get there. It'll be a beautiful sight on
the four-acre front lawn of the Mr. and Mrs. Eric
Homer Smith Estate and we're all requested not to scuff
up the grass. Filmer, I think it'd be nice if you went as a
young American boy of the Seventies with a wide collar
rolling a hoop. I'm making myself a costume. I'm going

as Mary Queen of Scots. I'm not like you; I'll tell anybody."

"Hoop?" Filmer said, with pain. "I'm not rolling any
hoop, thank you a thousand times, and you can't be Mary
Queen of Scots. When was she ever in America? After
she got her head cut off?"

"No; she couldn't," Cousin Olita replied. "Don't be
ignorant, Filmer. She's connected with the history of this
country of ours because her great-grandson gave Pennsyl-
vania to William Penn, and I think Charleston must be
named for one of her family. She's my favorite character
in all of history."

Filmer, thinking of what Antoinette Fry would be sure
to think, made heated gestures. "Mary Queen of Scots
wasn't supposed to weigh a hundred and sixty-four
pounds or something, was she? Can't you ever stop and
think a minute, Cousin Olita? Look, you're supposed to
be my cousin and if you go to the Welfare Fund American Costume Fair as Mary Queen of Scots, I and this
whole family——"

"Yes, Goody was talking like that, too," Cousin Olita
said peacefully. "She's going as some kind of a dolly
herself and——"

"What! A dolly? What's any dolly got to do with
American history?" Filmer was in despair. "If I haven't
got the battiest family——"

His remonstrances reached nowhere with sunny Cousin
Olita, and that evening he took his troubles to his mother;
spoke tragically of Mary Queen of Scots and dollies. He
went to the length of declaring that rather than be
publicly ruined by relatives he'd remain away from the

Welfare Fund American Costume Fair; he'd give up the whole business, he said.

Mrs. Little encouraged him to feel better. Goody was having a lovely costume made to wear as Dolly Madison, and probably Cousin Olita could be talked out of Mary Queen of Scots. In the meantime, what American historical character had Filmer in mind to impersonate? Surely he needed help about his costume, didn't he?

He declined the offer and refused to give information. "You'll see when the time comes," he said reservedly. "I've got a pretty big idea, Mother."

Then, before he went to bed, he gave himself a preview of his pretty big idea in the small mirror of his dressing-table. With a piece of burnt cork he depicted upon his cheeks, just forward of the rather noticeable ears, a pair of curved sideburns, typical as he believed of the American criminal most prone to massacre. Next he blackened his slight eyebrows, made black half moons beneath his eyes to indicate the ravages of night life, and drew two sinister lines from the sides of his nose to the corners of his mouth. After that, he put on an old jacket, turned up the collar, took from his clothes closet a heavy old cap of his father's and placed it upon his head.

The cap was too large for him and, pulled down, added to a winged look of Filmer's sometimes mentioned by his young friends when speaking of his ears; but this wasn't how he viewed the matter, himself. Not at all; and, though literal-minded people might perhaps have guessed that he was impersonating a mushroom, the mirror pleased him exceedingly. He clutched the water pistol, crouched, thrust his lower lip and inoffensive chin as far forward as their controlling muscles permitted, and spoke in the toughest tones his changing voice could utter.

"Put 'em up! Come out from behind that counter! This is a stick-up, see?"

Filmer's pretty big idea, in part at least, was to attend the Welfare Fund American Costume Fair as a national historic figure symbolically known (to him) as Big Shot, or Public Enemy Number One. There was more to it than that: "Big Shot" was the gist of it; but in the background of this conception was a phrase he remembered out of his father's table conversation, "The Fighting Whitings." There could be Fighting other people as well as Whitings, couldn't there? Certainly, and Filmer, in his mind, added this thought to his picture of himself as Big Shot, or Public Enemy Number One.

Wistful thinking being strongest in youth, Filmer usually believed his appearance what he hoped it was; his wish controlled his very eyes. Thus, as he peered into the glass from beneath the visor of the umbrellalike cap and beheld his sideburns, protruding jaw and blackened steely eyes, he couldn't help feeling that when he moved ominously among the throngs at the Fair he'd be about as much of a hit as anybody. He wouldn't tell a soul, beforehand—most of all not Antoinette. He intended, so to say, to burst upon her.

In his own room he rehearsed often, and, studiously practising the tough manner elsewhere, was twice embarrassed by the unsought observation of his father. "What on earth are you trying to do—look like one of those enlarged full-page photographs of an insect's face?" Ripley Little asked, on the second occasion; and

turned to his wife. "What's the matter with him? This
morning he was in the hall lavatory, all humped over,
with his jaw dislocated and his underlip looking as if a
bee'd stung it. He was whispering to the looking-glass
over the washbowl. Whispering to it! Right now I saw
him doing the same thing to his reflection in that window.
He won't speak. He's gone dead-pan; but have *you* any
idea what's the matter with him?"

Filmer silently withdrew, and Mrs. Little explained.
"It must have something to do with the historical character he's planning to be at the Welfare Fund Fair, Ripley.
He's keeping it a great secret because he wants to surprise
everybody. Won't let us help him, or even advise him,
about his costume. I can't imagine what he thinks he's
going to——"

"Wilkes Booth, likely enough," Little said plaintively.
"Maybe Quisling—or Dillinger. Most probably Dillinger. Well, *I* don't have to be there!"

His unfavorable prediction of his son's probable
choice, though not a bad guess, lacked comprehension of
Filmer's rebellion against the commonplace and the
threadbare past. To attend the Fair as one of the Alex-
ander Hamiltons, General Lafayettes, Forty Niners or
Roosevelt Rough Riders sure to be present would have
seemed to Filmer a concession to soft old Gay Ninety
ideals—to the pretty, the ignorant and the sentimental.
Ripley Little, moreover, would have been astounded had
he suspected that an utterance of his own, forgotten by
himself, was largely the inspiration of Filmer's present
doings.

XX

ANOTHER REHEARSAL, the final one, was also interrupted discomfitingly. This happened at a last moment, on the afternoon of the Fair, when already Filmer should have been making his entrance into that varicolored scene. In full costume, burnt cork and everything, he was still scowling into his mirror, convinced that Big Shot, Public Enemy Number One and the rest of it was written all over him; the door opened and two intruders walked in.

They were his two little second-cousins, Frankie and Francie, dressed for the Fair as Children of the Civil War Period, or perhaps thereabouts. They weren't twins but close to each other in age, both under five, and, though Francie was the boy and Frankie the girl, most people, including Filmer, seldom knew or cared which was, or who was, who. Loose in a house, Frankie and Francie were likely to be found anywhere, for their nurse, Lila, was a scatterminded girl; and Frankie and Francie, on the prowl just now at the Littles', found Filmer's door closed. Therefore they opened it and came in.

Seeing Filmer in old clothes and a funny cap, with his ears sticking out and with what they mistook for dirty marks on his face, they naturally laughed. When Frankie and Francie laughed they always did so aloud, meanwhile pointing with curved forefingers at what amused them.

"Ook!" Francie said, thus laughing and pointing. "Cuzzum Filla dirty! All dirty!"

"Dirty!" Frankie echoed. "Dirty face! Dirty!"

Their childish stupidity irritated Filmer. "Have you got any intelligence or not?" he asked sternly. Then, as Frankie and Francie both squatted, apparently to make their laughter more insulting, he advanced upon them crouchingly and threw open his jacket, displaying the water pistol secured near his left armpit by a schoolbook strap. Worse, he protruded his chin and underlip public-enemyly and hissed, "This is a stick-up, see! See this heater? Scram you! Scram!"

He had more effect than he wished. Francie and Frankie fell backward upon the floor, screaming with horror. Filmer would have been gratified except that from downstairs his mother, Cousin Olita and the scatterminded Lila began to call loudly for information. "Hush, can't you?" he pleaded with Frankie and Francie. "Look, I'll buy you candy at the American Fair. Can't you hush up? Candy! *Candy!* Look, if you'll hush up I'll buy you candy till you're sick!"

Unstable as the wind, Frankie and Francie stopped crying, rose and affectionately clung to Filmer. "Canny!" they cried. "Nice canny! Nice Cuzzum Filla!"

"Let go me!" Filmer said. "Let go me or I'll scare you again!" He reverted to Big Shot. "Listen! Take your paws off me if you don't want a slug o' lead through your gizzards, see!"

This time, unaccountably, Frankie and Francie weren't frightened at all but squealed with fond laughter. "Do some more!" they begged. "Make funny faces some more, Cuzzum Filla!"

Downstairs Mrs. Little was shouting earnestly. "Filmer! We've been waiting and waiting for you. Filmer! We're dreadfully late! Do stop playing with the children. Fil*mer!*"

Filmer appeared at the top of the stairs with Frankie and Francie trying to cling to his knees. "Playing with 'em?" he said, outraged. *"Playing* with 'em?"

He descended the stairway with difficulty, as Frankie and Francie wished to remain attached to him. Near the front door Mrs. Little, Cousin Olita and Lila waited impatiently; and Filmer didn't like their looks at all. Mrs. Little, with powdered hair, was supposedly a "Colonial Dame"; and Cousin Olita, saved from Mary Queen of Scots and also from Pocahontas, her second choice, wore black sateen with a white cap and white ruff. Thus she now rather strangely regarded herself as "A Puritan Priscilla", though she regretted having consented, after an argument with Goody, to remove a large scarlet A from her front. Lila was dressed simply as a children's nurse, and this added to Filmer's distress.

"Look at Lila," he said to his mother. "What's she going as? You aren't asking me to——"

"Yes, dear," Mrs. Little interrupted hurriedly.

"Cousin Lydia has a sudden cold; but she simply couldn't disappoint the children, so of course I said we'd take them. Lila's all right. A great many of the people aren't going to be in costume; they're supposed to walk around and look at the rest of us that are. Do let's get off, Filmer. Goody left an hour ago; but your father took the bus and left us the other car, so do——"

Cousin Olita spoke up urgently. "Filmer, is that black on your face part of your costume? I hope so, because if we have to wait till you go and wash——"

"*Sh!*" Mrs. Little warned her, aside. "It must be intended for make-up. I think he means——"

"Do you ever read the papers?" Filmer asked Cousin Olita, and with a significant gesture showed her the water pistol under his left armpit. "There! Big Shot, Public Enemy Number One, Torpedo, see—if you got to be told everything in words of one syllable."

"It's splendid, Filmer; do let's get off," his mother said, and placatively hustled the party of six outdoors and into the car.

Mrs. Little drove; Cousin Olita sat beside her, and on the back seat Frankie and Francie were placed between Filmer and Lila. Almost immediately Frankie and Francie began to have a fight. They poked each other, kicked each other, bit a little and squealed words unintelligible to Filmer.

"They're mad at each other again," Lila explained. "Frankie's mad at Francie because he's sitting next to you and she wants to, too."

Frankie wept piercingly, pounded Francie, climbed over him and sat clingingly upon Filmer's lap; but Filmer didn't like to have people there any better than his father did. "Here!" he said, attempting to dislodge her. "Get away!"

Cousin Olita looked over her shoulder. "No, no, Filmer. Let her stay; she makes such terrible noises when you——"

"Listen!" Filmer said. "Whether you've got brains enough to see it or not, I'm supposed to be Big Shot or Public Enemy Number One. What kind of a Big Shot would a Big Shot be with a gummy three-year-old child all over him? If you think I'm going to drive into the grounds of the Eric Homer Smith Estate with Frankie or Francie, whichever it is, sitting on me—— Get away, will you?"

"Canny!" Francie said, and also clambered upon Filmer's lap. "Nice Filla! I wuv you!"

Big Shot, or Public Enemy Number One, was driven into the Eric Homer Smith Estate with Francie and Frankie both on his lap, or partly so, and each trying to help him push the other off of it.

When the car found the last parking space in the enclosure allotted to automobiles containing people in costume, Filmer lived up well to the character he'd assumed. He didn't help anybody out; but, having determinedly shoved Frankie and Francie upon Lila, shot huntedly forth, slid between bordering shrubberies and emerged, successfully alone, upon the lively lawn. "Bums!" he muttered, alluding to Frankie and Francie.

Opposite him, across the broad stretch of turf, a uniformed brass band blatted and thumped upliftingly, and the music made him feel dramatic. Flanking the band were gay semicircles of booths attended by salesladies dressed patriotically, and upon the lawn some hundreds of people strolled or paused in groups, while others made benevolent purchases at the booths. About a third were in costume and all of the Colonial Dames, Puritan Priscillas and Children of the Civil War Period that Filmer saw seemed to him incomparably superior to his mother, Cousin Olita and Frankie and Francie. He caught a glimpse of Goody, too, behind the Red, White and Blue counter of one of the booths, and he thought she looked disgracing; there wasn't a doubt that Antoinette Fry'd be critical of her. Resolving to keep far away from all of his relatives, he pulled the cap visor a little more over his eyes, stooped crouchingly, thrust out his innocent chin, and with a sinister air began to slink hither and yon among the crowds.

In planning the Fair, enthusiasts had said much about living up to the costumes, and acting the types assumed, for the benefit of the uncostumed patrons; but after a time the efforts made in this direction were generally abandoned. Even Cousin Olita gave up going about chattily in her Puritan manner, though only by request: Goody hurried out from her booth for the purpose after being told by a friend that Cousin Olita'd said to him, "Prithee I bet it's going to rain, Mr. Ellers." Filmer was one of the few who conscientiously went on being the historical types they believed they represented.

Stooping, jaw and lip forward no matter how they ached, never lifting his narrowed eyes higher than people's shoulders, he went round and round the lawn, sometimes twitching back his jacket for a flash of the water pistol, and at intervals whispering, "Line up! This is a stick-up, see? Line up!"

Innumerable eyes seemed to be upon him and everybody to be thinking about him concentratedly; these were his sensations. No doubt his mind was a little vague upon the point of a general clear recognition of him as Big Shot, or Public Enemy Number One; but he was sure that the more intelligent spectators, unlike Cousin Olita, must see in him something very like it—at least a chief figure from the fighting hell of the underworld. To go about saying, "Look, who do you think I am?" and "Listen, I'm Big Shot, or Public Enemy Number One, Torpedo, see?" would have been a banality and a lowering. Antoinette Fry would understand who he was—so he believed perhaps a little mystically.

What he most counted upon, of course, was her astonished admiration and that of his whole Group. For some time his carefully narrowed and averted eyes, hampered by the overwhelming cap, didn't discover any of its members; but he felt that they must be looking at him from *some*where—especially that Antoinette, thrilled, must be watching him. The stirring drums and trumpetings of the band, continuing, made him feel heroic, singled out from the world; then, abruptly, he was somewhat let down. He bumped into Charlsworth Beck, who was dressed in an extinct military uniform.

"Yay, Filmer!" Charlsworth said. "Look, I'm supposed to be General W. H. Harrison in the War of Eighteen-twelve, afterwards President. My father wore 'em at the military academy he went to. Pretty hot, what?" He laughed fatuously. "Bill's only got a false face; says he's John L. Lewis. And Slops is just a gob in a sailor suit. Not so good! All these brass buttons and sword and chin strap o' mine—you ought to've seen their eyes pop! What you supposed to be, Filmer—kind of a gangster or something?"

" '*Kind* of?' " Filmer echoed scornfully. "Thought you had brains! Use your eyes, can't you?"

"General W. H. Harrison was a pretty great man," Charlsworth said; "but he certainly couldn't have minded warm weather much." He glanced about to see who was looking at him. "Well, sir, I tell you, Fil, these white gloves and sword and everything may be the cats; but they're certainly kind of warm to wear in the hot sun. Antoinette and Ellie and Bill and Slops are over yonder at the Ice Cream Booth eating cones. Let's go get us some."

"Don't want 'ny!" Annoyed by this friend, who seemed to be thinking of nothing except his dumb self and his ill-fitting uniform, Filmer went on his way. He guardedly allowed his glance, however, to wander in the direction of the Ice Cream Booth, and presently his stealthy criminal stride took him in that direction.

Antoinette and Ellie Turner were both Pocahontases or Indian Maidens or something; and Antoinette had seized the opportunity to mascara her eye-winkers stickily. She looked so gloriously Hollywoodish that she brought on a ringing in Filmer's ears. He made a circuit and came back, crossing the grass in a direction that would give her a rather close view of him in profile as he passed.

Marringly, it was just then that Frankie and Francie

got him again. They'd long ago shaken off Lila and they'd been hunting and hunting him.

"*Canny!*" shouted both little Civil War Children, and rushed for him. "*Nice* Cuzzum Filla! Canny! Canny! Canny!"

He made a pitiable attempt to seem to ignore them. "Get away from me!" he said, from the side of his mouth. "Get away from me, you guys!" The harsh undertones were ineffective; Frankie and Francie embraced his legs happily and demandingly. He tried a desperate kind of reasonableness. "Listen! Wait till after a while, can't you, and I'll buy you some. Listen, don't be such bums! Can't you even *try* to understand who I *am?* Look, if you keep on——"

"You p'omised!" Francie reminded him; and both squealed, "*Canny! Canny! Canny!*"

Agonized, Filmer turned to the Candy Booth close by, and, feeling himself scorched by the gaze of Antoinette, Ellie Turner, Bill, Slops, and Charlsworth Beck, he bought Frankie and Francie two paper bags of candy, twenty-five cents each. "There! Eat it!" he said, and, hopeful too soon, thought himself free to leave the candy counter unaccompanied.

He'd not gone three strides before Frankie and Francie, already obediently eating, each had him by a hand. "I *wuv* you, Cuzzum Filla!" Frankie said. "*Nice* Cuzzum Filla!" said Francie.

"Go '*way!*" But as fast as Filmer released his hands Francie and Frankie, delighted with the game, clasped him fondly by the legs. "Anyways for Sweet Mike's sake come away from *here!*" he begged, and, ruthless with them, dragged them from the near vicinity of those whose opinion was life and death. "Listen! I *bought* you the candy, didn't I? You've *got* it, haven't you? Now *can't* you——"

Francie, clinging stickily to his right hand, again told him that he was nice, and Frankie, affixed to his left, once more announced that she loved him. Then they began to have another fight. Nobody understood why Frankie and Francie had so many fights, and they never coherently explained; but the reason was that Frankie always thought that whatever Francie had was better than what she had, herself, and she wanted it, while Francie felt the same way about whatever Frankie had. Just now, Frankie wanted Francie's candy and her own too, and Francie wanted Frankie's and his own too. If they'd been older they'd have exchanged bags and probably regretted it; the trouble was, they weren't older.

Retaining Filmer's hands, they kicked each other before him and behind him, sometimes severely. Weeping un-attractively with filled mouths entirely open, they put themselves to the utmost inconvenience to tear holes in each other's bags, snatched therefrom, and kicked, slapped, shed tears and ate simultaneously. They got themselves smeared and sticky all over, did much of that for Filmer too.

Their passion so grew that physically he became able to leave them; but, observed by many, he had to accept a moral responsibility. Wishing that Frankie and Francie had killed each other good and dead in the car or in any previous fight, he had to act as peacemaker, revolting as the role was to him.

Frankie and Francie, having gone into a clinch with their candy bags between them, got him and themselves more smeared and sticky; then all at once, because they'd had enough fighting for the time being, they were placid again. "You're nice, Cuzzum Filla," Francie said, eating. "Make funny faces."

"Ess," said Frankie. "I *wuv* you, Cuzzum Filla. Make funny faces."

Even if he'd been alone, Filmer no longer had the heart to advance his jaw, not even to walk crouchingly. What good would either have been now? "Come on," he said, beaten. "We got to find that crazy darn Lila."

"Crazy darn Lila!" Frankie and Francie cried, accompanying him. "Crazy darn Lila! Crazy darn Lila!"

Doggedly Filmer sought and sought for Lila, but finally found his mother, instead; for she, as it happened, was looking for him. As he came to a halt before her, Francie sat down on the grass in order to use both hands for eating more busily. Frankie did likewise, and both, as they ate, leaned back trustingly against Filmer's legs.

"Filmer!" Mrs. Little said. "Really, dear, you oughtn't to let the children devour all that cheap donated candy; they'll be sick. Why didn't you leave them with Lila?"

"Why didn't I? Why didn't I leave 'em with Lila?" Then Filmer just looked at her.

"What's the matter, dear?"

"They fixed me," he said, referring swallowingly to the candy-eaters at his feet. "They fixed me!"

XXI

"Nonsense, dear!" The mother perceived the tokens of a collapsed morale; she comprehended. The lines from Filmer's nose to his mouth, the dark crescents under his eyes, the sideburns and the blackened eyebrows appeared to other people as an ill-chosen exhibition of burnt cork on the face of a harmless young lad; but Filmer, seeing himself as his realized design, was not only artist but the work of art, too—and both were ruined by the ignorant hands of Frankie and Francie. Mrs. Little offered a new hope. "You just wait till you hear why I've been looking for you!" she exclaimed. "Filmer, the *Morning News* is going to have a whole page of photographs of the Fair in tomorrow's paper and the photographer wants to take a picture of *you!*"

"What!" Filmer's chest found air again; he stepped forward, removing his support of Frankie and Francie. "Honest? He does?"

Life at almost fifteen is like the Stock Exchange, of which experts have announced that there is only one certainty: it goes up and it goes down. Filmer, having been down, made a new high for the season.

"Yes; he's waiting for you, Filmer."

"Well, my goodness!" Filmer said. "Where is he?" He stopped short as Frankie and Francie rose lovingly to accompany him. "Listen! If those bums think they're going to be in the newspaper with me———"

"No, no." Mrs. Little laughed, and called over her shoulder, "Lila!"

The laggard nurse joined them, and, herself eating candy, seized upon Frankie and Francie. They were left behind, having a fight with crazy darn Lila, thus naming her, while Mrs. Little took Filmer to a garden bench upon which Cousin Olita was sitting elegantly. Before Cousin Olita stood a middle-aged man with a camera and a tired young woman writing in a notebook.

"What's Cousin Olita doing?" Filmer asked his mother. "Does she think any *good* newspaper would———"

"They want us in a little group of three, dear," Mrs. Little explained. "You see, they've already done several of Goody because she's been awarded the Grand Prize for the most becoming costume and———"

"What? You say *Goody*———"

"Yes; it's a medal on a blue ribbon. Isn't that splendid! So now they want the rest of the family, too." She placed herself beside Cousin Olita on the bench. "You're to stand just behind us, Filmer, for a nice composition. Take your place, dear; we ought to be moving toward home pretty soon."

The implication that he was to be photographed because of Goody's prize somewhat dampened Filmer; and he didn't at all care to share the honor with Cousin Olita. Nevertheless, his picture was to be in the paper, a distinction never hitherto conferred upon him, or, to the best of his knowledge, upon any other of his Group, not even Antoinette Fry. The band played brilliantly, and, exalted again, dramatic intensely, it was the Big Shot, Public Enemy Number One, at his best who moved forward in character to the position assigned him.

"All ready?" the photographer asked.

Filmer twitched back his jacket, put his hand to the butt of the water pistol, and bent every effort upon keeping his almost worn-out chin thrust forward. "Shoot!" he said with difficulty.

"Okay," the photographer announced. "Hold it, please. Just an instant. Another shot, to make sure. Okay. Thanks. Now where's that next outfit?" He turned to the tired young woman with the notebook. "Got yours on this?"

"I think so," she answered. "Let me see. This is Mrs. Ripley Little, of course, and Miss Olita Filmer, I think, and——"

"Yes," Mrs. Little said, briskly on her feet. "As I told you—a Colonial Dame—and this is Filmer Little, my son. Now, Filmer, we'll have to collect Lila and——"

"Do they know who I am?" Filmer asked her, as they moved away. "Did you tell 'em?"

"Yes, I'm sure I did," she answered, laughing. "Come; it's late and we'll have to get those children home."

The shining thought possessed Filmer—his picture would be in the paper, dark, ominous, scowling from deep-shadowed eyes, hand on weapon. He felt noble, wished to be kind to everybody, a model son to his parents.

He wanted a word with Antoinette, Ellie, Bill, Slops, and Charlsworth Beck—just to mention that it might be worth their while to watch the newspapers—but, discovering at the Toastie Sandwich Booth that they'd all gone home, he wasn't downcast. Surprise might even add to the effect tomorrow, he thought; and, in the car, driving to Francie and Frankie's house, he was dreamy, gentle, enveloped in the proud bliss that makes us meek.

He spent the evening quietly at home; and, when in the morning he woke, there was a smile upon his face. Already, upon thousands of doorsteps his picture was waiting; at thousands of breakfast tables it was unfolding before the population. Antoinette Fry, overcome, might be looking at it this very moment. Charlsworth Beck and Bill and Slops, and Ellie Turner, were either staring at it openmouthed or would be, within the hour. In his mind's eye Filmer saw only the picture of himself—his mother and Cousin Olita were but blurs—and, beneath it, the words, FILMER LITTLE AS BIG SHOT, PUBLIC ENEMY NUMBER ONE. His feelings were those of an obscure aspirant to whom a great voice behind the clouds cries thrice: "This day Renown is thine!"

At the breakfast table he found only Cousin Olita, with no public journal in sight. "Goody's *so* upset!" she explained. "Your father had an early breakfast and took the *Morning News* downtown with him before any of us were up. Goody's sure that droopy girl with the photographer was getting everything all mixed up and it won't be a good picture of her. I expect the one I was in got spoiled, too, because your mother was in such a hurry I know I saw her moving when he snapped his camera. I shouldn't wonder if they left it out altogether, and I haven't had my picture in the paper for ten years. Just my luck!"

Filmer thought the exhibition of egoism sickening and refused to admit the possibility of a fiasco. "Look! Haven't you got brains enough to know a big active newspaper's got modern cameras too fast to throw a whole picture out just because somebody on one edge of it jiggled their arms or something? You take the modern camera and——"

Mrs. Little came in gayly just then, carrying two copies of the *Morning News*. "The pictures of the Fair are all lovely," she said, and placed one paper before Cousin Olita and the other before Filmer. "Hamilton Ellers bought out the drug store and's brought Goody ten copies, so you can each have one to keep. Goody came out beautifully, right in the center. The one of us three's splendid, too. It's good of Filmer and better of you than I expected, Cousin Olita, though I think it makes me look rather older than——"

Filmer wasn't listening. With hasty hands he brought to view the page of reproduced photographs of the Annual Welfare Fund American Costume Fair on the grounds of the Eric Homer Smith Estate. Goody, beautifully recognizable and distinctly wearing her medal and ribbon, confronted him, a single large portrait in the midst of the groups. Filmer's eye didn't linger upon Goody; it sped to the lower right-hand corner of the page and beheld his own likeness there.

It wasn't what he expected. It looked boyish unbelievably, and, as the water pistol was indistinguishable, his gesture of threateningly touching it seemed to imply that he itched. The sideburns hadn't taken well, either; seemed to be smut streaks. The cap appeared to be a giant's. Except for the title below the picture the whole darn thing might have been mistaken for the representation of a boy strangely untidy and scratching himself— but Filmer hadn't yet read the title below the picture.

His eye descended. He read, and the bottom fell out of his world: "Mrs. Ripley Little as a Colonial Dame, Miss Olita Filmer as a Puritan Maiden, and Master Filmer Little as an Urchin."

" 'Maiden'," Cousin Olita mused, studying her copy of the paper. " 'Puritan Maiden'. I told that girl three times I was a Priscilla; but maybe Maiden's just as well. Really I think the whole Fair passed off beautifully and the pictures are going to make nice souvenirs for all of us to keep. It's nice of you, too, Filmer."

"Nice?" Filmer, desiring no more breakfast, was on his feet; his burning eyes fixed themselves upon his mother. "Listen!" he said. "You told me you told that woman who I was! You said you told her I was Big Shot Public En——"

"I'm sure I did, Filmer. I'm almost certain I told her even before I went to look for you; but everything was in such a hurry just then and——"

"Did you tell her I was meant to be an *Urchin?* Did you? DID you?"

"Why, Filmer, of course I didn't tell her that; but what difference does it make, dear?" Mrs. Little tried to laugh soothingly. "I suppose they just forgot what I'm almost sure I'd said you were, and so they had to think up something in the newspaper office that seemed suitable and——"

"*Suitable!*" Filmer shook the paper at her, and his unstable voice became falsetto. "Do you think it's suitable at my age to be called Master? 'Master Filmer Little'! '*Master*'! That's a nice one, isn't it? You *knew* I was Big Shot, Public Enemy Number One. I told you before we started and you knew it! You can read, can't you? It says 'Urchin'; it says 'Master Filmer Little as an Urchin'! They claimed that Fair was for a worthy purpose; but if this is what they do to the parcipitants I hope they all drown! If *this* is what I get for trying to help the poor I——"

Mrs. Little tried to go on laughing calmingly, and Cousin Olita, too, strove to be soothing. Seldom have such efforts been of less effect and almost never has an adolescent voice sounded its variations more excruciatedly than did Filmer's during the next half hour. Its unexpected bass notes and pained flutings subsided intermittently; and during the latter part of this period were heard from his room upstairs, whither he retired to be alone with his emotion.

Opening his door, upon various afterthoughts, he would so address his mother as to be audible to her wherever she was, upstairs or down. "If you only *thought* you told 'em who I was, what'd you tell me you were *sure* you did for?" he inquired, in this way, more than once. "If you claim you know what the truth is, why couldn't you tell it to your own son before everything

got balled up and I could told 'em who I was, myself?
Were you deliberately trying to make your own son the
laughingstock of this city?"

He'd brought his copy of the paper upstairs with him,
and at times refreshed, so to speak, the paroxysm. Whenever Mother Nature partially restored his calm, he undid
her work by glaring again at the picture of himself. Over
and over, with accompanying miserable lip movements,
he read the libel, "And Master Filmer Little as an
Urchin." Thus he kept his grief alive until midmorning
when there was an addition to it from outdoors.

His open window brought him the sound of infantile
voices, and, looking down morbidly, he beheld Frankie
and Francie gamboling upon green grass, while the head
of Lila, rising from border shrubberies, conversed with a
man in overalls who mowed the Watsons' lawn. Filmer
went to the head of the stairway and shouted down to his
mother, who was in the living-room.

"What are those children doing on our property? If
you expect to saddle Frankie and Francie on me again
after what I been through——"

"No, no, dear!" his mother called from below. "Cousin
Lydia doesn't want 'em exposed to her cold and they're
just going to spend the day with us. They——"

"Spend the day? The whole DAY?" Filmer said, and
said no more.

He declined to remain upon the premises, went down
the back stairs and sought loneliness by way of a rear gate
out of the range of vision of Frankie and Francie. Strolling morosely, he was presently behind the garage belonging to the Fry family, and, pausing, heard young laughter

from the front yard. He listened bitterly; then spoke half aloud: "Well, I got to—*some* time—haven't I?" He meant that eventually he'd have to face the contumely of his Group; so why not desperately do it now?

He climbed over the Frys' back fence, and, walking slowly, passed round the house and approached the front yard. There, Antoinette and Ellie engaged in a running scuffle with Bill, Slops and Charlsworth. Antoinette and Charlsworth broke away from the others; Charlsworth flourished a crumpled newspaper, and Antoinette, pursuing, tried to snatch it from him. She was the first to see Filmer, and at once stopped running, stood still and stared at him. Charlsworth, too, stopped and stared. So did Slops and Bill and Ellie.

"Well, all right," Filmer thought doggedly. "Now it's coming! Well, I got to stand it."

"Filmer!" Antoinette cried. "Come make Charlsworth give me this newspaper that's got your picture in it. They're all mad 'cause I said I was going to cut it out and frame it!"

Charlsworth, Bill and Slops looked at him with unwilling deference. "Surprised you condescend to join us!" Bill said. "Got the big head this morning, I s'pose?" Slops, speaking at the same time, made a feeble belittling effort: "Whenever you get to thinking you're so famous and everything, don't forget the paper called you 'Master'. That part of it's not so hot, Filmer old kid!" Also, Charlsworth asked rallyingly: "How'd you work it, sport? Nothing but you and the Little family all over the page. Your father got stock in that paper?"

"Filmer Little!" fat little Ellie shouted. "Aren't you simply crazy about yourself?"

Antoinette took Filmer's arm cosily. "What I think was the beaniest of all, Filmer," she said, "it was your being an urchin. Now who in the whole world would ever think of that but you?" She leaned to his ear, spoke softly. "Didn't I always tell you you're different from anybody?"

Filmer began to perceive that people can have dazingly different views not only about world affairs but of even what is simplest. He'd kept his intended appearance as Big Shot or Public Enemy Number One so private and had been recognized in that capacity by so few—if indeed by anybody—that his debut into publicity as an urchin, instead, was being accepted not with derision but admiringly. His supposed impersonation of an urchin seemed even to imply a certain wittiness on his part—at least, Antoinette and Ellie plainly thought so. His Group was greeting him with envy on the part of the males and with a new tenderness on the part of the females. In a word, he was being received as their celebrity.

His insides completed some readjustments. "Well——" he said, swallowing. "I'll—I'll get you another copy of that newspaper if these heels spoil this one, Antoinette. I don't see why you want to frame it, though. Just having my picture in the paper don't amount to so terribly much."

He would have protracted this modesty, except for an interruption. Lila was still talking to the man in overalls; but Frankie and Francie had begun to study the neighborhood. Hand in hand they appeared before Antoinette's front gate, and, having opened it, caught sight of Filmer. *"Canny!"* they squealed, rushing toward him. "Canny! Canny!"

Filmer bellowed at them. "You go home! Go back out that gate! Go home!"

"No, no!" Antoinette cried, and, sitting upon the grass, took Frankie upon her lap. "I thought you were so cute yesterday, Filmer, when they were having their little fight and you tried to separate 'em. Do you think you could coax 'em to have another little fight, Filmer, maybe?"

There wasn't any trouble about that; Filmer didn't need to coax. Francie also wanted to sit on Antoinette's lap, and, almost before the request was made, Frankie and Francie were having another of their little fights— not such a little one, at that.

"Aren't they marvelous!" Antoinette exclaimed. "Just adorable!"

"Well—in their way," Filmer admitted; and he added, modest again, "Why they tag around after me so much all the time, I expect it's mostly because they're cousins of mine. The way they act so excited about me, it's likely more on account of being connected in my family maybe than anything they seem to look up to in me in particular about, especially, I expect."

XXII

"AREN'T YOU PROUD of Goody?" Mrs. Little asked, after greeting her husband upon his return from downtown, late in the afternoon. She'd gone outdoors to meet him, and they sat for a while in garden chairs. "The photograph didn't half show how lovely she looked at the Fair. Still, it wasn't really bad."

"No; not bad at all," he agreed. "Of course Goody's better-looking than that. Still, it was fairly like her—fairly. To me it's something of a puzzle about Filmer, though. All that practising he's been doing with his face—and muttering—I don't see how it qualified him to be an urchin especially."

"No, he didn't mean it for that, Ripley. Sometimes I think Filmer's almost as reasonable as a man fifty years old, and right afterward I just give up. There are whole days when you can't understand the workings of his mind much better than you can little Frankie's and Francie's." Thus she spoke of her son who, in turn, didn't understand Frankie and Francie, or his parents, either. To Filmer the behavior and conversation of Frankie and Francie, and his parents also, usually seemed inspired by unreason so profound as not to be worth even a speculative investigation.

"What's he done now?" Little asked. *"Now* what's he done?"

"Nothing—except this morning he was in such a state as never was about his picture in the paper. You were right about his intending to treat the Fair to a sketch of a desperado, Ripley. He meant himself to be supposedly a—— Oh, something about a Big Shot or Public Enemy Number One; but I'm afraid I must have forgotten to make that really clear to the reporter. Filmer was in *such* a state this morning over being called an urchin; then at noon he came home with six copies of the *Morning News* he'd bought and he spent the whole afternoon cutting out the picture of himself, pasting it on squares of cardboard, and then making and gilding little strips of wood into picture-frames. He's left one on his bureau, for himself; but I think he's still over at Antoinette Fry's distributing the others among his friends. How's anybody ever going to understand conduct like that?"

"It seems to be a different race," Little said. "Anybody between the ages of thirteen and twenty nowadays seems to belong to some other planet, like the new kind of politicians. All I know about either of 'em is I'm the goat; they've got me. Why, job jam my foolish soul, I ever let myself be whangboozled into buying that new convertible——"

"But, Ripley, think how much smoother our life's been

ever since. Don't you realize, yourself, how much peace-fuller your own nerves are, dear, than——"

"I realize I've had more sleep lately," he admitted. "But that's only because the car keeps her more away from home—out somewhere with that jobjam Norman Peel and——"

"Now, dearie," Mrs. Little interrupted, "you always seem to forget that it was you yourself got her interested in Norman."

"I did," Little said. "For my sins, I did. I thought he'd be a good influence on her and I totally overlooked the influence she'd be on him. He used to be conceited but quiet. *Horribly* conceited, but quiet! How long did it take her to turn him into the noisiest, yellingest, try-to-singest jam vase-breaker in the whole outfit? If I've got to have it thrown up to me for the rest of my life that I brought Norman Peel into this house I——"

"Now, Ripley!" Mrs. Little rose, and glanced toward the street. "There's Filmer coming home, so Antoinette must have been called in for dinner. I wonder what's delaying ours. I'd better skip in and see."

She went upon this mission, and Filmer, coming dream-ily into the yard, was surprised by a question his father called at him. "Well, did you get your gifts all dis-tributed?"

"Sir?" Filmer came nearer and stood, quiescent. "What gifts?"

"I was just curious," Ripley Little explained genially. "Your mother tells me you felt hurt this morning when you found the newspaper'd labeled your picture an urchin; but that later you went to a good deal of pains to mount and frame copies of it as souvenirs for your friends. I'd just like to get the idea; that's all."

"Yes, sir. They said they wanted 'em. You see, it'd turned out all right after all. Of course I didn't originally expect the photograph'd have that under it, and when I first saw it I thought it was going to do me some pretty tough dirt because the costume I went in represented something entirely different. What I went as——"

"Yes?" Ripley Little said, as his son paused uneasily. "You went as what?"

"Well—well—I intended to be Big Shot, or Public Enemy Number One, and——" He paused again; then, seeing that his father's face remained calm, Filmer became more confidential. "I kind of had another idea behind that, too; but I didn't expect to announce it or that anybody'd recognize me as it, exactly."

"Yes. What was it?"

Filmer rubbed his chin with the palm of his hand, somewhat embarrassed. "Well, I mean it was something I kind of pretended to myself that I was—something kind of more important than just simply being Big Shot, Public Enemy Number One. I mean I kind of had an idea behind it all, just to myself."

"I think I get you," Ripley Little said. "What was this idea that was behind the rest of it?"

"Well—maybe it was kind of foolish—— But the way I looked at it, myself, Father, besides being Big Shot, Public Enemy Number One, I was acting the part of—of something else."

"Yes? What something else, Filmer?"

"Well, just to myself," Filmer said diffidently, "I was being one of the Fighting Littles."

"One of the who?"

"The Fighting Littles, Father," Filmer explained. "You were telling us something once about the Fighting Whitings, so just to myself I was kind of being the Big Shot of the Fighting Littles. Of course I knew I *wasn't* the Big Shot of the Fighting Littles because of course you'd be that, yourself, Father; but this was just only dressing up like that and acting it for the Fair, so I thought——"

"The Fighting Littles?" Ripley Little stared at Filmer. "Just because a certain family got called the Fighting Whitings doesn't mean there were ever any Fighting Littles. The Little family have always been the most peaceable, quiet-mannered, unbelligerent——"

"What, Father?"

"What do you mean 'what?' " Ripley Little said with some testiness. " 'The Fighting Littles'! I don't know where on earth——"

"But didn't you have a grandfather that was this old General Little?" Filmer asked. "You were in the last World War yourself, too, weren't you, Father? You were in some of those trenches, weren't you?"

"What of it?" Ripley Little said. "That doesn't mean our family was ever called the Fighting Littles."

"Well——" Filmer looked regretful. "I didn't mean to get you cross again, Father."

"Cross? Not at all. I just don't happen to see where you ever could have got such an idea." The sound of a musical gong came from within the house, and father and son moved in the direction whence came the summons. Ripley Little was annoyed, but tried to keep this feeling out of his voice. "I suppose it's just as well, Filmer, that your publicity entitled you an urchin, especially as you seem to have felt that the actual Big Shot of the Fighting Littles was much the same as Public Enemy Number One."

"What, Father?"

"Nothing!" Ripley Little said. "Nothing whatever. Let's get in to dinner."

Filmer's peculiar idea remained in the father's mind, and, as a young-voiced song came from the distance in the after-dinner twilight to where the three elders of the family sat on the dimming lawn, Little told his wife and Cousin Olita of the talk he'd had with his son.

"Can't they *ever* quit singing that?" he added. " 'You're as pure as ice but a ball of fire!' If anything on earth could make a Fighting Little out of me *it's* going to if I have to keep on hearing it all summer. The Fighting Littles! Where'd he——"

"Oh, I suppose he's just picked up some old family stories," Mrs. Little said placatively.

"Family stories? What family stories? Not on *my* side of the family! What family stories?"

"Oh, nothing of any importance, of course, Ripley. I only mean maybe some time he's heard you telling, for instance, about the time your father threw both of his uncles out of the——"

"Nonsense!" Ripley Little said commandingly. "I

don't think I ever told it when he was present, anyhow. No, it couldn't have been——" He interrupted himself, seeming to detect an exchange of almost speaking glances between his wife and Cousin Olita. "If I know what you're thinking," he said, "and I think I do, you're wrong, because there never was a Little yet that didn't let himself be walked on more than half the time; but—well, for anybody who has the least understanding of what's going *on* everywhere——"

"What, Ripley?" his wife asked, as he paused.

"Just mumbling to myself," he said. "Forget it." He was silent, musing resentfully in the gathering darkness; then became aware that Mrs. Little and Cousin Olita were discussing matters of dress. "What do you mean what you're going to wear tomorrow?" he asked. "Why especially tomorrow?"

"For Goody's little Tea," his wife explained timidly. "Tomorrow afternoon Goody's having a little Tea for Miss Wanstreet."

"She's only in town for a few days," Cousin Olita said. "Goody met her at the Fair and had quite a long talk with her and was simply carried away. Gentry reports he can get Beulah to help serve, Cousin Wilma."

"Yes, Goody told me. She said Gentry said Beulah's coming, though she didn't much want to. But it seems Beulah's seen our new convertible and's trying to arrange with a finance company to buy one like it. Of course Miss Wanstreet——"

"Miss Wanstreet," Ripley Little echoed. "Who's Miss Wanstreet? Who's Beulah?"

"Beulah's a cousin of Gentry Poindexter's," Cousin

Olita explained. "Goody thought we ought to have at least three to make the serving smooth tomorrow, because of course she's awfully excited about Miss Wanstreet's coming. Gentry says Beulah's mother never got a lick of work out of her in her life; but he thinks she'll be all right for the Tea. He says she took fancy-dancing in high school and then got into a Federal ballet and thought she was fixed for life and——"

"Miss Wanstreet?" Little asked perversely. "Which are you talking about, this Miss Wanstreet or this Beulah?"

"Why, Gentry's Cousin Beulah, of course, Cousin Ripley. It was Beulah was in the Federal ballet and thought it was permanent."

"She did?" Little said. "In a Federal ballet? Just going to dance the summer hours away on our money the rest of her life, was she?"

"Yes, Cousin Ripley; so Gentry says. But it seems they've given up several of those projects on account of Defense and so Beulah's willing to take small commissions like serving at tea to help her buy her new car."

"I seem to have Beulah placed," Little said. "Who's Miss Wanstreet?"

"Why, don't you know?" Cousin Olita was surprised. "It's Miss Meta Wanstreet. Surely you've seen her name in the papers often enough, Cousin Ripley?"

"Yes; often enough," he said, emphasizing the third word. "Heads movements, doesn't she? I don't know what about, though. Somebody without much else to do, isn't she?"

"She's terribly important, Cousin Ripley. I saw in an

article on her her maiden name's Grofil; but her husband is a Mr. Horgish."

"What is all this?" Ripley Little's voice grew more impatient. "If her husband's name's Hoggish she's got to be Mrs. Hoggish, hasn't she?"

"No!" Mrs. Little made sounds of protest. "*Hor*gish. Her husband's name is Horgish and they're both mixed up in all kinds of deep movements that Goody says make her feel she's been wasting her life because she's never been intellectually social-minded enough. Now she wants to be and I think we ought to encourage it, Ripley; but you mustn't call Miss Wanstreet Horgish because she very naturally uses the name she first got famous by— Wanstreet. Goody asked me to be very, very careful to see that you keep calling her 'Miss Wanstreet', Ripley."

"Keep calling her? What do you mean keep calling her? I'm not going to call her at all."

"Please do, dear," Mrs. Little said coaxingly. "She got so interested in Goody she said she simply *must* meet her family too. Of course I didn't know whether you'd come or not—I was afraid not—but now that we're speaking of it, it seems to me it would be rather pointed if you stayed away after Miss Wanstreet said she hoped to meet us all, and especially you."

"Especially me? Why?"

"Why, because you're Goody's father, Ripley dear, and she's taken such a tremendous fancy to Goody. You will, won't you, Ripley? Everything's going so nicely and pleasantly just now, and Goody's really set her heart on your coming, Ripley. She told me so."

"Did she?" Ripley Little spoke somewhat drily; but in his heart he was pleased. He was a little flattered, in fact, by Goody's wanting him. "Well, we'll see. I don't know but I might if Goody thinks it proper for her new friends to meet both her parents. We'll see; we'll see."

XXIII

THIS PLACATED MOOD of Ripley Little's still reigned when he arrived for the Tea and guided his shabby car past the line of shinier ones in his driveway.

He went upstairs by the back way, and presently came down unusually dressed up and containing a hopeful heart. He wished to show Goody that he was interested in her branching out toward a more intellectual life—and maybe, oh, maybe, her new friends were going to be a great improvement upon Norman Peel, Ham Ellers, Bull Thetford, Ruggo Smart, Hot Toddy, and Cuckoo and Screwball!

The chatter of competing voices was loud, and, as he entered the living-room, he saw before him his wife, who looked strained, his daughter, who looked excited, Cousin Olita, who looked busy, several strangers, who looked fashionable, the abhorred Norman Peel and perhaps a dozen or so other people more or less known to him. Goody was talking rapidly to two of the strangers, one of them a fragile young woman with burning black eyes, and the other a handsome rather portly lady of forty, rosy of face and exquisitely dressed.

Little thought that the fragile, burning-eyed one was probably Mrs. Horgish—or, rather, as he ought to say, Miss Wanstreet—but his wife's flustered introduction of him proved the contrary: the big, richly dressed, handsome one of forty was Miss Wanstreet and the burning-eyed one was a Mrs. Pologa.

"So this is our baby member's father!" Miss Wanstreet said, in a voice so hearty that it startled Little. "Bravo!" she added graciously, he didn't see why, and she extended toward him at arm's length the half-consumed large champagne cocktail she held in her right hand. Thinking she meant him to set it upon a table for her, he tried to take it from her; but he'd mistaken her intention. She withdrew the glass quickly and drank from it, while he, confused, wasn't sure whether she was drinking his health or trying to make him look like a fool. He felt like one; everybody in the whole place seemed to be staring at him inquiringly, and his mortified neck, hot, swelled against his hard collar, he so repented his courteous gesture. "Bravo!" Miss Wanstreet gayly said again. "Mr. Little, I'm sure you'll be enchanted to know that we've decided to call your daughter our little Saint Joan."

"Is that so?" he asked in a polite tone, though already he didn't much like this Miss Wanstreet. "What for?"

Goody put a hand upon his arm. "Please go on with what you were saying before we were interrupted, Meta," she begged. "Father, do let Beulah give you some tea, and listen. It's all *so* exciting!" Little took a cup of tea and a Virginia ham sandwich from the young colored woman of unfamiliar face who proffered a tray. So this was the ex-Federal ballet dancer, was it, he thought, antagonized, especially as Beulah seemed to look at him contemptuously, thinking no doubt that as a dancer he'd be rotten. He hated tea, too, and so did his stomach, but not so much as they both hated champagne cocktails. Goody went on with her entreaty. "Please, please finish what you were telling us when poor Father barged in, Meta. I mean all about those exciting meetings you had during your two weeks of flying all over California."

"Exciting, rather!" Miss Wanstreet accepted a liquid replacement from the hospitable Gentry. "Flying from one of our drive-centers to another, I simply lived on exhilaration! One feels the impact of all these gorgeously fascinating new ideologies. I always land right in the midst of minds attuned to the vast changes that are going on, building for the days to come. You know of course, don't you, Mr. Little, that the old America that we used to live in has gone for good—all of it—and of course we'll never get back to it and naturally wouldn't if we could."

"Wouldn't we?" he said. "We wouldn't?"

Miss Wanstreet laughed. "Good heavens, no! What our new recruit, our little Saint Joan, will explain to you, Mr. Little, when she has a chance—because of course, you see, we count on her to bring you in—it's our plan for educating not only the common man but even the most obdurate samples of our old discarded and worn-out tory capitalism. Of course you understand we're anything but Communists, though—that silly old witch-hunting charge against anybody who tries to do anything modernly good in government! Yes, indeed, it's our task to educate pretty much everybody. You see, the very heart of our problem is what we're to do at the peace-table. What we're doing primarily, you see, it's preparing America to be ready for that."

"You are?" Ripley Little didn't understand what she was talking about; but he was sure that he didn't like it and he began to suspect that he'd walked himself straight into a Hot Spot.

"What's your own idea, Mr. Little?" Miss Wanstreet asked. "I mean what's your conception of America's precise place in the world-to-come?" He didn't need to answer, for she continued cheerfully, "You see, that's just the trouble; so few people have made up their minds and their ideas have to be formed for them. That's our plan, Mr. Little. That's what we're working for. We have to have a permanent peace and a permanent prosperity that will be universal. The fact that the problem's colossal doesn't mean that we don't need to settle it, does it? We have it on our hands, haven't we? So what are we going to do about it? We——"

"Who's 'we'?" he asked, and, to the ears of his hovering wife, he didn't sound reassuring. "I mean who is this 'we' you're talking about that's got to settle everything?"

"Let me explain it to him, Meta," the burning-eyed Mrs. Pologa intervened. "In the first place, Mr. Little, you surely don't ask us to stop *planning* for the new world, do you? Surely you don't want the world to go back to the Victorian days of Edward the Seventh and Harding and Coolidge, do you?"

"Do I?" Little responded. "Would I like to get back to

Harding and Coolidge? WOULD I? Listen, Mrs. Polo, I——"

"Ga!" Goody cried. "Polo-*ga!* What a man! He never does get anything straight. Not Polo, Father. Pologa!"

"All right, Pologa," he said. "What about we can't get back to Harding and Coolidge? I know that, don't I? Hitler wouldn't let us if we tried; so what about it, Mrs. Pologa?"

Mrs. Pologa looked at him coldly. "Have you read Laski, Mr. Little?"

"Who?" Little was now wholly confused. "Doesn't he have something to do with the movies?"

"I thought not." Mrs. Pologa smiled slightly. "I thought not."

Miss Wanstreet uttered a peal of good-natured laughter. "You're delightful, Mr. Little!" she said. "Our young Saint Joan warned us you were somewhat of the old order; but we're going to make a convert of you. Indeed we are! You haven't met my husband." She beckoned to a fair-haired slim young man, who obediently came and joined them. "This is Mr. Little, Freddie; and, Mr. Little, perhaps you ought to know that our Freddie Horgish is quite an important person because he's virtually certain to be head of the government's new questionnaire department as soon as we get it officially established. I'm afraid Mr. Little doesn't know much about our movement yet, Freddie. Explain it to him."

"It's very simple," Mr. Horgish said; and, even before he spoke, the fact that he had platinum-blond eye-winkers prejudiced Ripley Little against him. "In fact, nothing could be simpler. All of our vast social and economic changes have only scratched the surface. Our movement is to make certain that the factual voice of the common man is heard on all questions of government; but that's only a mere start, a mere start of course. I take it that like any other patriotic person you'd be enthusiastic for this ideal, wouldn't you, Mr. Little?"

"I don't know," Little said sulkily. "I might be and I might not be. Up to now I don't get you. What's it got to do with this Lasky?"

"Nothing, you dear man," Miss Wanstreet laughed. "I suppose it might be called revolution by consent, in a sense; but I'm afraid if we went into that it might only be rather confusing. You see, Mr. Little, radio quizzes and newspaper polls have already led the way in a stumbling fashion; but *we* hold that this work should be tremendously enlarged and become a governmental function."

"Function?" Little repeated, and began faintly to see a light. "You mean you're trying to pile up a new government bureau on us?"

"*What* a way to put it!" Miss Wanstreet continued to laugh at him amiably, as if he were a funny little boy. "Yes, Mr. Little, with a seat in the Cabinet at the top of it! How are we going to find out what people *want* unless we ask them? A system of fifteen to fifty million questionnaires a month, with a tabulation of the varying answers would—— Now, Mr. Little, don't ask me what that would cost! I see it coming in your eye; but don't ask, because of course it's really putting a foundation under the whole Defense structure. What's more, it's catching on like wildfire; we've organized groups up and down the land to write and wire Congress and hold meetings and collect voters' signatures. We're going to have yours, too, you know, Mr. Little."

"You are?" he said, in a tone that meant nobody was going to have his signature for anything. "Are you?"

"Father, sit down!" Goody cried. "You're spilling your tea and wasting Meta's time because you don't grasp what she's saying. Do sit down."

He obeyed, glad to be out of the limelight; for most of the guests had gathered about the central group formed by himself, Miss Wanstreet, Mrs. Pologa, Mr. Horgish and Goody. He sat in a chair against the wall and listened ominously while Miss Wanstreet, Mrs. Pologa and Mr. Horgish continued to explain their movement. He thought he was beginning to arrive at the gist of it, especially when he heard such bits as, "Oh, yes, we've got the economy bloc licked to death!" and, from Mr. Horgish, "Oh, yes indeed, Meta has done marvelous lobbying for me; it's really she that's put me over." It was Goody who shouted, then, "A thousand congratulations!" and Mrs. Pologa kissed Mr. Horgish while two or three other people patted his back.

Ripley Little ate sandwiches and drank more tea against his better judgment, imposing this discipline upon himself as a preventive. It helped to keep him from making a scene, something he more and more eagerly desired to do; but he didn't wish to begin a new war with Goody. She'd gone straight from swing to Hellespont; he didn't know which was worse but thought both were. The restraint he was putting on himself told on him: his face was red, his eyes were becoming bloodshot and protuberant, and intermittently his neck swelled out above his circumvallating collar. Over the rim of his tepid teacup he looked at the face of Mr. Horgish, who was explaining how many buildings would be needed for the official staffs of the projected new department.

"Dob dab him!" Ripley Little said in a low voice, meaning Mr. Horgish, not Pussy, though Pussy was present and seeking gifts of food from the guests. "Dob dab the job jammed bastinadoed son of a bullfinch!"

Miss Wanstreet, amused, had been watching her host with the tail of an eye, and, though she didn't hear the words he'd just used to define her husband, she comprehended that their purport wasn't favorable. "You'll come round, Mr. Little," she said smilingly. "We're leaving that to Goody; but we know that you feel the new ideas sweeping over you, baffling you, turning you heels over head, dazing you. That's natural, at first; but presently you'll find yourself swirling along with them as they break down your obsolete old system and——"

"My old system?" Ripley Little set his small plate upon a table beside him and put his hand upon his abdomen. "My old system?" He spoke in a rising tone that was a breach of manners and stopped all other conversation. "What do you mean my obsolete old system?"

"Don't pay any attention to him!" Goody was scarlet, but contrived to laugh. "I *knew* I ought to have had Mother keep him out because he was sure to do something! It was you who insisted on having him, though, Meta; you're really responsible."

"Don't be alarmed," Miss Wanstreet said cheerily. "Anybody can see he's really an old dear, you know."

"I'm not," Ripley Little announced. "I've been called a good many things in my time, but not that."

Breathing loudly, he was striding toward the door when words uttered by his daughter stopped him for a last moment. Goody was as infuriated as he; but she tried to sound indulgently amused. "Let him go! He's the very kind that bring on the revolutions!"

"All right!" her father said. "I used to understand street-fighting, and the sooner it comes to that, the better I'll like it!"

XXIV

His wife, fluttering after him as soon as she could coordinate her members, overtook him at the front door. "Ripley, Ripley," she said, lamenting faintly. "What in the world's upset you? What's your hat on for?"

"For my head," he replied. "For my head!"

"Now, Ripley, please!" she begged him. "Please, please don't go out on one of your——"

"One of my what?" he asked fiercely. "Have you known me to touch a drop of intoxicating liquor in the last eight years and seven months? I only wish I could, jab jam it, without the doctor."

"But, Ripley, you oughtn't to get so beside yourself just because Goody's new friends don't seem to think as you do about everything. I don't quite understand their ideals, myself, and maybe even Goody doesn't yet altogether; but she's *so* enthusiastic. I'm sure we both ought to encourage her all we can. Only the four principal ones are going to be here for dinner, and it'll be a short meal, Ripley, because they have to hurry away to hold an or-

ganizing meeting right after. So won't you please stay
and try to be nice for just a *short* dinner, please, Ripley?"

"Me?" he said. "'Not while my jobjam obsolete old
system's got legs under it! Goodnight, Mrs. Little."

"Now, Ripley, please———"

Her helpless plaint floated after him as he made his
way to the street and heaved on toward a descending cop-
pery sun harmonious with his own complexion.

He walked and walked; then dined (so to call it) at
the Daisy Dunker, although he knew that in his present
condition he oughtn't to eat at all and that in any condition he oughtn't to eat what he horribly did at the
Daisy Dunker. Afterward he went to a movie that was
all about slaughtering large wild creatures, including a
whale, and when he came out he felt good and sickish.

At home the only sound he heard in the house was
Pussy's growling at him from behind Goody's closed door
upstairs. Ripley Little came to the correct conclusion that
both Mrs. Little and Cousin Olita had accompanied
Goody and her new friends to their meeting; and, after
responding sotto voce to Pussy, as was his custom, he
looked about for his evening newspaper. He couldn't
find it and sat down to smoke a cigar that didn't taste anything like right. A cheerful whistler was heard approaching the house; but the melody whistled didn't help Little's
troubled digestion: "You're as pure as ice but a ball of
fire."

Filmer came in through the unlocked front door,
looked into the living-room, stopped whistling and spoke
from the doorway. "Good evening, Father," he said politely. "Is something the matter with you?"

"No, it's not. Do you *always* have to whistle that same tune, Filmer?"

"No, sir; I guess it isn't compulsatory," Filmer replied. "Look, Father, what kinds of goons were those Goody had here for dinner? Mother kept saying about a hundred times she was afraid you had an emergency call at the dentist's; but even if you did and he hurt you some I guess you were lucky, because I never did hear such a powwow and they might just about as well been talking Cherokee. I bet they don't understand what they're up to, themselves."

"I bet they do," Ripley Little said briefly.

"What, Father?"

"Get to bed, Filmer. Get to bed."

"Yes, sir." Filmer yawned, then whistled himself upstairs; but paused at the top to call down an apology. "I beg your pardon, Father; I forgot." He began to whistle the banned tune again, checked himself scrupulously and ceased to be heard.

His father's cigar had gone out and was not relighted, the house was still, and Ripley Little drifted into a half-sick state of dozing, from which he was roused to full wakefulness by the sound of two covert voices in the hallway. "Yes, I know she wanted me to," he heard his wife saying. "I know, I know; but I'm sure it'd be better if you did it. You know what he'll say if I try to. I'm sure almost anybody'd have a better chance than I would. Anyhow, try."

"Well——" Cousin Olita's voice sounded undecided. "Of course I'm always glad to do anything in the world for Goody."

"Try," Mrs. Little urged her. "Do try, Cousin Olita."

"Well—it seems somebody's got to." Cousin Olita appeared in the doorway, smiling. "Would I disturb you, Cousin Ripley, if I came in for just a teeny chat?" she asked ingratiatingly. "Would I——"

"Yes," he said. "You certainly would. I'm asleep. Stop waking me up. Go 'way from there."

"Yes but——" Cousin Olita said. "Couldn't I just a minute, Cousin Ripley?"

"No," he replied, and closed his eyes.

Cousin Olita withdrew; there was a hurriedly argumentative whispering in the hall, and Mrs. Little walked in and nervously affected surprise at the sight of him. "Why, Ripley dear, asleep in your chair? Don't you want something to eat, dear?"

He opened his eyes. "I do not. I certainly do not."

"But did you——"

"Yes, I did," he said. "Plenty. Too plenty and it's repeating on me. What were you trying to get her to do to me?"

"Who?" Mrs. Little asked incautiously. "You mean Cousin Olita? Nothing, dear. I just thought maybe you'd like to go up and be snugly in bed before they all get here. I'll bring you some soda and ammonia, dear."

"No, you won't. Before who all get here?"

"Why, it's like this." Mrs. Little began to be fluttery, very. "You see, it wasn't an especially large meeting, but was *ever* so enthusiastic and Goody's had quite an honor, Ripley. Coming on top of the prize at the Fair the other day, we ought to be *so* proud of her! You see, they organized tonight and elected Goody the head of it. She's to be this city's chairman, Ripley. It's really quite an honor at her age to be so prominent. Of course, too, it means that a great deal will be expected of her."

"Such as?" he inquired. "Such as?"

"Why, getting—getting the organization started here and everything, Ripley dear. Of course the first thing she'll have to do will be to get the—the subscriptions for keeping it alive and—and all that—to get them coming in—and she'll—she'll——"

"She'll what?"

"Well, of course—of course——" Mrs. Little looked genuinely frightened now. "Don't you really think you'd better get up to bed, dearie? They're staying a while to talk it over after the meeting; but they thought—at least Goody thought—it'd be nice if they'd all come here for a while afterward to—to rest and relax after the work of the evening. You see, Miss Wanstreet and Mrs. Pologa and Mr. Horgish and Mr. Berger are taking a plane at three-twenty——"

"Which three-twenty? A.M. or P.M.? Who's Mr. Berger?"

"Mr. Berger? He was the grayish-haired short one. Didn't you meet him, Ripley? He's *so* nice and seems to be doing quite a little of the preliminary financing, I understand. Three-twenty in the morning, dear. So Goody thought—that is, she thought——"

"Go ahead, Mrs. Little. What did Goody think?"

"She thought I'd better get here ahead of them." Mrs. Little sidled nearer to the door. "She thought maybe I'd better see if you wouldn't like to be in bed first and that I could have a—a little talk with you upstairs and then—

and then tell her. She's *so* enthusiastic and they—they all felt they ought to know something of what they could count on from—from the new organization here, and of course, being chairman, she'd be expected to head the list herself and they'd be *so* pleased to know the—the amount—tonight before they leave, and so Goody, being chairman, thought maybe I could find out for her and let her know and she could announce it to 'em while they're here and——" Breathless, Mrs. Little paused.

"Go on. Announce what to 'em?"

"Why—why, the amount. Now please, Ripley dear, don't look like that. Of course it wouldn't have to be paid now—any time, *any* time. What Goody'd *like* it to be, of course, would be in—in round numbers—on account of her being chairman; but if you thought—if you thought we couldn't afford that, even for such a good cause, or even five hundred or, say, four hundred or even three——"

"For such a good cause?" He rose, and, as he did so, she moved backward into the hall. "Three hundred dollars, did you say, Mrs. Little? I've been feeling sick all evening and what I ate isn't the dobdab half of it. Do you know how many causes we're subscribing to already? When a man's own daughter sicks his wife on him for a subscription to start pamphlets and broadcasts to get Miss Meta Wanstreet's Freddie a public job—nothing else in the jobjam world, I tell you, Mrs. Little, not another jobjam thing to it——"

"Oh, but Ripley!" she cried in protest. "*What* makes you say that? You couldn't be worse mistaken! You really don't understand, dear; they're all so——"

"Not another dobdab jobjam thing to it, Mrs. Little!
Yes, and planted it I'd be shown up as a dobdab obsolete
old tory capitalist if they couldn't work me. I'm a liberal-
minded man; but I'm getting jam tired of movements for
the jobjam Freddies, to get 'em salaries and stick 'em
up to run other people's business. Is that going to stop
Hitler, and what kind of 'peace-table' are they going to
have if we *don't* stop him? Why, job jam it, when a man's
own daughter falls for——"

"Now, Ripley, Ripley, please please! Goody's *so* anxious to——"

"Anxious, Mrs. Little? What do you think I am? Can
you tell me anything on this earth I'm *not* anxious
about?"

"*So* anxious," Mrs. Little repeated. "She did hope
that when they got here I could tell her you——"

"Not a cent, Mrs. Little. Not a jabjam cent for Freddie!"

"Ripley, Ripley, please!" she besought him, for he was
shouting at her. "Oh, dear *me!*" She was in a panic: cars
were blatting from the driveway. "Ripley, they're here!
Don't you think you'd really better——"

"Give Freddie my love!" Ripley Little said, as he
rapidly ascended the stairs. "Give the whole movement
my love and tell 'em that's all they'll get out of me! Give
'em my dearest love and tell 'em to go to the jobjam dobdab bastinadoed Hellespont's helm! Goodnight!"

. . . In bed he tossed and sometimes moaned, partly because of his indigestion and partly because of the sounds
of rest and relaxation that came from downstairs. The

poor old hunted piano had begun to call for help again; percussion instruments, in the wrong hands, were added to the piano, and ere long some form of primordial dancing or war between the sexes seemed to take place, encouraged by bellowings of Congo passion. Ripley Little recognized hated voices.

"By dob!" he whispered. "By dob, she's got *them* here, too. By dob, she has!"

There was a soft knock upon his door, and his wife came in apprehensively. "I wouldn't disturb you, dear, except I heard the bed creaking and knew you must be rolling around," she said. "Ripley dear, won't you please let me bring you some soda and ammonia?"

"No, I won't," he replied. "It's nine-tenths mental; my mind's getting diseased. If I didn't know she'd only brought her social and economic giants home to rest and relax, I'd have the delusion that she's got Ham Ellers and Bull Thetford and Hot Toddy and the rest of 'em with their drums and——"

"But Goody couldn't help *that*," Mrs. Little said quickly. "You see, she had them all at the meeting—to make it larger—and—and it seems Mr. Horgish plays the clarinet and had it with him and—— Ripley, I do wish you felt well enough to come down the stairway just far enough to peek in through the doorway and see Mrs. Pologa dance! Maybe you don't feel like believing it; but really I never saw more wonderful dancing. You'd get a totally different idea of them, dear, because you only saw them when they were all so serious; but if you could see them now when they've thrown all that off and are playing—just playing like children—really, Ripley, you'd get a totally different idea of them."

"Would I?" he said. "You seem to realize, yourself, that almost any totally different idea of 'em would be a better one."

"Oh, dear me!" Mrs. Little's sigh was a desperate one. "We had such a happy time while you and Goody were getting along so nicely; I just can't bear to see it stop and I'd do almost anything to keep it going. Her heart's so set on this, Ripley, that I don't know what'll happen tomorrow and from then on if we disappoint her. I know it seems to go against the grain with you, dearie; but wouldn't almost anything be worth while rather than let her down on this? If she could just announce to 'em—— Well, practically any moderate amount, say as little as a hundred, or even seventy-five——"

"Wait a minute!" Little sat up in bed, swung his legs over the edge. "Wait and I'll come down and announce it, myself. Just one moment, Mrs. Little, and I'll——"

"Ripley, Ripley, please go to sleep!" the defeated lady besought him, and fled. Before she'd quite closed the door he heard Goody's voice in the hall outside: "Mother! Did he promise he——" Mrs. Little said *"Sh! Sh!"* and from those two he heard no more that night.

Downstairs the stricken piano wires leaped in their tin death-song; a saxophone and a clarinet squealed exorbitantly; the percussion instruments rattled, boomed, banged and crashed; elephantine thumpings shook hardwood floors, and porcelain fell inconsequently upon a marble hearth. Upstairs, in Ripley Little's room, two moods fought for the mastery, and one of them, in spite of everything, was self-congratulatory. "Did their worst!" The sense of satisfaction became murmurously vocal. "Did their worst; but I stuck it out, jab jam it, I stuck it out!"

The other mood, opposing this, was one of anxiety for the future. He knew what Goody'd do. She'd never give up getting that subscription from him, never! Goody was going to raise the jabjam helm with him, and if she came down to breakfast in the morning it would start right there and then.

XXV

He was seldom more mistaken. Goody did appear at the breakfast table, just before he rose from it; her gentle manner and the unbelievable words she spoke set him into the midst of mystery. "Poor Father!" Goody said. "Mother told me you weren't feeling very well last night, and I'm terribly sorry if all that noise downstairs disturbed you; but I couldn't very well help it—for a while at least. I was afraid the rest would want to stay and dance some more after Miss Wanstreet and her party left, so I got them all to trail along and see them off at the flying field, and I do hope after that you got some sleep and feel better this morning. Do you, Father?"

Amazed, he responded, "Yes, Goody, thank you," and went to his work wondering when the attack would begin. It didn't begin at all. Another peaceful period of days elapsed; Goody looked thoughtful at times but was placid and in his presence failed to mention either a subscription or her flown-away friends.

"What's she up to?" he asked his wife. "I can't make head nor tail of it. I suppose she's putting in a good deal of time organizing for the great movement, is she?"

"Well—no, I don't think she is," Mrs. Little answered, looking noncommittal. "She's seemed rather to lose interest in it."

"But why? I never saw her more excited over anything. You mean she's let it all peter out?"

"Well—rather, I believe. You see, at her age, Ripley, they do get enthused rather easily and often forget it pretty soon afterward. I'd just forget it, too, if I were you, dear."

This was all the satisfaction his puzzlement obtained from his wife; but, baffled, he felt there was more to the matter. Goody's impulses weren't so hysterically brief as all that, and he wanted the answer. He got it from Cousin Olita, who never liked to keep anything to herself, and, alone with him for half an hour about a week after the visitation, asked herself, "Why not be really entertaining?"

"I notice, Cousin Ripley," she said aloud, "that you often look at Goody lately in a wondering sort of way. Is it because you don't understand why she made such a to-do over Miss Wanstreet and that movement they were talking so much about and then stopped all of a sudden right away? Is maybe something like that on your mind, Cousin Ripley?"

"Oh, well—I don't know but it might be sometimes."

"I thought Goody acted rather strangely about it, myself." Cousin Olita's manner was cosily confidential. "She doesn't know I know because she didn't suppose Cousin

Wilma'd tell me what she told her; but I happened to hear some of it while she was telling Cousin Wilma and so of course, later on, Cousin Wilma saw there wasn't any use not telling me the rest of it. But you'll have to keep it to yourself, Cousin Ripley."

"I will. Keep what to myself?"

"Why, all of it, Cousin Ripley. I mean from both Cousin Wilma and Goody. Myself, I simply can't see why Goody should have been so shocked and upset; but maybe it's because at her age they're really stricter in their ideas than the way they carry on would make anybody expect. But anyhow she was, Cousin Ripley."

"You say something upset Goody?"

"So it seems," Cousin Olita said. "It must be because at their age they don't see the romance of it when it happens to older people. When I was a young, young girl myself I remember that romances among anybody over thirty or thirty-five seemed to me terribly out of place. So when Mrs. Pologa told Goody——"

"Mrs. who?" Little interrupted. "You mean the one with the angry-looking eyes that Wilma said turned out to be such a dancer?"

"Dance!" Cousin Olita exclaimed. *"Did* she? I wasn't exactly supposed to be of the party when it got that late; but I simply couldn't tear myself away. First she danced and then she—— Well, there was a good deal of champagne left over from the tea cocktails and she—— Well, it seems she always needs a good deal to work up her best dancing on, and then afterwards it seems to kind of hit her and she gets sentimental. She got that way with Goody just before they left, and told her about the romance she's having. Really it ought to be a play and get put on the stage, Cousin Ripley."

"It ought? What ought?"

"Why, this situation she told Goody about. Think of the romance of it, Cousin Ripley—their all traveling round together working for the good of the public; I didn't quite understand that part of it—but you can see it's sincere anyhow."

"Yes; I don't doubt that," Ripley Little said. "Not for a minute."

"And think of what goes on under the surface!" Cousin Olita exclaimed. "You see, Cousin Ripley, Miss Wanstreet and Mr. Berger are absolutely devoted to each other and want to get married, and Mrs. Pologa and Mr. Horgish are head over heels in love; but they're all four the very best friends in the world and wrapped up in the movement and want to help each other. But you see Miss Wanstreet and Mr. Berger are the ones that have the money, and Mr. Horgish and Mrs. Pologa wouldn't have anything to live on, so they want to get Mr. Horgish established in a really important position of some kind, because he has such a remarkable mind, of course, before they go ahead and all get married the way they want to. You get the drama of it, don't you, Cousin Ripley?"

"Yes," Ripley Little said. "I think I do. You say Goody was shocked when Mrs. Pologa told her about it?"

"Yes. She told Cousin Wilma she didn't show it right then but got to thinking about it and decided she didn't feel so much like going ahead pushing the movement too energetically any more. You'll be careful, Cousin Ripley, won't you, not to let her see, or Cousin Wilma either, that now you know about it?"

"Yes, I'll be careful," Little said. A weight had been upon him; but it began to lift. Perhaps these young people nowadays had some sense after all; perhaps they sometimes even knew how not to be taken in by things their parents didn't know how to protect them from. It was a reassuring thought and remained with him until Cousin Olita, after a meditative pause, spoke again.

"Of course I wouldn't suggest it to Goody," she said; "but after all I don't see why she should be so critical. Love's always understood to be the highest function of man, isn't it? But the different ages don't seem to understand each other when they have it. For instance, the other day I mentioned that Mrs. Watson's uncle had lost his wife and was coming to spend the rest of the summer with her and Mr. Watson—a really lovely man named Mr. Carol Ladd Wheeling from Maukegan, Mrs. Watson says—and when I merely mentioned that when he gets over his loss he might think of marrying again, both Goody and Filmer hooted with laughter at the idea, and the only reason on earth they were so amused is he's a little over sixty. Yet Goody doesn't think it's the slightest bit funny, the longing way Norman Peel looks at her through his spectacles, and Filmer'd be furious if I dared to say a single word about how he runs to Antoinette Fry's the minute he finishes every meal. Don't you think that's terribly inconsistent, Cousin Ripley?"

"Norman Peel!" Ripley Little said. "Antoinette Fry!"

These were the only words he uttered in his present

parting from Cousin Olita; but they conveyed all of his unjust thoughts about the two persons mentioned.

Goody might have borne with him if she'd heard him; but Filmer'd have been sore stricken had he been made aware of the inflections used by his father whenever pronouncing the loved name of Antoinette Fry. Filmer thought that name rich and tenderly sonorous, and, at the very moment when his father now uttered it, Filmer was slouching, chewing nothing, and arm-swinging along the old familiar sidewalk that led to the third yard northward of his own.

"Antoinette Fry," the lad coincidentally said to himself, in a tone as different from his father's as a rose from a dead fish. "Antoinette Fry!" Then, at a distance of about sixty yards from Antoinette's gate, his advancing steps came to a tentative stop: a large and shining automobile was standing at the curb before that gate, and an imposing elderly woman was just stepping into this impressive car.

A liveried chauffeur helped her, and Filmer stood watching reverently. Filmer had no personal acquaintance with the enclosed cold-looking white-haired lady; but in her he recognized a terrifying yet blessed being—Antoinette Fry's grandmother. All of Antoinette's relatives had become for him august, dismaying and yet inexpressibly dear. As the car moved away it seemed to ride in a golden haze shot with lightnings.

Filmer, emotional, walked on, and as he came to the Frys' hedge he heard voices that he knew and others strange to him. Then he saw the charming small blonde head of Antoinette, the uncouth heads of Charlsworth

Beck, Bill and old Slops, but not the head of Ellie Turner. Instead, he beheld two unknown shiny brunette heads, female. Moreover, Antoinette caught sight of the advancing tousled head of Filmer, and came skipping to the gate in the hedge.

"Filmer Little!" she cried softly. "Does your ear ever pain you, Filmer? I mean the one that happened the Fourth of July? I want you to meet my two darling cousins from Hammondsville, Myrtle and Cora. They're *awf'ly* cute gals, Filmer, terribly witty and you'll just adore them!"

Filmer already had doubts. "I don't know if I will, Antoinette. I'm not—not exactly like all these other guys, Antoinette; I don't make a goon of myself over every new dame I see."

"But you will over Cora and Myrt, Filmer. They don't care what they say and they're terribly severe. Ellie got mad and went home because she heard Myrt telling Cora she thought Ellie was common. You mustn't get so goofy over 'em, though, that you forget *me,* Filmer. Come on in and meet 'em."

Filmer, serious, came through the gateway, and she performed the ceremony: "Myrt, this is one of my very best friends, Mr. Filmer Little, and you too, Cora. He had the most awful time with his ear I was telling you about; but it's all well now."

Myrtle was sixteen, Cora only fourteen, neither being very pretty; and Filmer, standing before them, enfeebled by a suitor's bashfulness, felt that they were looking at him satirically. Charlsworth Beck, Bill and old Slops, already familiar with Myrtle and Cora, laughed crudely,

bumped into Filmer, pushed their knuckles into his back
and ribs.

"Curtsy or something, can't you?" they said to him.
"Shake hands with Myrt and Cora; they won't bite you.
Tickle 'em; they're both ticklish. Show 'em which ear
you got the skyrocket in; they'll be crazy about you."

Bill and Slops and Charlsworth made utter buffoons
of themselves; and the afternoon, beginning thus poorly,
did not improve. Antoinette invited the four boys to
accompany her and her cousins to the movies; but when
the little party reached the sidewalk Filmer found himself shunted to the rear with young Cora. She walked
dawdlingly, humming loudly, picking dandelions from
grass plots beside the pavement, forming a wreath of
them, and paying no attention to Filmer. She made him
feel criticized and uncomfortable just when he was doing
his best to be sociable with her because she was Antoinette's cousin.

"Well, well!" he said, laughing unnaturally in order to
sound cordial. "So you're related to Antoinette, are you?
Well, well!"

"What's funny about that?" young Cora inquired in
a hard little voice. "Give us a tell."

"Oh, nothing," he said. "I didn't mean it was funny.
I just meant so you're Antoinette's cousin."

"Oh, so I am, am I? I am so, am I? Well, well!"

"What?"

"Nothing, Big Boy."

She began to hum again and there was no further conversation during the walk to Zorky's Rialto Neighborhood Theater. Inside, he and Cora couldn't get near

Antoinette, Myrtle, Bill, Slops and Charlsworth, but could see that they were all having a happy time together and eating something. Afterward, the walk home was similar. Filmer, though he made every exertion, again found himself—he didn't know how—walking behind with young Cora, who renewed her interest in dandelions and grass plots.

"In Hammondsville where Myrt and I live," she told Filmer, toward the close of their silent companionship, "the boys all got zig—anyways a little!"

"What's zig?"

"It's what prob'ly you back numbers over here still call pep. In Hammondsville it's zig and the boys in our crowd show some."

"Well——" Filmer said, suspecting that she meant to cast reflections upon him, "Well, let 'em!"

Cora suddenly darted ahead and ran into Antoinette's yard, where the others, already arrived, were making merry. Filmer, following, saw Cora "whispering secrets" to Antoinette and Myrtle; then all three looked at him and giggled. Myrtle and Cora repeated this derisive effect often: they would confer together behind their hands, watching him with bright malicious eyes; then they'd laugh half-hiddenly. Myrtle and Cora, in fact, didn't enjoy being mere satellites and took it out on Filmer. He seldom spoke, or even moved, without hearing the spiteful little sound of their giggling. Longing to be elegant, romantic, aristocratically humorous, he could only endure. To the rough twitting of Bill, Slops and Charlsworth Beck, and to their jocose manhandling, all he could do was to respond, "Can it, can't you? Listen, can't you can it? Can it, can't you?"

"That's dated," Cora announced. "In Hammondsville we don't say 'can it' any more—not since about sixty years ago. Why'n't you learn something, sweetie?"

"Foolish question Number One," Myrtle said behind her hand, yet so that everybody heard her. "Haven't you noticed the shape of his head?"

Animal-like, Bill and Charlsworth and Slops thrust hands in Filmer's hair, rocked his head, yelped of discoveries there, while doggedly he asked and asked if they never tired of clowning. Myrtle and Cora laughed persecutingly.

XXVI

By THE TIME Mrs. Fry called Antoinette and the two sisters indoors Filmer had a burning feeling in his stomach, not imaginary. Then, all at once, the world changed.

Myrtle and Cora ran into the house; Charlsworth, Slops and Bill went whooping ahead down the street; but Filmer, lingering, saw Antoinette turn at the front door and come back for a handkerchief she'd left on the grass. He approached her sadly.

"Listen," he said, swallowing with some difficulty. "Antoinette, listen. Listen, Antoinette. Antoinette, it looks like you've forgot that day you said—you said I— said I was different from anybody. You—you—— Listen, Antoinette, you treat me the worst of everybody."

"Why, Filmer Little, I don't either!" Antoinette, perfectly a belle, knew how to keep them going; and it may be that after all she really did rather like Filmer best. "What you think I left that handkerchief out here for?"

"Not—not so I——"

"Yes!" she said enrapturingly. "So's maybe you'd notice it and wait till I came for it."

"Oh, Antoinette!"

"I wanted to tell you good-by, Filmer."

"Good-by? What for, Antoinette?"

"Because Grandmother's going to take Myrtle and Cora and me to Lake Opako for a month. We're leaving tomorrow morning. It's awf'ly nice up there. Will you be sorry, Filmer?"

"Sorry? Oh——!" He began to swallow again, sand apparently. "Antoinette, is this the last time I'll see you, the last time for a—for a month?"

"It looks like it, Filmer."

"Oh, my!" he said. "Oh, my!"

"I tell you what you do, Filmer," Antoinette charmingly suggested, stepping close to him. "In a few minutes Myrtle and Cora are going over to Grandmother's for dinner and stay all night and I'm going for dinner but coming home afterwards. You come over there about half-past nine and come in the house like you just came to call on Myrt and Cora, and for heaven's sake don't say you're there on purpose to walk home with me! Grandmother's awf'ly strict; she lives in the past and'd have a fit! But pretty soon after you get there I'll say I haf to be going, so then you get up and say you haf to, too, and live right a couple doors from me, so then I'll say all right, Grandmother won't need to send me in the car, and she'll prob'ly say all right; so then you can bring me home, Filmer. Doesn't this make it all right with you that I honestly think you're different, Filmer?"

Filmer's chest seemed to become a beautiful balloon,

lifting him. "Where—where's your grandmother live, Antoinette?"

"Sixteen-four Buchanan Avenue. Be sure to be there by nine-thirt', Filmer."

"Will I! Oh, Antoinette!"

Breathing heliotrope and violets, treading a musical sidewalk under gilt-edged shade trees, Filmer went home to dinner. Antoinette was going away—for a whole empty, empty month—but tonight, tonight he'd be with her, free from Bill, from Charlsworth, from Slops. He'd be alone with her in the summer night, all the way home from her grandmother's. At the table, his father and mother, Cousin Olita and Goody looked altered; they seemed to be heavy insensitive creatures grubbing dully through underprivileged lives. He had scarcely a word for them, heard nothing they said, and, at about half-past eight o'clock, as he went upstairs to make improvements in his attire, he saw before him a kind of floating radiance labeled in gold, "1604 Buchanan Ave."

Dressing in reverie, at intervals sitting on the edge of his bed for as much as ten minutes with his mouth open and a garment partly on or nearly off, he finally had himself into a fresh "sport shirt" open at the throat, proving him an athlete, a thin blue jacket and his cleanest and least bulbous white flannel trousers. Eventually he drew upon his feet his whitish buckskin shoes. That is, they were here and there whiter than elsewhere, and, wishing to appear at his very best, he was troubled by observing that they were streaked with grassy greens and blobbed with dried oil that had been all the way through an automobile.

Filmer owned no remedying powder or fluid, but, re-membering that his sister did, went into her pretty room and turned on the light. Indignant, he found that the closet where Goody kept her whitening was locked; then his eye fell upon her dressing-table and an amethyst glass bowl containing face powder and a large white powder puff. Relieved, he sat upon the stool before Goody's dressing-table, dabbed the puff and powder lavishly over his shoes, and was unduly satisfied with the temporary result.

After this he did a number of things that would have seemed odd to his father, for instance, and yet were en-tirely natural to Filmer's age and sex.

Filmer, looking at himself in the clear mirror of the dressing-table, applied the powder puff to his face and to most of his hair. He made himself not so white as a clown but comparable. Then, solemn, he several times used his fingers to turn up his nose and widen his mouth to the last possible extremity. After that, he examined lengthily the maplike inner linings of his lips and the under side of his tongue; then he just sat looking at himself.

Here was nothing either of vanity or of a deliberate purpose to make use of his face as when preparing it for the Annual Welfare Fund American Costume Fair. Only during the last year or two had Filmer discovered, so to speak, his face. He didn't think of his face either as beautiful or as lacking in beauty; it just interested him. Also, he found a fascination in experiment; that is, in seeing what could be done with and to it. Sometimes he wouldn't think of his face for days, and then without warning, alone with a mirror, he would have the spell upon him.

Seated at Goody's dressing-table, he wasn't thinking about what other people thought of his face, not even thinking about what Antoinette Fry might think of it; he was so lost in looking at it he didn't think of Antoinette Fry at all. For the moment, even on the eve of her departure, she was out of his system, as it were; and here was a difference between him and his sister. When Goody thought she was in love with anybody she thought so all the time. Filmer was in love with Antoinette Fry only when he happened to think of her. Just now he had no thoughts except about his face, and, although they were amorphous, he was absorbed in his purely visual experience.

He opened an enameled box on the dressing-table and took from it an eyebrow pencil with which he gave his upper lip a slight moustache. Then he blackened his unimportant eyebrows and lashes with the pencil, used a lipstick heavily and was also liberal with rouge upon his cheeks. Fascinated by the alteration, seeming to have an almost entirely new face, he strained his neck trying to see himself in profile. Nevertheless, here was no effeminacy; Filmer was thoroughly masculine and what he did this evening to his face he didn't do to be lovelier. The final thing he did to it was with the lipstick: he dreamily converted the lower part of his nose, when seen full front, into a large round coral-colored polka dot.

After that, he thought perhaps he'd better wash off the artificialities; but Cousin Olita was on her way upstairs singing, "In the gloaming, oh, my darling——"

He jumped up, put out the light, and, not wishing to answer inquiries about where he intended to go at this hour, or what he was doing in Goody's room, waited for Cousin Olita to pass the open door. At the top of the stairs, however, she paused to reply to a question from his mother below. "Going to listen to my radio in bed," Cousin Olita called. "It's twenty minutes after nine and the What They're Wearing program comes on at half past."

"Oh, gosh!" Filmer gasped. "Twenty minutes after nine! Oh, my gosh!"

Cousin Olita didn't pass the doorway. Instead, she felt a draft, came into the lightless room and closed an open window. "Not *too* much air, dearie," she said aloud, lovingly addressing the absent Goody, and, while Filmer shrank against a wall, resumed her song. "Tum-ty-ump-ty, best for you and best for me."

Singing, she went out, passed down the hall, entered her own door, closed it behind her and sang louder, having given the unseen Filmer two nervous shocks of a strength almost sufficient to erase from his mind the sense of his present appearance—or, at least, anxiety about what that appearance would be in a lighted place. Especially in hurried and eventful moments, as his father often said of him, Filmer could be careless about anything whatever, even things of the utmost importance to himself; and he could go on being careless about them afterward.

"Twenty minutes after nine! Oh, my gosh!"

He dove into Goody's bathroom, fumbled for a towel, found one, wet it at a spigot, scrubbed his face hard but too briefly in the dark. Then he hurried silently to the back stairs, tiptoed down and diplomatically left the house by means of the kitchen door.

... Having run most of the way, he came into Buchanan Avenue pantingly. This was the town's most celebrated uncommercial thoroughfare; its lawns were broader than elsewhere, its trees and shrubberies more impressive. Through trembling leafage, lighted windows seemed to gleam from noble heights; haughty residences appeared retired to intensely private distances from the street, and Filmer unexpectedly found himself disquieted.

Thus far unthinking, eager and bold, he now seemed a stranger, a small one, in a chilly neighborhood presided over by a dear but disturbing grandmother to whom Antoinette might never even have mentioned him. Thoughtless confidence began to leak out of him and a dreadful self-consciousness, anything but sustaining, to take its place. He ceased to hurry, walked lingeringly.

At Antoinette's grandmother's would a foreign hostile type of manservant open the door and inquire his business —or would Antoinette's august grandmother herself perform that office? If so, in what words was he to explain himself? Was he to say, if able to speak at all, "Listen, I'm paying a call on Myrtle and Cora?" or, more economically, "Look, where's Cora and Myrt?" And if the manservant or the grandmother said, "Cora and Myrt WHO?" what could he reply, since he didn't know?

The little plan impulsively sketched by Antoinette in the afternoon now all at once appeared formidable. Antoinette's grandmother was hers, not his. Antoinette was accustomed to her grandmother and to 1604 Buchanan

Avenue. What appeared simple to Antoinette—dashing into 1604 Buchanan Avenue and asking for Myrtle and Cora—began to seem to Filmer like the Charge of the Light Brigade with nobody at all to ride back again.

He came to stone pillars, one of which bore a metal placard, "1604", faintly glittering under the white-globed light of a street lamp; and from here a driveway curved dimly between trees and clustered bushes to the lighted doorway of a house that looked intentionally larger than people's houses ought to be. Swallowing slowly and irregularly, he passed between the gateposts and moved sluggishly toward the house; but, at a distance of about thirty feet from the stone front steps, a sensation that began at the back of his throat passed down his spine, reached his feet and stopped their forward movement.

Antoinette was there, not far within that lighted doorway and the lighted windows on both sides of it—and—and who else was there, too? Cora and Myrt, certainly—Cora and Myrt with their bright ratlike little eyes and spiteful titterings—and who else? Maybe there were callers in there, grown people, maybe old people, maybe people forty and fifty years old—maybe the grandmother was having a party. Filmer's voice was glued down flat in his throat; but his still too warmly colored lips faintly formed stricken words.

"Oh, my!"

Could he go in there and sit down among Antoinette's grandmother and old people and wait for Antoinette to say it was about time to be getting home? No, he could not. Maybe, though, there wasn't any party and maybe—

just maybe—Cora and Myrt and the grandmother had gone to bed. Filmer's breath came back fitfully. Maybe Antoinette was sitting in there all alone, waiting for him to ring the bell. Maybe! His legs wouldn't ascend those steps until he knew, even if the rest of him wanted to.

The shade of the open window nearest the doorway was up an inch or so from the sill, leaving a bright horizontal strip crossed by vertical slim shapes, the legs of a chair or table. Filmer crept forward, and, standing tremulously upon tiptoe, applied one eye to this brilliant aperture. Immediately his stomach seemed to fall away within him.

His appalled eye beheld not one but two populated interiors. In that nearer to him, eight ladies—all old, all severe and all dressed up, including the grandmother— sat silent at two card tables; and beyond, through an open double doorway, Antoinette, Myrtle, Cora and two youngish grown women, probably aunts, were seen to be solemnly drinking lemonade and eating cake.

Filmer's supporting toes relaxed; so did his fingers upon the stone window sill, and his eye descended from that overwhelming sight. If Antoinette had thrown her glove into a cage of lions—well-trained sea-lions—Filmer might have retrieved it for her; but she had giddily asked too much of him. Like the traveler fascinated by horror who takes one last look over the rim of the active volcano's crater before fleeing, he raised himself again and set his eye to the horizontal strip of bright window.

He was unaware of a slight rustling in a clump of bushes a little distance behind him; but the sound was made by a large, middle-aged man named Rennert, professionally a neighborhood night watchman. This Rennert was sensitive about never having made an arrest; and of late, as it happened, he was doubly so because of special complaints on the part of his clients. He had become electrically upon the alert, when, from across the street, he'd seen the slight figure of Filmer furtively entering the driveway gates of 1604.

Officer Rennert, as he had once or twice been called because he possessed a badge and a holstered weapon, had followed the hesitating white trousers of Filmer through the shadows, and, nearing the house, had concealed himself among hydrangeas. The second time Filmer applied his eye to the window, however, Officer Rennert stole forward; then leaped. Shouting hoarsely in the quiet night, he encircled the neck and body of Filmer in ponderous, compressing arms, which to their owner gratifyingly seemed to hold almost nothing.

"*Got* you!" the watchman shouted. "Got you, Peeper! Tried your little game in my territory just once too often. Knew I had you soon as I first seen you, Mr. Peepin' Tom!"

"Don't!" Filmer said in a whispering voice. "Don't make such a noise! I am not! I know her! I'm calling on her! Don't make such a noise!"

"Who won't?" the night watchman asked, naturally expansive in this his almost only success. "Who won't make a noise? Claim you're callin' on Mrs. Minchester Thomas, do you? Tell that to the Sergeant! Now just let 'em try to keep on sayin' Rennert ain't no good to his customers! Just let 'em try to say it after this! Stop that! You want your wrist twisted?"

"No," Filmer said. "You let me go! What you——"

"What'm I goin' do? I'm goin' to take you in there and 'phone headquarters I——"

"You're not! Me in *there!*" Filmer's squirming, inspired by a supreme revulsion, surpassed the human. Harder to hold than even Pussy, he broke away, ran for more than life, and the night watchman, cursing, followed. If Filmer hadn't been wearing white trousers he might have made good his escape; perhaps he could have done it if the back door of his father's house hadn't been found open by Almatina, who locked it. As it was, he wasted time on the door, and the hard-panting Rennert laid hands on him there.

"Listen!" Filmer entreated. "This is Mr. Ripley Little's house and he——"

"I know doggone well it is," the night watchman said. "I'm goin' to take you in here first and give Mr. Ripley Little a chance to charge you; then I'm goin' to drag you back to where I got you and show you to Mrs. Minchester Thomas, and then I'm goin' to call headquarters, and then——"

"Don't!" Filmer begged. "Don't!"

"Won't I, though!"

XXVII

WHAT DINNED LOUDEST into Filmer's wakeful mental ear after he'd been sent to bed was the word "arrested". This was partly the effect of the number of times his father'd said it, keeping it up long after the officious Rennert's grudging departure. The different ways in which the word had been said were also repetitive in the sorely plastic mind of Filmer: "Only fourteen years old and already he's been arrested!" "Our only son, arrested!" "The only member of the Little family ever arrested!" "Out in the night without permission and gets himself arrested!" "Arrested at Mrs. Minchester Thomas's!" "Arrested for peeking in Mrs. Minchester Thomas's windows!" "Arrested! Arrested! Arrested . . ." The doomful word, uttered interminably in his father's voice, became an ache in Filmer's head upon the unrestful pillow. From downstairs he could hear at intervals sounds that suggested distant oratory and discussion; he was willing to bet they were all still jabbering, "Arrested! Arrested! Arrested!"

They weren't confining themselves to that, however. His father paced the floor, talking straight along no matter how often interruptions were attempted by his wife or by Goody, who'd just come in, or by Cousin Olita, who'd rushed downstairs in a rose chiffon wrapper upon hearing the uproar made by Ripley Little, Rennert and Filmer when the night watchman dragged the son of the house into the front hall.

"I fail to comprehend your expression," Ripley Little said, pausing before Goody and referring to a risible movement of her facial contours. "I don't care to see you looking as if you were trying not to laugh. I don't care for it, understand; I don't care for it! That jabjam night watchman may have exceeded his duty because, as he said, there'd been complaints of a Peeping Tom in that neighborhood lately; but the fact remains that getting arrested isn't a laughing matter. He swore Filmer told him he was paying a call upon Mrs. Minchester Thomas. Upon Mrs. Minchester Thomas! Was that sane, at his age, to tell anybody such a story? Was it?"

Goody's lips quivered. "Father, how often must we tell you she's Antoinette Fry's grandmother?"

"Was it sane?" Ripley Little continued vehemently, pacing again. "Even at his age was it sane? That night watchman insisted again and again that Filmer swore to him he was calling on Mrs. Minchester Thomas herself. Then look at the state he was in! Calling *any*where with no necktie and his face smeared with every color of the rainbow. He claimed he'd washed; but who could believe him? Then what was his answer when we asked him why—*why* he had to go peeking in at Mrs. Minchester Thomas's windows? To see who was there, he told us—to see who was there! What's the jabjam sense in that?"

"*I* know," Cousin Olita said. "At least I think I do. Filmer wouldn't say so; but *I* think he wanted to find out if Antoinette Fry was there."

"Why, jabjammit," Ripley Little said, paying no attention to Cousin Olita's theory, "if I'd ever thought I'd live to have a son that an officer of the law would drag into my house, smeared all over with mascara and lipstick and arrested—*arrested!*——"

... Filmer, coming down late in the morning, purposely very late, met Cousin Olita in the front hall, and, observing that she looked at him oddly, stopped and spoke sharply to her. "Listen, are you or aren't you supposed to be the well-bred woman? Weren't you ever trained not to stand in a person's way goggling him in the face?"

"Poor Filmer!" Cousin Olita said. "Filmer, did you know little Ellie Turner's aunt lives next door to Mrs. Minchester Thomas and that nosey-parker night watchman is a friend of Ellie's aunt's cook and went back there last night and told this cook all about what happened and she told Ellie Turner's aunt and *she* told Mrs. Turner by telephone, and so Ellie heard all about it first thing this morning, and so, Filmer, young Charlsworth Beck and your friend young Willie Hormer and that singsong-voiced young Ellers boy you call Slops and——"

"What about them?" Filmer said. "What about them?"

"Why, they've all been here looking for you, Filmer,"

Cousin Olita informed him. "I thought you'd better know because I'm afraid most likely they're feeling anxious to talk it over with you, your getting arrested and everything."

"When?" Suddenly Filmer was filled with fury. Here, he thought, was something he could deal with. *"When* were they here? Where are they? Where's any Bill and Slops and Charl———"

"Well, I wouldn't bother with them, Filmer, if I were you. When I came in just now I noticed they seemed to be laughing and joking on the sidewalk a little way up the street; but———"

"Oh, they are, are they?" Filmer, reckless with anger, forgot his breakfast. "Out there, are they? I'll show 'em!"

Cousin Olita thought she ought to tell him something she hadn't yet mentioned, and she put forth a detaining hand; but he rushed stormily by her and from the house. After all, she felt then, maybe it was just as well that she hadn't spoken. "He always gets so mad at me," Cousin Olita thought, "whenever I'm the least bit critical of him." Humming "In the Gloaming", she went upstairs for her knitting, came down again, went outdoors and sat in one of the garden chairs. Sounds of mingled altercation and gaiety came soon to her ears, and then whoopings and cacklings from nearer by. Filmer was returning home, accompanied by a group of active young associates, three boys and a joyous little fat girl. He was walking backward, of necessity, because the others were all trying to dance into him.

He'd misguided himself in hurrying out of the house

before Cousin Olita had been able to impart what no doubt she'd have mentioned eventually. Upon retiring last night Filmer had felt no desire to see a mirror, and, when he rose this morning, he'd been too preoccupied for even the slightest customary ablution. Until a few minutes ago he hadn't any idea of what his face still looked like—something that Charlsworth Beck, Bill, old Slops, and Ellie Turner were telling him and telling him and telling him.

It was hours before Filmer remembered that he had one alleviation to console him somewhat in his troubles: Antoinette Fry had been motored away by her grand-mother, Mrs. Minchester Thomas, with Myrtle and Cora, at five o'clock that morning, too early to hear of the awful things that had happened to him and were con-tinuing to happen to him. He had a bad day and spent the whole evening of it in his room composing a letter, sometimes applying himself to a dictionary he'd brought upstairs under his coat with as much care as if it had been Bokakio. He'd obtained Antoinette's address from her mother, by telephone.

Dear Antoinette

I would not wish you to think I did not come because I got over there but not having the information of Cora and Mirts last name to announce my call at the front door with I decided I better desist so do not think I did not wish to. There is no news around here since you left here except I can not recommend the conversation of some of my friends though I would prefer to designate these individuals as so called acquaintances instead as their conversation is nothing but so called witticisms and dumb cracks like you had to listen to yourself so often before going. Their incorrigibility of dumbness brings me fatigue and there are times when anybody would like to get out of this old town a good while. The way I am feeling that is what I would prefer. When are you coming home Antoinette? In frankness this town makes me sick. I am going to ask my mother to influence my father to let me go to a camp maybe the same Slops Ellers is going to for August though his intelligibility is so weak and incorrect I certainly do not expect to enjoy his conversation during the trip or while there.

I hope you are having a nice time at Lake Opako but I am not having any here Antoinette—but I hope in the midst of it all you remember what you said about your noticing about me being you know what Antoinette if you meant it as I doubtlessly hope you do Antoinette

Cordially yours
FILMER LITTLE

Filmer's proposal of camp life for the remaining month of summer was at first received by his father with skepticism and denial. Filmer wouldn't know how to take care of himself, Ripley Little insisted—a boy who began to get himself arrested before completing his fifteenth year would probably land in jail even on his way to the camp. He wouldn't know how to travel such a distance; he didn't know how to do anything at all without getting himself into trouble. The plan, however, was warmly pressed, not only by Filmer's mother but by Goody, who had now become Ripley Little's favorite. Goody said she happened to know all about the Pine Trail Boys' Camp, where Filmer's friend, young Slops, was going; it was one of the best in all New England, Goody announced authoritatively, and the two boys traveling together would be safe.

She carried the day; and Filmer, after a last stroll in the twilight and a final lingeringly wistful gaze over the Frys' hedge into a speaking emptiness, came home to interfere loudly with his mother's and Cousin Olita's packing for him. He made such a fuss that Cousin Olita abandoned her share of the task: she'd have to stop anyhow, though, she explained, because she was already late for an appointment to make a fourth at bridge with Mr. and Mrs. Watson and Mrs. Watson's uncle, Mr. Carol Ladd Wheeling. Bridge, Cousin Olita said, a little consciously, was the only thing that now distracted Mr. Wheeling's mind—at least so Mrs. Watson told her.

Filmer's parting with his father was almost formal, both being too manly not to conceal whatever emotion they experienced, and Filmer was relieved by the fact that Ripley Little, curbing himself, didn't even once introduce the word "arrested" into his expressions of farewell.

XXVIII

Aｕｇｕｓｔ ａｒｒｉｖｅｄ upon the city, bringing along its customary record-breaking wave of humid hotness. Prostrations were as usual, people with the best of tempers lost parts of them, and, at half-past eight on the third morning of the great heat, Ripley Little rose from his breakfast and struck the table a blow that made silver hum and porcelain clink.

"Dot dabble it!" he shouted. "Stop trying to excuse it! Helen's belts, this bob dand house is too much for me, all busted up again! If he ever sets another foot in it—— Well, take your choice, either him or me, Mrs. Little; either him or me!"

"But, Ripley, please! He's really the nicest of——"

"And the best-looking, too," Cousin Olita added. "I've always thought Goody was making a great mistake in preferring Norman Peel to him. He's so good-natured and has such a nice figure and hair and——"

"Take your choice, that's all!" Ripley Little said. "Him or me, Mrs. Little! I'm going down to my place of business and stay there night and day till either I get dragged to Leavenworth for leaving out a comma or you can think of some jam good reason why I should return to such a hod banned wrecked home as this. I bid you good-by, job jam it, Mrs. Little, I bid you good-by!"

He stamped out of the room and, still talking, out of the house. Mrs. Little followed him, twittering, as far as the front door; then, when the reverberation after its closing gave way to shocked silence, she stood looking at the formerly graceful newel post of the broad stairway. This post, splintered, leaned at an unpleasant angle, and so did the adjacent balusters, giving the whole stairway a drunken appearance.

"Oh, my!" Mrs. Little murmured.

"The carpenter promised he'd be here by ten," a sweet voice called reassuringly, from above, and Goody, in pajamas, descended the stairs. "Was the newel post what he was jobjamming about, in particular, Mother?"

"No. Heavens, no!" Mrs. Little sank upon a stiff-backed hall chair. "Goody, he said if Hamilton Ellers ever sets one single clumsy foot on these premises again——"

"That's unjust!" Goody cried. "His feet are not, and my sympathies are entirely on his side. I let him try to back into the garage last night from an acute angle because everybody was taunting him with being a rotten driver and he bet two dollars he could do it. The only reason it wasn't a success and made the cracking noise Father came to the upstairs back hall window about was it was dark and the rest were all yelling, trying to make him lose his bet, and they did. It was a pure accident and so was everything else, because when we came in the house they were ribbing him about the door and he got into a broil with Bull Thetford and Cuckoo and Screwball and——"

"With Cuckoo and Screwball?" Mrs. Little interrupted, shocked. "Fighting with girls?"

"No! Not fighting, Mother; it was all just fun. But he reached up for something to hold to when they tried to throw him down and happened to catch Father's grandmother's picture's frame and it just accidentally hit that ugly old vase on the pedestal and got the little hole in her face when it fell down. So then they caromed out into the hall, all scrabbled together, and landed against the stairway balustrade—and that newel post is bad architecturally anyhow because it's too slim—so these other cracking sounds began—and that's when Father chose to commence his awful roarings upstairs and we looked up and saw him starting down in his nightgown, blaming poor Ham for everything, and everybody hurried off home because they certainly didn't want to stay and hear me mortified."

"Your poor father!" Mrs. Little said. "Goody, he says now that of all of 'em not Norman Peel but Hamilton Ellers is the worst and he——"

"That's simply Father's patter!" Goody cried hotly. "They aren't any of 'em the 'worst'!" She uttered a sound like an angry sob. "Father's practically driven him out of town!"

"Who, Goody? Who's he driven——"

"He has, Mother! Ham just telephoned me he thought he'd better keep out of Father's sight a while and said

he didn't believe he cared to stick around and listen to
the new nicknames the crowd's worked up on him out of
what Father said he was last night. Ham's going on a
long visit right away to stay up to when college opens,
and by now he's practically out of town. I never knew
anything more unjust than his being made to feel that
way!"

"Your poor father!" Mrs. Little said again. "I can't
remember seeing him in such a state."

"But he is every week or so, Mother. When a man's
got a temper like——"

"I know, Goody; but it doesn't have much chance to
get better. He says what with Hitler not stopped yet over
there and Ham Ellers and Norman Peel the same over
here, even a man's own stairway isn't safe. He needs a
change and I wish I could get him away."

"Away?" Goody was heartily encouraging. "That's a
great idea, Mother! Splendid! Get him to take a nice
long motor trip somewhere with you."

"He wouldn't," Mrs. Little explained. "I know what
he'd say. He'd ask me what we'd find left of the house
when we got back. You'd have to come, too, Goody."

"*Me?* On a motor trip in the same car with *Father?*"

Goody's laughter was derisive; but Mrs. Little was
sometimes, in her own flaccid way, a persistent woman,
and the weather helped her. After three more days of it
Ripley Little, bogged down and melting behind his ears,
was willing to go anywhere else. Goody, yielding suddenly, consented to a motor trip on the condition that it
be through quaint old New England.

For one thing, she urged, they could look in on Filmer

at the Pine Trail Boys' Camp and see if the water he had to bathe in was as cold as he said on the postal. New England, thus, was settled upon; though Goody was overruled in another matter. Ripley Little declined to travel in the new convertible on the ground that in hot weather it was too narrow for any party inclusive of Cousin Olita, and upon this point Mrs. Little sided firmly with her husband. At the last moment, however, Cousin Olita decided not to go because the house needed to be looked after by somebody more responsible than just the servants, she explained conscientiously, and Mrs. Watson had been begging her not to leave because it would make the neighborhood so lonely.

"So there!" Goody said. "Now there's no reason we can't take the convertible."

She lost again. Her father declined to use the convertible because it was green, because it was a gas-eater and he didn't intend to have the government and Mr. Ickes accusing him, and because Goody'd want to have the top down in the hot sun.

All in all the pleasure journey didn't begin serenely. At the hour set for departure Ripley Little, in fast-wilting white clothes, stood beside his middle-aged sedan, making a speech to Cousin Olita about women—the numbers of bags, baskets, thermos bottles, pasteboard hatboxes they can't travel without, even after the baggage compartment's choked with luggage—when Goody came brightly from the house, leading Pussy by a new green leather leash. Between Ripley Little and Pussy the feud caused by fundamentally opposing ideologies had never much abated; Little at once declared that he wouldn't go

if Pussy did. Goody said she wouldn't if Pussy didn't—
she couldn't risk leaving him because Cousin Olita was
certain to be too busy over that old gentleman next door,
and Gentry, unwatched, might try to get even with Pussy
for a lot of things. Goody further insisted that there'd
be plenty of room because Pussy could sit next to her on
top of the two suitcases beside the driver's seat, which of
course she was going to occupy.

"Drive?" Little exclaimed. "You expect to drive? I
wouldn't go a step. I wouldn't——"

"All right!" Goody said, and added that if she didn't
drive she, twice as much as he, wouldn't go a step.

He made another speech: subject, Young People's
Driving—Goody's in particular. "I wouldn't sit in a car
with you or any of your friends at the wheel for money
the size of this week's government budget!" he said,
approaching his climax. "Every public highway's your
private race track and you're convinced that nobody else
has any business to use it. What courtesy do you ever
show other vehicles? When do you ever realize that a
little patience and courtesy would avoid an accident? If
somebody's in front of you, you honk your job jammed
horn as if he didn't have any more rights than a spider;
then you zizz round him so close you take his mudguards
off and send the bill to Father! If it's the last thing I
ever swear, I won't go if that jam Pussy does, and either
I drive every inch of this trip or I don't start. Why, dob
dab it——"

"Now, Ripley, please!" Mrs. Little begged. "Look
what you're doing to your collar!"

She proposed a series of compromises, and, after half

an hour, both father and daughter thought they'd won; the overheated sedan rolled crossly out of the driveway. Little sat at the wheel, repulsing with his right elbow the sidling advances of two suitcases and a hatbox, and, in the rear, Goody was already telling him which way to turn. Mrs. Little, silently gymnastic, was trying to keep a guarantee to hold Pussy on her lap the whole way, and Pussy was showing his determination not to sit there.

Before noon Goody had often said that the next time her father insulted her she'd get out, and Ripley Little had told her again and again that if he heard one more word of backseat driving, or if that jam Mongolian screech-hound couldn't be quiet, he'd stop at the next railroad station and go home by train. Pussy was, in fact, a poor motorist. There are dogs who love traveling by automobile; but he wasn't one of them, couldn't accustom his nerves to it, and, moreover, had a bedrock conviction that he ought to bark terrorizingly at everything unfamiliar to him. As everything he saw after he left home was unfamiliar, and as not even Goody had any real influence with him, he gave himself infrequent intervals of rest.

"He's a jobjam Nazi," Ripley Little said bitterly. "He thinks he has to soften 'em first by barking his dobdab black heart out!"

When the travelers reached the destination they'd appointed for the first night away from home, Ripley Little, his ears ringing with Pussy and his whole being worn down with repulsing advice and sliding baggage, announced that although the town they were now in was notoriously uninteresting he intended to remain there for the rest of his vacation. Mrs. Little, pleading, proved to him by the map that within another twenty-four hours or so they would be in the heart of Old New England, with all its quaint inns, odd characters, rambling country byways and old sea captains. He told her to tell her old sea captains to go sit on a tack and said he was jam well tired of odd characters in his own home town. However, after keeping him long awake with gentle-voiced persuasions, she prevailed upon him to promise that if she'd quit whispering and go to sleep a few minutes he'd do any jobjam thing on earth.

It was on the second day after this that the Littles found themselves fairly in the midst of the land they'd sought, though only the map said so. What they seemed really to be in the midst of was a large part of the populations of Ohio, Illinois, Arkansas, Michigan, West Virginia, Wyoming and other states, in automobiles, looking for quaint inns, odd characters and old sea captains, though by no means for rambling byways. The three-ply road was one long purgatory of cars going and cars coming as fast and as insultingly as they could. The weather was hotter than it had been at home, and the afternoon air was burnt gas mixed with fried-clam smell. The scenery consisted of signboards, filling stations, overnight cabins, lobster restaurants, antique shops, small graveyards, front-yard displays of red and yellow toys, hitch-hiking soldiers, beer shacks and fried-clam stands.

Ripley Little had eaten fried clams for lunch, and the incessant vapors that came from others being fried had begun to help his own to disagree with him, when Pussy tried twice to jump clear over him because a dog looked out of the rear window of the next car just ahead. Mrs. Little fought Pussy, won temporarily, and muffled him under a writhing rug. "Oh, dear me!" she said. "Goody, he put his hat back on without a single word. It's a bad sign."

Goody was preoccupied with a map. "Milford," she murmured, and looked up. "It's only thirty miles ahead. The map's blurred; I thought it was eighty. Now it's only the middle of the afternoon; but we've simply got to make him stop and stay overnight at Milford."

"Milford? What for, Goody?"

"Because Milford's not so *very* far from the Pine Trail Boys' Camp, and besides that it's the very rarest old New England village there is, Mother. It's got a darling old inn and furniture and elms and ocean and everything!"

"He won't," Mrs. Little said. "Fernvale's fixed in his brain for tonight. He won't."

"You've got to make him, Mother!" Goody looked excited but kept her voice lowered, though Pussy had his head free and was incessantly vocal again. "Milford's just as near Filmer's camp as Fernvale is and—well, frankly, Mother, Milford's the most important place on the whole trip."

"Why is it? I never heard of it before, Goody."

"Mother, I might as well tell you now, confidentially, and get it over: there's a really lovely summer crowd at Milford and they're having a party for me tonight at the Milford Inn. Milford's really where I've been heading this trip for all along. Hamilton Ellers is getting the party up, Mother."

"Who? Oh, dear!" Mrs. Little said, losing her breath. "Oh, dear me!"

"I've been in—in communication with Ham pretty often," Goody admitted, emotionally. "He's visiting a quaint old uncle of his at Milford and the truth is it's why I consented to take this trip. His uncle simply dotes on him because he's named for him, and Ham always visits him when something disagreeable happens at home. I was talking to him over long distance while I took that walk with Pussy in Tidport at lunchtime, Mother, and he told me about the party he's been getting up for me at Milford and said he'll stay out of Father's sight until we get him to bed or something."

"He'll see him," the dismayed mother predicted. "I just know he'll see him! Goody, I'm all confused: I'd been thinking—— We'd all been thinking it was Norman Peel you——"

"Never mind!" Goody said primly. "Never mind, if you please, Mother. Norman's all very well in his way. That is, he has his good points; I mean he's very nice."

"For your father you mean?" Mrs. Little's voice quavered. "Oh, Goody, I do hope he'll never find *that* out!"

"Why should he?" Goody asked, surprised that Mrs. Little even raised this point. "Everything will be completely jake if you merely manage to make him stop in Milford, Mother. Besides the party, Ham's arranged a surprise that——" Here Goody, feeling that she'd already told her mother enough, checked her tongue abruptly, yielding the floor to Pussy.

"A surprise, Goody?" Mrs. Little got the rug momentarily over Pussy's head again. "A surprise besides Ham Ellers? Oh, dear! What?"

"It wouldn't be one if I told you! It's partly for you, too, Mother."

"Oh, dear me!"

"The important thing," Goody said, "is all up to you. It's simply when we reach Milford you've got to make him stay there."

"Oh, dear!" Mrs. Little fought Pussy and looked woefully at the sturdy and discouraging shoulders of her husband. "Oh, dear me!"

XXIX

THOSE STURDY SHOULDERS heaved; one arm and hand, reaching backward over the top of the front seat, sought blindly for Pussy, but missed him. "Can't you keep him quiet just *one* minute—out of all eternity?" Little said. "If I ever take a jabjam motor trip with a dog again and two suitcases in my ribs and a hatbox falling on me every seven seconds, may Og, Gog and Magog strike me dead in my tracks!"

His temper had been accumulating, so to speak, ever since he'd left home. Moreover, the heat was not to be borne, especially not by a stoutish man. He sweltered, itched and hated—hated the clams within him and the frying ones outside. He hated Pussy, the cars that edged him over and those that he edged over; he especially hated those that cometed out, going in the opposite direction, and missed him by microscopic miracles. He hated bicyclists who insolently forced him to spare their lives by risking his own; he hated bullheaded pedestrians who walked in the roadway as if they didn't give a cuss whether he was coming or not. The glaring world seemed full of crazy speeders, spiteful barkings and honkings and hotness and fried clams, and he was getting good and dobdab ready to try to do something about it.

Fernvale, a hundred and forty-five miles ahead, had soldered itself into his mind as the next stopping place. From Fernvale, next day, they'd go to Filmer's camp for an hour or so; the map had convinced Ripley Little that Fernvale was the center from which to make that excursion. He yearned for Fernvale and a hotel room with an electric fan; but now, in a solid procession of cars headed by a semi-crippled truck the size of a cottage, he'd been moving bitterly for half an hour at a rate that would bring him into Fernvale some time tomorrow morning.

Obeying an impulse suddenly, he turned off to the right upon a side road. Goody, alarmed, asked him if he'd lost his mind. He replied that he knew what he was doing; this detour would take him back to the main route far ahead of where he'd have been if he'd stayed behind the truck, and would she kindly for the first and only time in her whole life stop backseat driving?

The rutted road wound snakily through the countryside; nevertheless, for the next twenty-five minutes or so the car made an average of slightly over sixty miles an hour, borne by Mrs. Little with heroically speechless horror. Then Little turned left into a shaggy lane, expecting thereby to return to the main-traveled route, and, after a bumpy interlude between hedges, arrived at a closed gate beyond which were a barn, chickens, pigs and a harrow, all enclosed in a delightful old New England stone fence.

He had to back most of the way out of the lane, while Goody insisted upon an apology for what he'd said when she warned him not to turn into it. She had to speak piercingly—Pussy was convulsing himself because of three farm dogs who talkatively escorted the sedan till it was on the snaky road again.

Ripley Little said nothing in response, another bad sign.

Beyond the lane the rutty road became narrower, with high soft shoulders between ditches; but, to make up for time lost in the lane, and to bring Fernvale nearer, though mostly for other reasons, the speedometer now went up to 65. Some moments after it touched this figure, the Little family, tilting, came round a sharp bend and found themselves facing a disheartening obstacle—a hay wagon overflowing widely and loftily with fragrant greenish hay and moving at a speed of three miles an hour. Mrs. Little's nose and much of Pussy pressed into her husband's upper back before he contrived to suit his pace to the hay wagon's. The hay wagon, self-centered, occupied precisely the middle of the road. Ripley Little honked passionately.

The hay wagon, majestic, continued to move upon the middle of the road.

For almost a mile Little drove behind the imperturbable hay wagon, and honked at intervals—shorter and shorter ones. Then he honked continuously, producing one long unbroken war-trumpet summons exciting to Pussy and assisted by him. Mrs. Little, with her hands over her ears, told Goody she wished she was dead, and Goody reminded her father of what he'd said about young people's honking. Ripley Little paid no attention, for he was now immersed in the fateful mood that leads men on they utterly care not (for the time being) whither. Either love or fury may become wholly possessive of the person in whom the passion lodges, and Ripley Little, in these dooming moments, had no love left in him. Particularly he had none for his fellow men, least of all for farmers.

The hay wagon stopped and so, necessarily, did the seething sedan behind it. There was a pause; then a farmerish face under a brown straw hat looked down from the top of the rearward hay. "If you're so certain you're Hitler," this face asked harshly, "where's your mustache?"

"You pull over!" Ripley Little said in his worst voice. "You pull over and give me half of this road or I'll——"

"Oh, so you ain't Hitler!" the farmer returned. "Only jest a common everyday road hog. Listen, bub! I ain't a-goin' to pull over and go off the shoulder and leave my hay in this ditch."

"Hay?" Little pointed at it. "Call that hay? It's green and two-thirds weeds. Farmers in my part of the country wouldn't feed it to a jobjam hyena. Pull over, dob dabbit!"

"Cursin'," the farmer said. "Cursin' right in front of your own women. Shame, bub! I ain't a-goin' to."

"You ain't? Why, jab my soul, that left hind wheel of yours wobbles five inches out of plumb every time it turns round. I'm going by you and when I do I'll take that wheel off for you!"

"Take my wheel off?" The farmer, abruptly horrid, threw Little a kiss. "Jest try it—Claudie!" he said, and, retiring over the hay, disappeared from the Littles' sight.

They heard him speak to his horses; axles creaked and the hay wagon resumed its journey—jeeringly at a lesser speed per day than before.

"Now jab my soul," Ripley Little said, "I *will* take his wheel off for him!"

His head was down as in a butting position. The car charged forward. *"Father!"* Goody cried. "Remember what you said about other people's rights and courtesy to——"

"I'll take it off!" Little said. "I hope to die if I don't!"

The sedan veered to the left in its desperate attempt to pass the hay wagon. In spite of his declared intent, Little didn't deliberately try to detach the wobbly wheel; there was no deliberation about him. Possibly he may have thought that he could pass without real damage, even if he had to press the right side of his car somewhat into the overhanging hay. He must have understood that he was taking a chance; but he couldn't bring himself to be further delayed by a person who'd called him Claudie. The right side of the car butted into the hay; there were metallic protests, cracking sounds and two loud female screams.

The hay wagon stopped massively; and the automobile, in a careened position and oppressed with hay, ceased to operate. It was still behind most of the hay wagon, which now had a list to port. The wobbly wheel lay flat and undeniable upon the ground.

Vocalizings insufferably nasal were heard from ahead;

the farmer was descending. "You sit where you are!"
Little said fiercely to his womenkind. "If this isn't lesson
enough for him I'll give him another!" With a violent
hand he opened the door beside him, jumped out, and,
before his wife could finish her second scream, strode forward and was lost to her sight beyond intervening hay.

"We ought never to have come!" Mrs. Little gasped.
"Get out, Goody; let's get out. Oh, me!"

Already she could hear the voices ahead—rough,
rough voices—growing rougher. There were three of
them; and Ripley Little's was easily the roughest. Mrs.
Little and Goody slid down from the car, scrambled
round the hay wagon and its two aged horses, and then,
with womanly loyalty, tried to play a part in a fast, confusing scene; but couldn't, for this was man's work.

Not only the hay wagon and the Littles' sedan occupied the road. Another sedan, a lusterless twelve-year-
old, had just come out of a grassy driveway; and it
stood vacant some twenty yards before the hay wagon.
A frowning, brown-faced fat man, shabby but with dull
brass buttons upon his old blue waistcoat, had emerged
from this sedan and at once taken part in the altercation. Ripley Little seemed to be but the more stimulated
by the intrusion; and, as if he welcomed it, was first
shaking his fist close to the farmer's face and then even
closer to the fat man's, outbellowing them both unques-
tionably. Bits of what he said were distinguishable.

"Show you one jobjam American citizen that knows
his rights . . . Yes, pay for every jam scratch on my
car . . . See both you dobdab bullfinches in the Hellespont . . . You lay one bob dand greasy finger on me

and I'll . . . Just you try it, you hot dabbled bastinadoed Yahoos and . . ."

"Father!" Goody screamed. "Be careful! That fat
man's got a badge on his vest and he's got brass buttons.
He's a constable!"

"You're under arrest!" the fat man shouted, and with
a large soiled hand grasped at Little's shoulder. "You're
under——"

Mrs. Little shrieked and shrieked again. Little hit the
fat man in the stomach and the farmer on the ear. For
half a minute Ripley Little was in extravagant action,
then perhaps he realized that the Law was upon him; the
fat man and the farmer certainly were. Unceasingly
vociferous, all three, twining and untwining, Ripley Little,
the farmer and the fat man wrestled toward the twelve-
year-old sedan. Little was heaved into its rear seat,
where he sat with the farmer's arms about him. The
fat man jumped in, took the wheel, and the car fled
down the road.

Mrs. Little and Goody, shouting plaintively, ran after
it.

Upon its license plate, for some moments, they could
plainly read the inviting word VACATIONLAND; then even
this encouragement was denied them. The car, dwindling
with distance, turned leftward and disappeared. Mrs.
Little said she was going to faint, and sat down in the
dust.

Two miles ahead, at the end of the snaky road, a
Christopher Wren steeple rose above clustered elms, and
plain white houses with green shutters wore lovely

speckled blue shadows from the trees. Slightly outflung from this settlement a large gray shed bore on its front a partly obliterated circus poster and the sign "J. Ellers Wilson Garage & Repairing". On a bench outside this shed, Mr. Wilson himself, with an oily screwdriver on his tapestrylike lap, sat asleep in hot afternoon sunshine. He was awakened by an investigative Chow and two dusty ladies, one of whom seemed to be in a state of collapse.

In response to rapid questions put by the younger of the two, J. Ellers Wilson looked at his screwdriver for a time, then said slowly that yes, this was Milford and that there wun't no courthouse in Milford; but the jail, if so be they was lookin' fer it, was in back the Fire De-pattment. Further pressed, he said that he didn't keep no cazz fer hire and they didn't need none to git to Mil-ford Inn in anyhow, on account it was no more'n a couple hundud yadds ahead; and that yes, soon as Joe come back he himself would see if he could go fetch their sedan from where they left it, bring it in and see if he could see what was wrong with it. The two ladies de-parted, the older leaning on the younger, and the leashed Chow going round trees the wrong way, insisting on being dragged, and making all the trouble he could.

The Milford Inn, white in an open green yard, faced the village street, on the opposite side of which were half a dozen two-story buildings, all with shops on the ground floor, except one that bore over its closed doors the sign "Ellers L. Thompson Memorial Fire Depart-ment". The long verandah of the Inn was furnished with settees and wicker chairs, all vacant; but Mrs. Little couldn't ascend to them. She sank upon the steps.

"I can't," she said. "Miles and miles in this sun with my knees shaking all the way—it's too much! I'll have to be carried. Oh, listen!" She clasped her head convulsively. "Goody, it almost seems to me I hear your father's voice somewhere."

"My soul!" Goody whispered. "So do I! It's over there!"

She pointed at the open upstairs windows of the building next to the Memorial Fire Department. From these windows came sounds that fascinated an enlarging group of natives upon the sidewalk below. Mrs. Little, on the steps of the Inn, across the wide street, was sure she heard the words "bastinadoed", "jobjam" and "Hellespont"; then, suddenly, the voice that uttered them seemed to be extinguished. Heavy feet trampled noisily; doors slammed powerfully.

"Oh, Goody!" Mrs. Little murmured. "What are they doing to him? What *are* they doing to him?"

There was silence. The group of natives under the open windows apathetically dispersed, and one of the doors of the Memorial Fire Department opened. A fat brown-faced man who had greasy brass buttons upon his blue waistcoat came forth, looking gratified. He saw the two ladies and the dog upon the steps of the Inn, crossed the street and approached them.

"You couldn't find a nicer place," he said. "Milford Inn fer food and bed, there ain't no bettuh. It's run by kind of a cousin o' mine; you'll like her." He laughed meditatively. "Well, ladies, if so be you're a mite anxious 'bout the prisoner, it's no great mattuh—and anyhow the way I'll tell it to you there wun't be no call fer excitement. Fust he's got to pay the bill fer that wheel and exle, practically ruinin' my brothuh's hay cat and spillin' good hay. My own hay it is, too; my brothuh was jest goin' to turn into my place and d'liver it to me. Yes, sir; as you might say, Judge socked it to him."

"To my father?" Goody asked gulpingly. "What——"

"Thutty days," the tactful fat man said. "Dun't git excited; I'll tell you easy. Fust he socked the prisoner a hundud dolluhs fine, with costs, fer drivin' t' the public danger, and course the bill fer the hay and hay cat. Then give him the thutty days fer sayin' beforehand he'd take Lem's wheel off, next doin' it, and on top o' that resistin' an officer of the law. Next, Judge had to give the prisoner thutty days dishnal fer what he says when he got the fust thutty—out-and-out contempt o' court and profane and obscene language. Sixty days in all."

Mrs. Little couldn't speak; but Goody stamped a furious foot. "Profane and ob——" she cried, and interrupted herself. "You're crazy! He never in his life——"

"Profane and obscene language," the fat man repeated. "I nevuh heard wuss since 'leven years ago come Septembuh, the day I had to take my father-in-law to the 'Sane Asylum. Only reason you can't hear the prisoner now it's account the cell he's in, it's down the back stairs from the Judge's office, in back the Fire Depattment. Claims he ain't goin' to pay no fine, no costs nor no hay bill. That'll make it ninety days more."

Mrs. Little murmured the name of her Maker and

seemed to stretch herself upon the steps, whereupon the deputy sheriff, for such was his office, spoke sympathetically. "Take it easy, lady. The prisoner's a-goin' it now; but come the end his fust sixty days, he'll pay. Don't worry; they all do if they can raise it. No, sir; say what you will, nobody livin' ain't nevuh heard such language in a courtroom nor see Judge Hamilton Ellers git insulteder. He——"

"Who?" Goody said. "Judge Hamilton Ellers? Where's the Post Office?"

"Jest round the next corner t' the right, lady. What you——" The fat deputy closed his mouth and marveled. Goody thrust Pussy's leash upon him, ran out to the street, turned to the right and was gone.

"My 'Orry!" the deputy said. "Look at that girl run! I don't want this dog. Lady, fer Godfrey's sake git up!"

XXX

Mrs. Little sobbed feebly and said that before the trouble began she was wondering how to get her husband to stop just overnight in Milford. She thought she must be in a dream, she said. Then, realizing that several people were leaving the shops across the street and coming to look at her, she lifted a wavering hand toward the deputy. He took it, got her to her feet and supported her as she leaned against him, murmuring and almost unaware of him except as a crutch. He helped her up the steps, across the verandah, and through a doorway into a barroom vacant now of everything except bottles, glassware, the bar, tables and chairs.

"You set here," he said, as she slid down him, as it were, into a chair. "Summer people's all at the sailbut races and tennis tunnament; but this is a good nice cool quiet place and you got your dog." He affixed the loop of Pussy's leash to the chair. "She must had mighty important mail directed here; but she'll be back, likely. Me, I got duties to p'form. You'll feel bettuh when you git your full senses back, lady, like I've often told many. Good-by till next we meet up, lady."

Alone, except for Pussy, Mrs. Little made efforts to rise and become efficient; but she couldn't do either. She could only sit with her eyes closed while her lips moved almost soundlessly, repeating strange words: "Sick in a barroom and my husband in jail, sick in a barroom and my husband in jail, sick in a barroom and my husband ——" Thus whispering to Pussy and herself, Mrs. Little knew not how long it was before she again heard the voice of the fat deputy.

"Open up them eyes, lady," he said, standing before her. "You got a suit on the second floor with bath. Dog allowed."

"Suit?" she asked. "Dog? What——"

"Suit o' rooms with bath, lady. From the young lady and Ham Ellers I collect it would seem it turns out you're friends o' Ham's. It would seem now he was to be waitin' fer her at the Post Office and was. It's why she run. He——"

"Who?"

"Ham Ellers, lady. His branch the family left Milford during McKinley but summers always visited back here loyal. Kind of a cousin o' mine, Ham is—same's the Judge, natchly, him bein' close kin to Ham, his uncle. Me, I scarcely got away from you when her and Ham and the young boy come runnin', tuck me with 'em up t' the Judge's office. Courtroom we us'ally dub it. Ham persuaded till we fixed up a compamise, you might call it, 'mongst us. So, after all, it's only been a moneytary loss t' the prisoner, lady. He——"

"Who?"

"The prisoner. When I unlocked him out and up t' the courtroom again and he see Ham Ellers, and your daughter says hush it's Ham gittin' him his lib'ty, he's the Judge's nephew, why, the prisoner commenced goin' it wuss'n even durin' receivin' sentence; but Ham kep' tellin' everybody to notice how if you listen close it ain't so much profane and obscene such as what reg'lar men might employ but more kind o' baby-talk-like that the prisoner uses. So then the Judge says that seemin' to be the case he begin to see he can rescind them sixty days. You bettuh let me git you up t' the suit I told your daughter she bettuh take fer you. Lady, you'd really ought to git up there before they come."

"Why?" she asked. "Before who come?"

"The prisoner, or your husband as maybe he ought to be called now, lady. Ham Ellers's got him out, and he see, himself, he bettuh settle costs, fine and hay cat. Ham and the young lady they're walkin' one each side of him, coaxin' him along, as it were, to git him here, and tryin' to quieten him so's not to cause no distubbance in the Inn lobby. You can see 'em and the young boy with 'em, too, if you look out the window right 'side you. So hadn't you bettuh git up to your suit 'fore they come in—jest for quietness' sake, lady?"

Mrs. Little looked out of the window and saw Goody and Ham Ellers arguing, as it were, with Ripley Little on the sidewalk. He seemed to be telling them that he wouldn't soil his soul by remaining in such a dobdab bastinadoed town another jobjam second; and they seemed to be trying to tell him that the garage man said

that he'd just towed the sedan to his shop and couldn't yet
say how much was wrong with it. Mrs. Little's dis-
traught attention was centered upon these three; then
she became aware of a smaller figure devotedly interested
just behind them. Again she seemed to find herself wandering in a dream.

"That boy——" she said. "Why—why, it's my—it's
our son. It's Filmer."

"Yes, lady. It's the young boy Ham had, I was tellin'
you, lady. I collect it would seem this young boy belongs over t' Pine Trail Camp with young Lidgcomb
Ellers, Ham's young brothuh—nice place they got there,
eighty-six acres of wood lots that's still in Ham Ellers's
branch the family. I collect Ham went and brought this
young boy this mornin' so's to be a good nice supprise fer
you and the prisoner, since it turns out he's your son
and Ham wanted to cause you joyfulness with him."

"It's Filmer!" Mrs. Little moved uncertainly toward
the outer door. "It's Filmer. I must——"

"I wouldn't, lady," the deputy insisted. "Honest, I
wouldn't. Give 'em a little time and they'll git your
son up to your suit, along with the—with your husband.
You can see from the window there's a good many of
our citizens edgin' up to listen in, and if you go out there
it'll only excite more distubbance. Bettuh leave it to
Ham and the young lady; they're workin' on him and
they'll git him up there. From the looks of you, what you
need's to lay down where you can stretch out, lady."

Mrs. Little let the fat deputy conduct her to an
elevator.

. . . By eleven o'clock that night, music at the Milford Inn had drawn a dozen or so of the village's pleasure-loving natives to the verandah windows, to watch the summer people dancing. One of the spectators was an elderly man in white flannels, and after a time he was joined by a brown-faced fat friend.

"Good evening, Cousin Ellers," the man in white said graciously. "Fine taste, Ham has. Never in my life saw prettier dancing or a prettier girl."

"Sing'lar father, though," Ellers Smith, the deputy, returned. "Course it's all come out favorable: town gits the fine and costs, brothuh Lem the new exle and wheel and the hay damage, and Cousin Euphie's got her nicest-priced suit rented. On tops o' that, thanks to Ham, the summer residents and young folks receive all this music and crab salad and dancin'. On the othuh hand what a contrast!"

"Contrast?" Judge Ellers repeated. "Where?"

"Upstairs," Ellers Smith said. "Upstairs in Euphie's best suit. Tuck kind of an interest—curiosity you might call it. Been kind o' standin' round on the soft cappit outside their door. Couldn't help hearin' a good pat of it. Ham can claim all he's a mind to it's jest some kind o' baby-talk; but if I was to hear a baby usin' it, Judge, honest, I'd run like a deer. That's what makes I say what a contrast. All this festival downstairs and at the same time, in the suit right ovuh their heads—my Godfrey! Unreasonable, he is, unreasonable."

"He is?" the Judge asked. "Still?"

"Is he! Why, look, Judge, all in the world he'd 'a' had to done this aftanoon, if he'd waited two more

minutes Lem'd 'a' been turned into my driveway with
that hay cat, and the road'd been clear. He'd 'a' been
in Fernvale right now where he wanted to be; but think
his wife can git him to b'lieve it?"

"Can't she?"

"Fer one thing," Ellers Smith said, "there was its
natchly comin' out in the courtroom that lucky fer him
you're Ham's uncle. Fer anothuh, it seems he's drawed
wrong conclusions from Lem and me bein' brothuhs and
Ham's relations, and in dishnal's got kind of a strong whiff
of everybody in Milford bein' more or less Ellerses, as
you might put it. It would seem he claims his wife's
crazy if she thinks he can't put two and two togethuh
it's a plot."

"Plot? What nonsense!"

"So 'tis; but by 'Orry I heard him tellin' her he jest
about b'lieves now Lem's hay cat got in his way a-puppose
so't he'd haf to ram her and bust his cah so't he couldn't
git out o' Milford."

"But that's ridiculous!" the Judge said. "Ridiculous!"

"So 'tis." Deputy Ellers Smith looked through the
window benignly. "Graceful couple, ain't they? Nobody
ain't told him yet that the garage man workin' on his cah,
not knowin' how long the job'll take him, is Cousin
Ellers Wilson. Course Cousin Ellers Wilson bein' 'gaged
to Euphie and her promisin' him she'll marry him come
Indian fall if she gits a good enough season, and Ham
always sech a great favorite with Cousin Ellers Wilson,
why, who knows but somethin' might come of it? No,
Judge, like you says, *up* to now it certainly ain't been no
plot—but from now *on* I wouldn't like to say! That cah

might haf to stay in Cousin Ellers Wilson's garage quite some days."

Gudrida Little and Hamilton Ellers swung harmoniously out of the gay ruck of dancing couples, ran to a pair of chintz-and-wicker chairs secluded in an alcove of the Inn's lounge, and sat, laughing together—laughing for several reasons but mostly because they were their age. After a moment or two, however, Goody told her young friend seriously that he was this world's supreme marvel.

"But you are!" she repeated. "I mean truly. Nobody else on earth could have had an uncle that was actually the only person anywhere that could save Father! So you're really the person who saved him, Ham, and I think—I do really think—an inkling of that is working itself into his perceptions. Anyhow, while we were having dinner in our rooms and he was walking up and down, he admitted it *would* have been worse if it'd been Norman Peel, instead. Poor Norman! Father said he couldn't have stood that."

"Neither could I," Hamilton Ellers said. "It'll be a great advantage for me if there gets to be at least one of us more unpopular with your father than I am. I don't believe he actually wants to murder any of us, though— not really, Goody."

"No, not exactly murder," she agreed. "Maybe it's only that he makes more fuss about things than most fathers do. Ham, I'm afraid I'm awfully mean to him sometimes."

"Are you?"

"Yes, maybe it's the Little temper."

"Might be," Hamilton Ellers assented. "Temper's all right unless it's misapplied—as it usually is, Dean Murphy told our class. I've been thinking about your father, Goody."

"You have?" The seriousness of both had increased as they talked. "Thinking about Father? What?"

"Well, I'm only twenty, Goody, and it isn't so easy at that age to understand much about what goes on in the feelings of a man as old as he is; but I've been wondering if one of the reasons he seems jumpier than most people—— Well, don't you think it might be, really, because he's got more sense than a good many have?"

"More sense, Ham? Father?"

"It may sound funny," Hamilton Ellers admitted. "There's such an awful lot to get sore about all over the world and it's been like that a good while and keeps getting more so, worse and worse—— Well, maybe at our age we don't know that in the same way he knows it. Maybe we don't know it as *much* as he knows it. He's more out in it than we are, so it gripes him more than it does us."

"More out in it?" Goody said. "But if next year you get called up and have to leave college——"

"I know, I know. All the same, while nobody can deny your father's pretty irascible—and who knows that better than I do!—yet after all I can't get the notion out of my head that he's a pretty grand old party."

"Can't you?" Goody said, and he was pleased and surprised by the warmth with which she spoke. "That's a coincidence because it's what I told him, myself, just before I came down to dance with you tonight."

"You did, Goody? How'd he take it?"

Goody laughed. "I was afraid to wait to see!"

. . . Mr. and Mrs. Ripley Little were seated upon the otherwise deserted long verandah of the Inn, their eyes refreshed, when they glanced upward, by cerulean patterns seen between the tops of wineglass elms, while a cool breeze came in from the adjacent sea.

"Nobody's about because it's the bathing hour," Mrs. Little said. "They have it here at noon. Goody and Filmer and Hamilton say the water's cold but very stimulating; the beach is only about half a mile away. Did the man say the car'd be ready for us after lunch today, Ripley?"

"He said at two o'clock. That means four."

"Well——" she said regretfully. "I suppose we *could* be packed up by then, and Hamilton could take Filmer back to the Camp this afternoon, too. In certain respects, after one walks about and looks at it, this does seem quite a fascinating old place. Anyhow, don't you think it's cooler than the other places we've been, Ripley?"

"It might be that," he admitted, frowning. "Nowhere could be hotter than the other places we've been. Nowhere!"

There was a stir within the Inn, the sound of voices and a distant clamor of dogs barking. "The other guests are coming back," Mrs. Little said. "They come in by the Inn's other entrance when they get back from the beach. I think I hear——"

"Yes; it's Pussy all right, job jam him! I'd know his voice in a hundred—in a thousand—in a dobdab million!"

Summery-looking people began to appear upon the verandah, and, exhilarated by recent immersions in salt surf, paced briskly up and down, awaiting the sound of the musical gong that meant lunch. Filmer was among them. He walked briskly, too; but presently approached his parents with some diffidence. "It's great," he said. "I swam out to the float they've got there four times. Father, you ought to try it. This is a great place. Father, they wanted me not to talk about it or mention anything, and up to now I haven't and don't intend to, except there's simply one question I'd like to ask you: Father, just before you got arrested——"

"Filmer!" Mrs. Little spoke sharply. "You promised both Goody and me you wouldn't make use of that word!"

"Word?" Filmer repeated. "You mean the word 'arrested', Mother?"

"Filmer, you promised——"

"Never mind," Ripley Little said. This was a moment he'd dreaded; but, with a sunken heart, he stood up to it. "Let him ask what he wants to."

"Thank you, sir." Filmer faced his father and spoke out. "Father, when you socked those two men, before you got arrested, where did you land on 'em? Which one'd you hit first? The cop or that big farmer, and where?"

Ripley Little's gaze rested upon the face of his son. It was plain there had been nothing invidious in Filmer's repetition of the word "arrested"; he was not trying to avenge himself. On the contrary, in Filmer's eyes there was only the glow of a profound admiration, just acquired. Those eyes were worshipful.

Ripley Little was already aware that the workings of Nature are unfathomable; but here was a new one. Seldom in his life, as he well knew, had he so misapplied the heat of his temper as in his lawless assaults upon the hay wagon, the farmer and the deputy; and yet that very misapplication had given him a higher stand with his family than he'd ever before attained. Nay—it had brought to him the love and respect of the two beings for whom, in all the world, he most deeply cared.

The sun of summer was bright yet gentle in the blue above the elms; away from a few lovely such spots the earth suffered and most of it was hell, madness and mas-sacre; broiled lobsters were on the menu for lunch, he'd seen the headwaiter and would have two; the breeze carried a smell of the ocean and also another—a smell of salt-marsh hay that brought him no regret.